Sign up for our newsletter to hear
about new and upcoming releases.

www.ylva-publishing.com

To Sharon,
Happy Pride !
Wendy
x

FOUR STEPS

[signature] 7/18

WENDY HUDSON

DEDICATION

To my mum, Sweet Caroline

Acknowledgements

Firstly, I'd like to thank my amazing editor, Andrea Bramhall. Publishing your first novel can be scary and daunting, but she made it enjoyable and in the process made me a better writer.

Thanks to Astrid Ohletz and everyone else at Ylva Publishing who believed in my manuscript and worked hard to get me to this point, with a special mention to Adam Lloyd for the excellent cover art.

Love and thanks to Lynsey Duguid for being my first reader, for the gold star, and for the push I needed to submit. You always had faith and believed I could do it even when I doubted myself.

Thanks to all my friends and family who have supported me and listened to my endless book chat. There's too many to name you all, but special thanks to Sarah Hodgetts for providing junk food and beer on creative Saturdays and Pamela Mackay for her ridiculous stories that inspired.

Lastly, thanks to my mum, Carol. For leading by example and showing me it's never too late to try new things and fulfil your dreams.

Prologue

The edge of the verge collapsed under the old man's weight. He stumbled sideways and grabbed at the barbed wire fence that ran alongside the drainage ditch as he fell in. Snagging the palm of his hand on a barb, he cursed aloud at the deep gash that opened up and the stinking water that filled his boots. He pulled a greasy handkerchief from his hunting jacket and wrapped his hand to stem the blood flow. Digging in a metal-capped toe and grunting, he took two attempts to hoist his weight out again. As he tightened the rag with his teeth, his breath puffed out with the pain, inducing an alcoholic cloud into the calm night around them.

He cursed again and glared ahead at the back of his son, who continued moving on without him, oblivious. The stony track that ran parallel was too noisy underfoot so they trudged through the mud, maintaining a silent approach.

As they cut the final corner through a copse of trees, the dark outline of the farmhouse came into view. A bulb shining low on the front porch was the only sign someone was home.

His son held up a hand, signalling them to stop. Their eyes, already well adjusted, scanned the house for security lights and sensors. Convinced there weren't any, his son signalled again, directing him to follow on.

They pressed themselves against the wall of the barn, then skirted along in its shadow until, after a short sprint across the drive, they were crouched next to the side door of the house.

His son raised a hand again. They held still and listened.

The only noise louder than the trickle of water from the nearby burn was the gentle snorts of sleeping horses and an owl purring in the distance. No cars on the track, no barking dogs, only silence from the house and their heartbeats in their ears.

The old man watched as a smile spread widely across his son's face. So far, so good. This wasn't just revenge, stealing a bit of jewellery and giving a fright to some stuck-up bitch who thought she was too good for him. No matter what his son said, he was relishing every second of this.

His son stifled a whoop when the small rabbit statue by the side door gave up its hidden key; his eyes widened in triumph, and he mouthed, "Too easy." Laying down his gun, he took a breath and steadied shaking hands before slowly inserting the key, turning the lock, and pulling down the handle.

By the light of a pen torch in his mouth, they moved through the house a few steady steps at a time, keeping low and stopping periodically to listen for movement. The living area led them to a long corridor lined with doors. They turned each handle painfully slowly, both holding their breath, expecting a squeaky hinge as they inched the doors open, looking for their prize. There were only empty beds in the first two rooms; it was third time lucky. The master suite.

Thick carpet muffled their heavy boots as they crossed to the bed. The old man edged around to the side farthest from the door and on a silent count of three clamped his injured hand over the sleeping woman's mouth. The blood-sodden handkerchief muffled her cry as he grabbed her tightly around the neck with his other hand, pinning her back into the pillow.

His son pulled a double-edged knife from the sheath on his belt and followed suit on her sleeping husband. He pressed a heavy knee into his chest and held the serrated edge of the knife to the man's neck, stilling him instantly. The whites of his eyes glowed in the dark, and he held them until satisfied he wasn't going to be a problem. He propped his gun against the nightstand, the butt resting on the floor, then flicked on the bedside lamp.

The couple blinked rapidly at the sudden brightness, eyes flicking between the two masked men and to each other before fear took their features and the woman began to cry.

The old man watched his son draw blood from the husband's cheek and growl low in the man's ear, "Not a fucking sound", making clear his intentions should they try to fight back.

Shock and their weapons easily won the couples' silence, and neither attempted to struggle as they were bound and gagged where they lay.

Taking out his own knife, he stood sentry over them as his son began ransacking drawers and cupboards. Despite wearing a balaclava, he took care not to look either one of them in the eye, knowing they weren't stupid and would recognise him from their earlier confrontation in the village bar.

The plan was only to scare them shitless and leave them a few quid lighter. If he was to believe his son, no one was going to get hurt and the couple would have the good sense to call it even and let it go.

As he watched his son searching through their belongings, a young girl edged into his peripheral vision. She quickly crossed the room and picked up the shotgun standing on the other side of the bed to him. Her eyes never left his. He hadn't even noticed the gun there until she reached it.

She had picked it up and cocked it before his son, with his back to the door, noticed her in the room.

Her mother tried to sit, furiously shaking her head at her daughter. She only stopped when his knife forced her back onto the pillow.

Her father pleaded through the gag that she put the gun down and do as the men say, his cries muffled and almost unintelligible. Eventually, he simply shouted for her to run.

Undeterred, she pointed the gun at him even though he was holding a knife at her mother's throat.

He held her stare and watched as her nose wrinkled. Through the balaclava he could smell his own sweat and the sour fumes of alcohol coming heavy with his breath and felt the grimy layer they seemed to have cast over the room.

She stole a glance at his son frozen still to her left, but the gun remained pointing his way.

He'd fired a twelve-gauge weapon plenty of times and wondered just how well she could handle it. Her slender arms trembled along with her voice, a mixture of fear and the weight of the weapon.

"Put the knife down, or I'll shoot."

The old man glared at his son, determined not to panic and maintain his authority. She was just a girl and they could deal with her.

"Now what?" he barked.

His son ignored him, didn't even glance his way, fixating on the girl. Sizing her up in the same way he had. He glanced between the two of them and tried to calculate how many steps and how long it would take for his son to reach her. The bed prevented any element of surprise from him.

Or maybe it wasn't the threat that had his attention. He gritted his teeth and watched as his son's gaze travelled up and down the young girl. The tilt of his head as he admired her lean legs before lingering on small, pert breasts covered with only a thin vest made him cringe.

Bile rose in his throat. She was young enough to be his granddaughter, and he knew she was in trouble if he didn't intervene.

"Beth is it?" He spoke softly and slowly drew the knife away from her mother as an act of good faith. "We don't want any more trouble here. Lower the gun and let us leave quietly. This doesn't have to go any further." Slowly, he lifted his hands into the air, refusing to look away as her wide eyes changed to slits, suspicious of his movements.

"What the fuck are you doing, old man?" His son started to move, but she had already swung the gun towards his gruff words.

"Put the knife down, or I'll shoot." She repeated her earlier instruction, only this time it wasn't aimed at him. She was speaking to his son.

He licked his lips and tasted the saltiness of his own sweat. Even without seeing his son's face, he knew he was smiling under the balaclava, relishing the challenge, sure this was a fight he would win.

Keeping his hands in the air, he glanced between the two of them. Her parents remained still, their breaths coming fast and panicked through their gags.

His son's roar broke the silence as he charged with his knife still drawn.

Her father lunged toward them, falling from the bed.

Her mother squeezed her eyes shut and screamed through her gag.

The old man shouted to stop, reaching out over her mother. Futile.

Four.That's how many steps it took to reach the girl.

Then the gunshot deafened them all.

CHAPTER 1

Aging hinges groaned as Lori Hunter pulled open the thin wooden door of the bothy. She'd hoped to find it empty, and the intricate cobweb woven across the threshold told her no one had been there in at least a few months. She swiped them away with one of her hiking poles before ducking under the low door frame into the chill of the musty hut that promised her shelter for the night.

Her hike through the glen had taken almost an hour longer than the online guide had suggested – her fault, not the guide's. Caught up in her surroundings, she'd dragged her heels, unable to put her camera away.

Now, conscious of time, she hurriedly dug unnecessary items out from her rucksack, aware that if she wanted to summit the mountain and make it back to the bothy before dark, every minute of daylight counted.

Wiping what dust she could from the wafer-thin mattress, she laid a sleeping mat on the top bunk, followed by her goose-down sleeping bag. This, she hoped, would reserve the bed for the night. It was always a bonus to find an empty bothy, particularly one with a cot or bunk, because no matter how thin the mattress was, it still beat lying on the floor of a tent.

After unloading her cooking items, she stuffed spare clothes inside her sleeping bag before folding down the hood to keep out spiders. She looked around the small hut and smiled.

At five feet ten inches, she could reach a hand above her head to easily touch the ceiling. Apart from the metal-framed bunk beds, the only other furniture was a small, square table in one corner and an old fashioned three-legged milking stool. She chuckled at the absurdity of the door mat considering three steps covered the space from one end to the other.

A previous occupant had strung a line of green garden string along one wall and hammered some chunky nails next to the door for hanging wet socks and coats to dry. It was back to basics Scottish style. Compared to her hectic, noisy lifestyle in London, Lori loved every minute of it.

When she used the cuff of her bright red jacket to wipe the filthy window at the end of the bunks, it revealed uninterrupted views of the stunning Maoile Lunndaidh, the Scottish Munro she was about to climb.

Lori surveyed the mountain, a patchwork quilt of lush greens, browns, burnt orange, and yellows. Her eyes quickly found the faint line of a path already cut through the grass and heather by previous climbers. She traced it to the bottom, pinpointing where her ascent would begin.

She pulled her favourite hat down over long, wavy, chestnut hair and made a final check of her gear before heading out and securing the bothy door behind her.

Following the dirt track from the bothy door as it zigzagged marshy land, she eventually reached the river that stood between her and the mountain, in hopes of finding a passable shallow section to save her feet from the frigid water. She should have known better. After surveying up and down for a few minutes, she sighed and resigned herself to the only remaining option.

She squatted on a rock to remove her boots and gators, tied the laces together, and used their weight as momentum to swing them across to the other side. Then rolling up her trouser legs, she braced herself, took a few short breaths for courage, and took her first step.

"No going back now," she muttered as she plotted her course and slowly waded into the river. As the icy mountain water rose to her knees, she gasped and couldn't stop herself shrieking. She paused a moment until the tingling sensation passed, then gritted her teeth, used her hiking poles for balance, and carefully picked her way across the slick rocks. "Do not rush. Do not. The last thing I need is to slip and end up soaked on my arse."

Once she was safely across, she rubbed her feet furiously with the outside of her thick socks. "Merde, il fait froid!" She shook her head at the memory of her aunt telling her that swearing in another language wouldn't stop her getting in trouble for it.

She tugged her boots and gators back on, picked up her pack and the faint dirt track again, and finally began her ascent.

The terrain was boggy, making the going tough, but the adrenaline soon started to pump, powering her legs to keep a steady pace. The first hour flew by and brought her to a natural rest point at the edge of a steep crevasse. When she found a suitable rock, Lori dumped her pack and sat down to take in the awe-inspiring views before her.

Below, the bothy had disappeared, easily blending in to the brown heather-covered hills behind it. She could just make out the faint path of the old railway line that the guide said ran through to Achnashellach Station. Lori loved how small and insignificant everything became at this height, but by far her favourite thing about climbing mountains was the absolute quiet.

As an interpreter constantly and repetitively conversing, she craved the quiet while lying in bed at night. Unfortunately, the constant buzz of a city always awake surrounded her, every noise manufactured and fake. Today the only sound was a waterfall roaring into the crevasse she perched alongside. It filled her from the inside out with a sense of calm relief.

She ate a banana and sipped lukewarm tea from a small flask, holding it close enough to allow the steam to tickle her nose. A square of Kendal Mint Cake slowly dissolved on her tongue. Instantly, she felt the much-needed energy boost. Revitalised, but still conscious of the time, she set off again with purpose, attacking the steep, muscle-busting climb.

After a couple of hours, she stopped to survey what looked like a minefield of rocks and boulders. The last thing she needed while alone on a mountain was a turned ankle or a stuck foot. She steadied herself again with the hiking poles, concentrated on her balance, and carefully wove her way through the last obstacle between her and the mountain's peak.

Half an hour later, she closed her eyes and blew out a long breath, feeling the welcome rush of pleasure and adrenaline that came with touching the cairn at the summit. Another mountain conquered and scored from the list. The cairn underneath her palm felt reassuring, sturdy in the vast space that surrounded her.

Hot from exertion despite the drop in temperature, she ditched her hat, poles, and rucksack against the cairn and unzipped her jacket. Next, she grabbed her camera and circled the peak, taking in the stunning views. To the northwest, the iconic Torridon Mountains were instantly recognisable, including the imposing Beinn Eighe and Beinn Alligin. One day she hoped to take them on; maybe her brother would be persuaded to join her. To the southwest, she found the unmistakable sharp summit of Bidean a Choire Sheasgach watching over the beautiful Loch Monar in the South. If the weather held, as well as her muscles, her plan was to climb it, along with the adjoining Lurg Mhor, the following day.

She tried the names aloud, remembering her dad making her repeat them on their occasional climb together and his frustration that, despite all the languages she could speak, Gaelic seemingly wasn't for her. The distant memory made her sigh.

A familiar feeling of peace settled over her as she took picture after picture, even knowing she would never quite capture the scale and beauty of her surroundings. It was cathartic. It was her therapy.

The light began to fade fast, and ominous clouds building in the west were her cue to get moving again. Deciding the descent would be easy enough to take pictures along the way, she stuffed the camera in her jacket pocket, threw on her hat and rucksack, and set off back toward home for the night.

CHAPTER 2

Lori picked up the pace, crossed the rock mine without incident, and watched as the clouds drifted closer. From her altitude, she had the surreal visual of watching the rain fall in the distance whilst the sun still shone low behind her. She took out her camera, snapping photos of a rainbow spanning the glen that the rain had left in its wake.

It wasn't long before she reached the crevasse, stopping briefly to rest her thighs from the downward impact. Drinking the rest of the her already doctored tea to take on some sugar, she continued to zigzag down the narrow dirt track until she was low enough to eventually pick out the bothy from its vast backdrop. She aimed her camera in an effort to capture its insignificance and squinted as her eyes picked up movement. Given the royal blue colour, it couldn't be any animal she knew of.

Human.

"Verdammt," she swore aloud in the direction of her fellow hiker, watching the bright dot close in on the bothy as it stood out so easily against the dull hillside. It was exactly what she didn't want.

Company.

She quickly threw on her waterproof trousers in case the rain caught up with her, and continued the descent. It was relatively quick and, in less than half an hour, all that stood between her and the bothy track was one last careful river crossing.

Safely on the other side, it was then the heavens chose to open, raining the only way it knew how to in Scotland.

Hard.

She knew the bothy was only another quarter mile away, and the thought of hot food and a warm sleeping bag motivated her into a light jog despite the burn in her thighs.

Hood up and head down against rain, she didn't spot the dog until it was under her feet barking. He jumped up and around her with such excitement, she couldn't help but laugh when the rucksack on her back coupled with the springer spaniel at her front, toppled her back onto the sodden track. Her reward for a muddy arse was an enthusiastic face licking that had Lori shrieking worse than at the river crossing. She couldn't move and was relieved when she heard a female voice in the distance shouting, "Frank!"

Lori freed her face long enough to shout back, "Over here!" before "Frank" resumed his assault on her face.

Two blue arms suddenly wrapped around his body, lifted and unceremoniously plonked him aside. "The blue dot in the distance" now hovered above her, peering down at her through mischievous eyes. They shone against her flushed cheeks and the way she bit on her lower lip, Lori could tell she was torn between guilt and laughter.

The stranger's gaze was so enthralling that it took a moment before she realised she was still lying in the mud getting rained on. "So are you here to lick my face too or are you going to help me up?" she said, and laughed.

Relief flooded the woman's face. She stepped back, and offered Lori a hand. Lori was pulled to her feet and couldn't help but notice how soft and warm the young woman's skin was.

"Oh no." The woman surveyed the damage Frank had done. A panicked look slid across her lovely features and darkened a pair of stunning green eyes. "I'm so sorry. Let me see what he's done to you. Oh God, your rucksack is covered and your arse..." She made a swipe at the mud with her jacket sleeves. "Do you have spare clothes? That flipping dog, honestly I'm really sorry—"

Lori raised a filthy hand to stop her. She wiped it on her trousers then held it out in front of her. "Lori Hunter, nice to meet you."

The woman smiled again, visibly relieved, revealing a ridiculously cute dimple in her left cheek. She wrinkled her nose and held up her own filthy hands.

Lori shrugged, grabbed hold, and shook one anyway. "Alex Ryan, same here."

She was half a head shorter than Lori and, although petite, the ease with which she had pulled Lori to her feet showed she was strong. After a moment Lori realised she was still holding her hand and staring. She quickly dropped it and looked toward Frank, who was now chasing something unseen near the river.

She nodded in his direction. "Frank, I presume?"

"The one and only," replied Alex with a grimace. "I'm so sorry again for what he did. He's good as gold at home, but once he's released into the mountains, all manners go out of the window and he's unstoppable. Not that he would hurt anyone, or anything for that matter, he just likes the chase and meeting new people. It's so remote out here I let him have his fun."

Lori waved her apology away. "It's the mountain air. It can get to the best of us."

As they both turned to head in the bothy's direction, it seemed Lori's initial thought had been right. She wasn't going to be alone in the bothy tonight. "So I take it you're my bothy buddy for the night then?"

"Oh!" It had obviously just dawned on Alex. "Aye, I hope that's okay? I hope you don't mind sharing with Frank too? He is an outdoor dog but normally has a barn and the company of other animals, and with the rain and..."

Lori placed a hand on her arm for reassurance and stopped her mid-flow. "So long as he doesn't want to share my bed, I think I'll cope."

Alex offered her a cheeky smile and turned toward the river. "Why not? I thought you'd already fallen for him?" Alex glanced back over her shoulder, a grin covering her face.

Lori returned her smile. "He certainly has a way with the ladies." She looked across the water and the last known location of Frank.

Alex craned her neck clearly looking for her pooch.

The rain had let up so Lori freed herself from the restrictive hood and took the opportunity to properly survey the woman she would be sharing her evening with.

She couldn't have been more than five feet five and clearly took care of herself. Alex was obviously comfortable in outdoor clothes and boots. Wisps of black hair had escaped the hood of her jacket, sticking to her rain-soaked face. Only a few small freckles high on a cheek bone seemed to interrupt a perfect complexion, now tinged from the wind with a pinkness to match her lips. Her left cheek maintained the slight indent of the dimple Lori had already seen.

Lori saw Alex's lips moving, but it wasn't until those shining eyes caught hers again that she realised she was staring. "Uh, sorry, in my own little world there," she said, quickly dropping her gaze before looking across the river, scanning the area for Frank. A tingle crept up her spine and she shivered involuntarily. Suddenly aware that she was soaked and covered in mud, she gave Alex a nudge and nodded toward the bothy. "C'mon. Let's go get warmed up."

"Aye, you must be freezing! He knows better than to stray too far and I'm sure will come back when he's hungry. He always does."

CHAPTER 3

Lori stepped into the bothy with a sigh of relief just as the rain picked up again. Alex looked around some more for Frank but soon closed the door, blocking the wind out along with him when there appeared to be no sign.

"Look at the state of us." Alex yanked down her own hood and pulled her hair back. The tendrils sticking to her face earlier, too short to be caught in her ponytail, were quickly drying, going wispy around her face. She took her outer jacket off, followed by waterproof trousers and a thick outer fleece, and hung them on the nails by the door.

Lori found herself suddenly conscious of her own appearance. She pulled off her hat and quickly ran her fingers through her hair in a vain attempt to make it look respectable. Next she stripped off her own muddy jacket and waterproof trousers, but, kept the warm fleece on as she was feeling chilly.

"Dinner?" asked Alex.

Lori was already digging in her bag when her stomach rumbled. "You read my mind."

"Okay, what have you got? Mine is boil-in-the-bag mince and tatties. Sorry, minced beef and potatoes," she corrected herself.

It was a nod to Lori's soft English accent that told Alex she wasn't even northern, never mind Scottish. "Don't worry. I've spent enough time in Scotland to know what tatties are. I even know what neeps are too," she said, referring to the common name for turnip.

"Phew," said Alex, dramatically wiping a brow, "I don't need to translate myself then?"

"No, don't worry," said Lori, laughing as she talked, "I'll tell you if I don't understand. If you were from Aberdeen we might have a problem, but your accent isn't too strong, so I think we'll be fine."

Alex chuckled. "Aye, even I struggle with the Aberdonian folk. I spent the first year of University sitting next to a girl from Mintlaw. Let's just say I spent a lot of time nodding and smiling when she spoke. I only started understanding her when we became pub buddies. I find beer is a great language leveller."

Lori waggled two miniature bottles she pulled from a side pocket in Alex's direction. "As is red wine."

Alex's eyes widened in obvious delight. "I think you're my new best friend. I can practically taste it already."

"Well my bag has a questionable version of chicken tikka masala so I find the wine necessary to wash it down."

Alex crinkled her nose as she caught the silver pack Lori threw towards her, eyeing it suspiciously. "I personally don't need a reason for wine but that's as good as any."

They busied themselves gathering pots, gas canisters, water, and sporks, until all that was left was to wait for the water to boil their dubious dinner packs.

Lori broke the silence as Alex added another layer of clothing. "So is this your first time here?"

"No it's a bit of a favourite spot of mine that I discovered quite a few years ago with my ex. It's my first time here on my own though." Her head popped through the top of her fleece. "It's been a while."

"Oh right." Lori was mildly surprised to get such a candid answer. "Trying to get rid of the ghosts by making some memories of your own?"

"Aye, something like that." Distracted, she poked at the bags in the pot. "I decided I gave up enough for that relationship and places like this are far too special to forget." Alex went quiet at that, her eyes darkening like rain soaked moss. She blew on to her chilled hands, her eyes still on the bags bobbing in the boiling water.

"We kind of made it our place. We came back loads of times. But what started out as a great adventure to be shared together, huddled on one bunk, talking and kissing the night away, soon became more of a chore. Our last time here was also the last few days of our relationship."

Lori raised her eyebrows as Alex took a breath. The words had seemed to tumble out of her in a rush. "Wow. I'm not sure what to say apart from I'm really glad to be sharing with only you and not some giggly, smooching couple." She stifled a smile, hoping her humour wasn't misplaced.

Alex seemed taken aback for a moment, but then threw a smile her way to Lori's relief. "Don't worry, you're safe. It was long enough ago that I can laugh about it now."

Lori watched her continue to absentmindedly poke at their dinner bags and hoped it was true. "So it just didn't work out then or did something happen?"

Alex seemed to size her up before speaking again. "Okay, let's get the morbid talk out of the way before our delicious dinner is served. Something did happen and that something was somebody else. For my ex, not me."

Lori drew out a long "Oh," leaving it open for Alex to carry on if she wanted. She studied Alex's face, her eyes had glazed, and she stood still with her hands over the steam from the boiling water. Clearly, Alex had drifted away, slipped into her memories. She wanted to bring her back, ask what had happened or say something reassuring. But she didn't think Alex would appreciate a stranger prying any further into her business, particularly out here where there weren't many distractions if things got uncomfortable between them.

Suddenly Alex blew out a long breath and blinked at Lori. It was clear she had forgotten someone else was there with her. "Oh is right." She sheepishly rubbed her hands together. "Sorry, not sure where I went there."

Lori smiled reassuringly and joined her at the stove. "Funny how an ex can do that to you, eh?"

Alex nodded. "Aye. I was just thinking I'd come a long way since we split up. It's taken me a while to feel as if I could spend a night here alone without getting scared, sobbing into my whisky, and becoming a snotty mess. It would have been a terrible time for Frank."

Lori gave her a wry smile, appreciating her attempt at humour despite the hurt she could see written all over Alex's face. She reached past her and turned off the gas, satisfied the food was heated well enough. "So I should be bracing myself for a potentially snotty time then?" She opened the packs and started spooning the mushy food into mess tins.

Alex shrugged. "Listen at this point I can't promise anything but good intentions. I'll admit it helps having someone else here so you're probably safe. Frank will be most grateful."

Lori took her opportunity to find out more. "You don't seem the type to scare easily and need someone around for protection, well apart from Frank obviously."

Alex settled on the bottom bunk. "Ah, well you would have me pegged right, then. Her name was Rachel and she was a bigger scaredy cat than me. Scared of spiders, scared of the dark, and as it turned out, scared of commitment."

Lori's hands stilled at Alex's words, unsure why her stomach had just done a small flip-flop. She was glad she had her back to Alex. She poured the wine into their tin cups and finished serving, and then turned with the steaming mess tins and a smile. "Dinner is served," she announced and handed one to Alex before setting the wine at her feet.

She was about to sit on the wobbly milking stool when Alex patted the space on the bottom bunk next to her. Her legs engaged before her mind and, suddenly, she was sitting next to her, close enough to feel the warmth radiating from Alex's thigh.

She felt Alex glance sideways at her, obviously waiting for a response about Rachel. She picked up her drink and held it out in a toast. "To sharing wine and secrets with strangers."

Alex's shoulders seemed to drop in relief. "Cheers to that." She toasted and took a large gulp. "I should say I'm not normally so quick to out myself, but I figured sharing with a lesbian surely can't be worse than getting dripped on in a soggy tent on your own?" She winked at Lori with a half-smile.

Lori returned the smile. "Hey, I'm a big city girl, Alex, you're not the first lesbian I've ever met. Besides, Frank seems like a good judge of character, I mean he likes me, so I'll trust him on this."

Alex held her eye. "You have one of those faces."

"Those faces? I'm not sure if that's a compliment or not?"

"It is. It's the kind that makes someone want to spill all their secrets."

Lori peered at Alex over the top of her cup and watched her take another sip of wine. "Well after tonight, you never have to see me again so what's the harm? Spill."

Alex shuffled back in the bunk. "You better get comfy if we're doing this."

Lori hesitated a moment, conscious already of their proximity, but joined her leaning back against the side of the bothy. "So why would being alone out here have you worried if spiders aren't a problem?" she asked, turning slightly to face her.

Alex stared at her wine before giving her what was obviously the short answer. "Because being alone meant time to think about how unhappy I was."

The sadness written all over Alex's face made Lori want to pull her in to a hug. She had even started to reach out an arm when a loud bang on the door made them both jump. Wide eyed, they looked at each other in panic until frantic scratching indicated that it was just Frank trying to get in.

Alex got up to let the dripping wet and muddy mad dog in. His tail wagged uncontrollably, but he obviously knew better than to jump at them in his current state. He instead waited for Alex to unroll a thin, padded mattress from her rucksack that turned out to be a makeshift dog bed. He circled twice in the middle of it and then collapsed in an exhausted heap.

Alex pulled a small towel from a pocket and then gave him a rough rub all over to help warm him up. Pouring water into another mess tin for him, she returned to the bunk promising to feed him just as soon as her own now lukewarm mush was finished.

The moment now passed, Lori decided it was best to leave the 'ex' subject, not wanting to see Alex upset again and not really wanting the tables turned. She'd come up here to get away from the ex-not-ex question after all. She finished her dinner and decided to play it safe instead. "So what are your plans for tomorrow?"

"My, my, aren't you forward. I haven't even finished this delicious dinner you made me and you're already planning our second date," she said, smirking, "I mean, I was planning on climbing a mountain, but, you know, if you want to take me out, I could be persuaded," she winked.

Lori couldn't help the heat that crept up her cheeks at the flirty words and the deep dimple that creased Alex's cheek. To hide her embarrassment, she picked up her mess tin and started tidying up after their dinner. Her mind whirled. One wink from a girl she'd known an hour, half a cup of wine, and she was acting like a bloody fool. In her mind she chastised herself, *it's just because she's a she, and you're not used to girls flirting with you that's all. She's just having fun with you. Get over yourself and have a laugh.*

Her back to Alex, she laughed and decided to play along. "Wow, well who knew a solo trip to a bothy in the middle of nowhere would get me a date with a hot local." She turned and returned the wink. "If I'd known, I'd have done something with my hair."

Lori calling her hot was obviously not what Alex had expected, evident by her own blush. "So it's a date then? Seafood is my favourite, in case you're wondering."

Lori smiled at the comment, pleased at her ability to make Alex shift uncomfortably just as easily as she had. "As tempting as that is, I'm not sure my boyfriend would approve. But maybe we could go climb a mountain together? That's if you're up for the company?"

"Ah, there's always a boyfriend." Feigning disappointment, Alex shook her head sadly. "I guess I should have known someone as gorgeous as you wouldn't be single. What's his name?"

Lori was determined not to let Alex see the effect being called gorgeous was having on her and also not really wanting to get into boyfriend territory, she began to organise her bed and sleeping clothes on the bunk above where Alex was sitting.

"Andrew. He's back in London, not really the roughing it type, which works out well because I like the time away by myself..." she trailed away hoping the subject would be dropped.

Jumping at a prod to her side, Lori looked down to see Alex peering up at her mischievously "I'm sorry. I didn't mean to make you uncomfortable, teasing you like that about a date. I'm told I'm a massive flirt when the notion takes me and you straight girls don't always appreciate it."

Lori sat on the stool opposite the bunk. "Trust me, it's not that at all, although you do seem to have a knack for making me blush. I just hadn't thought about him all day. I've been distracted by the climb and the view, and then meeting you and Frank." She sighed and rested an elbow on her knee, chin in hand. She guessed talking to a stranger had to be more productive than to her best friend. Stella would just profess what a bore Andrew was and pour her more wine. To be fair, she was right. "I kind of came here under a bit of a cloud. Andrew and I argued about yet another weekend spent apart. It's getting boring and I'm tired of it."

"The arguing is getting boring or he's getting boring?"

She could have played along when she heard the humour in Alex's voice, instead she gave the honest answer. "Both, I guess. When we first started seeing each other, having walking in common was a big plus. Turns out my walking and his walking are two very different things. But, anyway, we have much bigger problems than that and I guess I've just finally taken my head out of the sand and seen them." It wasn't just an argument. It was a full-blown shouting match that had ended with Lori declaring it was over between them. Again. "I guess I just can't take his selfishness anymore. Or his complete disregard for my career and my hobbies. In fact, the more I think about it, his disregard for anything that makes me happy. Andrew wants a housewife, and a housewife I most certainly am not."

Alex blew out a breath. "Well high five for the sand-free head. It took me three years to do the same and realise the only thing Rachel cared about was Rachel. How long has it taken you?"

Lori's shoulders slumped. "Don't be so quick with that high five. I've wasted the best part of seven years on Andrew."

"Wow," Alex said, eyebrows raised. "It surely can't have been all bad if you've stuck around that long?"

"No, you're right. That's not fair. We had our moments. I suppose these days I'm struggling to remember what they were."

When they first dated he had understood her work would involve travel. As an interpreter, she would sometimes be out of the country to work freelance at the European Parliament or to personally accompany an MP or diplomat to a summit or meeting.

It was normally only for a couple of days at a time but sometimes longer, depending on the event. He was happy that her interest in politics and international issues had swayed her away from signing on with one of the many businesses that had courted her, avoiding a potential permanent move out of the country. He also said it was perfect because it afforded them plenty of freedom to do as they pleased, particularly with the hours he would have to put in as a junior broker in the city.

At twenty-three, they were still young and, although committed, they wanted to retain some independence, including keeping separate homes and their own group of friends.

On paper, they were a good match and Andrew ticked all the boxes she thought a good future husband was meant to tick. He was handsome and career driven, he came from a similar wealthy background to her, and was headed for big things. They could have the picture postcard life. House, kids, cars, pets. They could give their kids all the traditional, stable things she never had.

After five years together he started to change. In the last two years, he'd become possessive and demanding, deriding her for staying away and 'deserting' him despite it being necessary for her job. Suddenly her handsome and easy-going boyfriend had turned ugly and emotionally manipulative.

Despite the fact that they didn't live together, he expected her to be waiting for him at his place, with dinner on the table and an open ear ready to listen to him drone on about his day when he got home. Whether it was after work or a day on the golf course, he didn't care.

If she wasn't there when he expected her to be, she was grilled about her whereabouts. Who was she with? What did she do? What did they talk about? She had even caught him once checking her phone messages although he had denied it, making up some lame excuse about wanting to check a date in her calendar. She was sure it hadn't been the first time.

He made her feel guilty for wanting to spend time with other people without him, to the point where even a drink after work with her best friend came with a barrage of questions. It had taken a while for her to realise part of the problem was Andrew didn't have friends. He had colleagues and golf buddies, but any real friends he had kept through University and his first few years at the bank he had let drift away or they'd moved on. He made no attempt to find new ones and had become more and more reliant on her for a social life, for attention, for everything, and she couldn't be everything for him. It was exhausting.

His solution? Get married, have kids, move to a soulless commuter town and plan dinner parties.

She had spent years studying languages and politics, gaining her postgraduate degree in conference interpreting. She'd worked long and hard, freelancing in order to build relationships and a solid reputation. It had enabled her to secure a permanent position in the Westminster Parliament and a place high up the list of people willing to travel. She couldn't believe Andrew expected her to give it all up. Just so he could play out some old fashioned fantasy that the old boys at the bank seemed to encourage. He'd been watching too many episodes of Mad Men.

Seven years was a long time though, and it would be hard to make the break, despite everything, she missed him.

However, she was resolved to end it and wasn't going to feel guilty for taking control of her own life and living it her way.

"Let me guess," said Alex, breaking into her thoughts, "his walking involves a golf course?"

Lori burst out laughing. "And four of the most tiresome men you've ever met in your life. Andrew included."

Alex licked her finger and scored one for herself in the air. "I remember when I was younger, my granddad was a mad golfer and my grandma could never understand him spending four hours walking around a course when he could be at the top of a mountain in that time."

"Well, no more," Lori declared, jumping to her feet. "I hope he and his golf clubs are very happy together. May they keep him warm in the night."

"Wow, so it's actually over?" Alex asked, clearly confused. "A minute ago he was your boyfriend."

"Yes. It's over." The realisation that she truly meant it this time suddenly hit her. So many times these past two years had she uttered those words, knowing Andrew would talk her around. But this time felt different. She grabbed her rucksack and dug around, hoping she'd remembered to pack what she needed right now.

"A wee nip to keep the cold away?" she asked, attempting a Scottish accent, triumphantly holding up a miniature flask.

Alex's eyes lit up. "Ah, wine and whisky. I knew you were a girl after my own heart. I'll take that as an apology for fobbing me off with what is actually an ex-boyfriend."

Lori smiled and sat on the bottom bunk again, unclipping the top of the flask to release two small silver cups, she handed one to Alex and poured.

Alex looked impressed. "Very sophisticated." She sniffed it and closed her eyes in obvious delight. "Glenlivet?"

Now it was Lori's turn to be impressed. "Right again, a favourite of my dad's." She touched her cup to Alex's, looked her in the eye, and raised it in another toast "To exes and to ridding ourselves of their crap once and for all."

"To exes," Alex echoed before they both swallowed the amber liquid down in one.

Lori felt it burn a satisfying trail down to her stomach and, with a smile at both their empty cups, she topped them up again.

Alex shivered and sat back against the wooden bothy wall, pulling her sleeping bag across her legs, before tossing the other side of it over Lori's. Lori followed, sitting close for extra warmth. She took another sip of whisky, its calming effect immediate as she sunk down lower under the sleeping bag. They were both quiet and lost in their own thoughts. The only sound was Frank softly snoring.

"What are you thinking about?" Lori asked. "Rachel?"

"Nah, this trip was about forgetting her. Wiping her memory from this place by making new ones of my own. I was actually thinking Frank obviously isn't interested in his dinner and so far, I've never enjoyed sharing a bothy with a stranger so much as I have with you."

Lori glanced across at Alex, smiling at her honesty. "I think you might have been right about me and you being good friends, you know. We have mountains, whisky, and a hatred of golf in common. What more do we need?"

"Well, right now, I need more whisky." Alex held out her cup for a third time. "And while you top that up, I have something else to finish this impromptu little dinner date of ours."

Lori cocked her head and raised an eyebrow. "Why am I worried?"

"Relax." Alex smirked, handed Lori her cup, and then shuffled to the end of the bed to rummage in her rucksack. "I'm over you already." She grinned over her shoulder. "Ah ha! Dessert." She pulled out a zip lock food bag with what looked like Frank's dinner in it "Jess's homemade brownies. I promise looks are deceiving, they got a bit mashed in my bag."

She got up and retrieved their sporks before crawling back next to Lori on the bunk and pulling the sleeping bag back over them. She opened the food bag and offered it to Lori first. "Go on, I swear they're amazing."

Lori dug in, never one to turn down chocolate. "Oh my goodness, that's delicious." She groaned. "Okay, you win with dessert. Well, Jess wins, whoever she may be."

"Best friend," Alex mumbled through a mouthful.

The brownies didn't last long and one more refill each finished the whisky.

"Yep, I was definitely right about us being friends," Alex murmured, leaning in to rest her head on Lori's shoulder, the whisky seemingly making her sleepy. "I think I was meant to meet you."

Lori tensed a little, surprised at the familiar gesture, then relaxed into it. A few minutes later, she realised Alex's breathing was matching Frank's and that she was out for the count.

Rousing Alex long enough to take the cup from her hand and lie her down, Lori laid the sleeping bag over the top of her. She figured Alex would soon crawl inside when the cold started biting.

The temperature had dropped dramatically and Lori could see her breath cloud in the small space. Stealing herself for the chill outside, she manoeuvred around Frank and left the bothy for nature's bathroom.

The sky was clear and the sheer number and brightness of the stars never failed to hypnotise her. She always took a moment to stand and stare, letting her mind clear before bed. Only tonight it wasn't working and, for a change, it wasn't because of Andrew.

She thought about the 'hot local' sleeping inside and smiled. Why was that? Yes, she was funny and cheeky and easy to talk to but there was something more. She couldn't put her finger on it. Suddenly exhausted, Lori headed back inside.

Alex's walking trousers on the stool told her she had taken the time to change before climbing into her sleeping bag. The hood was pulled tight around her head against the cold and Lori stood a moment studying the serene looking face lit softly by the lantern on the table. She couldn't help but admit Alex was beautiful.

Lori moved around quietly so as to not disturb the sleeping woman while she changed into thick thermals. The ladder groaned under her weight as she climbed up to the top bunk and slid down deep inside her own sleeping bag. Closing her eyes, she let the whisky do its work.

CHAPTER 4

Alex awoke early, shivering in the damp, morning air. The whisky had initially wiped her out so she hadn't bothered with thermals on her top half before crawling into her sleeping bag. Not sensing any movement on the top bunk, she eased herself gently from the squeaky bed.

Frank's head perked up from his bed, tail wagging when he realised he was about to be let loose. She stretched her arms above her head and up on tip toes, her fingertips just brushed the ceiling. She felt good after yesterday's walk, stiff from the cold and the wafer thin mattress but the stretch was satisfying. She pulled a pouch of dog food from a side pocket in her rucksack, then grabbed Frank's bowl and her toothbrush before pushing her feet into cold boots and creeping quietly outside.

Frank wolfed down his breakfast as she surveyed the mountains and weather whilst brushing her teeth. Light drizzle fell and the peaks were invisible behind low-hanging cloud. It was still early so she had time to wait and see if the sun would burn it off, but a decision would have to be made soon whether bagging another mountain this weekend was worth a potentially wet and miserable climb.

She didn't mind climbing in the cold and snow, but rain was just depressing and there was no reward of a view at the summit. Besides, she'd climbed them before and this weekend was more about putting another memory of Rachel firmly in the past and enjoying one of her favourite places again on her own. Well, almost alone. She heard movement inside the hut and quickly relieved herself before heading back in.

"Good morning." Lori smiled brightly as Alex entered. "Bathroom free?" she asked, grabbing her own toothbrush.

Alex chuckled. "Sure, it's all yours. Weather doesn't look great. I'm not sure I'm up for the masochism a climb would be today but..." She pointed to a narrow case about a foot long attached to the side of her rucksack and said, "Telescopic fishing pole. I thought I'd maybe head to the river instead for a while and then take my time walking back out to the car."

Lori stopped in the doorway, she looked out towards the peaks still shrouded in cloud then back inside where Alex sat rubbing Frank's belly. "Is that an invitation?"

"Only if you happened to have brought coffee and plan on making me breakfast when you get back from the bathroom."

"You did hear me when I said I wasn't the housewife type last night, right?"

"Trust me, my little English muffin, I don't plan on being anyone's husband either." She shrugged and lifted her hands innocently. "I'm merely trading goods and services with you, coffee and breakfast for the use of my fishing pole and the joy of my company. I mean, I'll happily make my own and head off solo..."

"Okay, okay," Lori held up her own hands. "Just making sure we understand each other. Besides, you had me at English muffin." She laughed with Alex. "I will accept your terms and be right back to hold up my end of the deal."

Alex busied herself with packing up both her and Frank's beds before pulling out sachets of porridge and a couple of battered bananas. When Lori reappeared, Alex sat on the bottom bunk and watched her put water on to boil and ready their cups for coffee.

"Will this do, your majesty?" she asked producing two sachets of 3-in-1 instant coffee from her pack.

"That would be amazing, but I don't suppose you have any 2-in-1 hiding in there? I'm sweet enough without sugar."

Lori laughed. "I'd disagree, but I'd be lying," she said, pulling out a sachet of 2-in-1 and holding it up as if she'd found gold.

Alex smiled. "I don't know if I'm happier at the compliment or the sugarless coffee. So how did you sleep?" After an initial couple of hours of sleep born mainly of whisky and exhaustion, Alex had woken with the cold and struggled to fall asleep again. Her mind had played tennis thinking back and forth between her last time at the bothy with Rachel and the girl asleep in the bunk above.

There was no doubt she was a beautiful woman. Alex warmed inside thinking about the day before when Lori had quite obviously been checking her out. However innocent it may have been, Lori's good looks had not gone unnoticed by Alex. Since she'd pulled down her hood to reveal a funky hat covering hair she later discovered matched her rich amber coloured eyes, Alex had been stunned. Add to that a sprinkle of freckles over skin that looked as smooth as syrup and the widest, most genuine smile Alex had ever seen, she imagined men and women always gave Lori Hunter a second glance.

Maybe it was the close proximity of sharing such a small space when they had only just met. Maybe she was feeling vulnerable expecting to be out here alone, but the realisation she was single and attracted to this girl was unsettling.

She'd kept anyone remotely interesting at arm's length for a long time and was working hard not to let the panic of actually liking someone set in.

But she had to admit she'd never felt so instantly comfortable with someone, yet so nervous at the same time. She also knew she didn't mind the close proximity of Lori and the tingling feeling in her stomach that came with it.

"Earth to Alex." Lori was clicking her fingers and laughing.

Alex shook herself back to reality and spun around to face Lori, feeling like she'd been caught with her hand in the biscuit tin. Her reaction caught Lori by surprise, startling her and causing the unstable milk stool she'd been perched on to tip sideways. Before Alex could stop it Lori was deposited in a heap of arms and legs on the floor.

The roar of Alex's laughter obviously piqued Frank's interest, within seconds, he was inside the bothy and on top of Lori again, licking and fussing around her face. This only encouraged Alex as she rolled around on the bottom bunk, tears flowing freely, and holding her stomach as she struggled to breathe. Lori played along, shrieking and frantically moving her head from side to side trying to avoid Frank's wet kisses and dog food breath.

"Help me! Don't just lie there, get him off! I can't breathe! Please, Alex, help!"

Regaining some control, Alex stood and hooked a finger in the dog's collar pulling him toward the door. She bumped his backside playfully with her foot and sent him on his way, closing the door behind him. Lori still lay in a heap on the floor, wiping her face with her sleeve and trying to catch her breath.

Alex stood over her and reached both hands down in an offer to pull her up. Lori eyed her, feigning disgust, but took them and instead, pulled Alex to the floor along with her. She quickly overpowered the smaller woman, getting her own back with tickles to Alex's sides and stomach. Alex squealed with surprise trying to stop Lori's hands, breathe, and shout "Mercy!" all at the same time. Eventually Lori stopped, pinning Alex's hands above her head, bringing their faces close.

"Give in?" she asked with a smirk.

Alex's chest heaved as she tried to catch her breath. She stared off into space as if to consider her predicament. "Hmm, for now," she said, finally looking at Lori. "Although I can't say it was all bad."

She couldn't help but stare into Lori's eyes, so close she could see small yellow flecks, like autumn leaves floating on a pond. A moment of stillness passed before Lori broke the eye contact and seemed to realise their position. She was straddling Alex, hands still pinned up behind her head with her face only inches away.

"Oh crap, the water!" she said, jumping up.

Alex lay a few seconds longer trying to catch her breath again, but not from the laughing. What had been a bit of innocent flirting suddenly didn't feel so innocent. Her heart had jumped into her mouth when she'd turned back and met those deep pools of amber, their lips so close she could feel Lori's breath on hers and smell a hint of syrupy sweetness she couldn't quite place.

Yes, Lori was gorgeous and funny, but she was also straight. And straight in Alex's world of dating was spelt d-r-a-m-a. Anyway, she'd clearly freaked Lori out and scolded herself for taking it too far. She'd made her uncomfortable and spoilt the easiness between them. Getting to her feet she brushed herself off while Lori fussed with adding water to the porridge and coffee cups, keeping her back to Alex.

Alex sat on the bottom bunk again, deciding some inane chit chat and a bit of humour would go a long way to break the awkward silence that had fallen over them.

"So you got me drunk last night before I had a chance to grill you on the usual subjects. You know family, friends, and career?"

Lori turned and smiled, and Alex felt the awkwardness pass. She took the offered coffee as Lori made to sit on the stool again to wait for the porridge to thicken.

"Uh, do you really want to risk that again?" Alex chuckled, once again patting the space beside her on the lower bunk.

Lori seemed to hesitate for a second but sat down. Alex couldn't help but notice she put a bit more distance between them than the night before.

"Okay sure. What do you want to know?"

"Hmm." Alex stroked her chin striking a thoughtful pose that gave her instead a mischievous look.

"Within reason," Lori said with an arched eyebrow.

Alex held up a hand and laughed. "Okay, then. Let's start easy with the basics. Tell me about your family?"

"Ah, the family question. Where to start?" she said, thoughtfully tapping her chin. "Well, I'm a twin. My brother Scott is a photo journalist and doesn't like to stay in one place very long. He's got a base in London though so we do get to catch up every now and then, even if it's just to grab dinner or a drink before he jets off again."

"Wow. That must have been cool growing up with a twin?"

"Not so much when we were younger. He tormented me like crazy and always got me in trouble. He's eight minutes older and never lets me forget it. But as we got older, we grew closer. Well, as close as we can be when we're rarely in the same country. He's completely self-centred and arrogant, takes after my Dad for sure. But he's not a bad listener for a bloke which I tell him is his only saving grace."

Alex nodded her agreement. "Definitely a rare breed. What about your parents?"

"My dad is also a journalist and travels all the time. He writes for a couple of broadsheets, but he's currently researching for his latest book. I think that's where Scott and I got the travel bug. Cancer took our mum when we were only five and Dad didn't cope well with it. Our Aunt Emily pretty much took over until we were old enough to go to boarding school. Initially, we were in Switzerland, then Edinburgh for our final years."

Alex rested a hand lightly on her arm. "I'm so sorry, Lori. That must have been awful for you both, losing your mum so young."

Lori took a deep breath and audibly swallowed, but Alex had heard the crack in her voice at mention of her mum. She stayed quiet allowing her the time to continue at her own pace.

"Ah, you know, it was me and Scott against the world. We looked out for each other and came out the other side in not too bad a shape." She smiled and glanced down at Alex's thumb gently rubbing back and forth on her arm.

"Sorry, got a bit maudlin there. I guess no one's asked me that question for a long time. I have a very small circle of people in my life that I talk to. I don't get out much."

Alex squeezed her arm, then got up to top up their coffee cups and add banana to the now thickened porridge. "No, I'm sorry for being so nosy," she said and handed one of the tins to Lori and sat back down, a little closer than before. "And I'm the queen of staying in so don't say that as if it's a bad thing. We can't all be social butterflies."

"You're right." Looking at Alex, she smiled gratefully. "I'm not sure why, Miss Ryan, but I have an urge to tell you all my secrets. In fact, the only thing stopping me is that I'm not sure you'd still like me if I did."

Alex cocked her head. "What? You mean under that sweet and innocent face there lurks a dark, maybe even naughty side?"

Lori played along, knowing Alex was trying to bring her out of her funk. "I'll never tell, so don't even try. You'll just have to keep wondering."

"Hmm, you don't play fair. Hinting at something like that and then not even giving me a story."

"It keeps me mysterious," she replied with an attempt at a brooding look.

"Okay I'm clearly not going to get anywhere with this so I give up for now. But just wait until I have a chance to get you drunk."

"I do believe that's twice in one day you've given up." Lori smirked, referring to Alex's cries of mercy just a short while ago.

Alex laughed and nudged her shoulder. "Come on, smart arse, and eat up so we can go fish."

CHAPTER 5

Once breakfast was finished, it didn't take long to pack up their belongings and change for the easy walk. With the fishing rod in hand, they followed a dirt track that would eventually bring them alongside a deeper, wider part of the same river Lori had crossed the day before. They'd been walking in silence, Lori not making conversation as her mind reeled over what had just happened in the bothy.

She'd become uncharacteristically self-conscious when she realised she'd have to get undressed in front of Alex. Lori'd turned her back and tried to hide at the end of the bunk while she exchanged her thermal sleeping clothes for regular underwear and light, waterproof layers.

Alex seemed to sense her discomfort and had turned away to get undressed. This wasn't what was bothering Lori. What bothered her was the fact that she'd peeked.

She'd bent down to put on her socks looking up just as Alex had pulled a light green T-shirt over her head. She caught a glimpse of creamy, smooth skin and the profile of one perfectly formed, braless breast, the nipple erect from the cold. It wasn't seeing this that had her reeling, she'd been in her fair share of women's changing rooms, it was the way it had made her feel and the overwhelming urge she'd had to reach out and touch her. To trace fingertips down her side, over her stomach—

"Lori? Hey!" Alex nudged her, bringing her back down to earth.

Her face flushed, as she stopped and pulled her backpack off. "Sorry, I keep doing that on you," she said, dropping it to the floor. Lori squatted down, still not looking at Alex. "My rucksack isn't sitting comfortably. Just give me a second to shift some things about."

She took a few deep breaths and made a show of removing and repacking some of her gear before hoisting the bag back up and adjusting the straps. She managed to calm herself enough to be able to look Alex in the eye again.

"Is everything okay?" Alex asked, a worried look on her face.

"Yes, of course. I'm sorry." Lori smiled. "Why don't you continue the grilling you started back at the bothy?"

"Okay, if you insist. I'll try not to upset you this time," she said with a reassuring half-smile.

"I'm sure you won't, go for your life."

"Right then, I have an obvious one which, hopefully, you'll find easy enough. What do you do to pay the bills?"

"Phew. That's an easy one." Lori grinned, dramatically wiping at pretend sweat on her forehead. "I'm an interpreter. I work for parliament in Westminster, but I do some freelance as well.

"Cool. What kind of freelance stuff?"

"Well, I took the tests a few years ago to get on the books at the European Parliament which takes me between Strasbourg, Brussels, and Luxembourg. I fill in at conferences and summits and sometimes accompany politicians or embassy officials to meetings, that kind of thing. I'd like one day to do some work with the UN in Geneva or, ideally, New York. People tell me how much money I could make with big businesses, particularly in Asia, but it doesn't interest me. I don't just want to translate. I want to be where the decisions are made that affect so much and so many of us. I want to be intrigued and feel something when I'm speaking the words, as if I'm having the conversation and I care, rather than relaying meaningless words. Do you understand what I mean?"

Alex nodded. "I think so. You don't want to be a machine or used as a search engine?"

"Exactly. And you shouldn't get me started on so called Internet translation tools. Touchy subject."

Alex held up a hand. "Noted. So why the UN? Are there no other organisations or charities?"

"I have done some work with charities. Mostly over summer holidays in medical centres abroad and I've taught English as a second language. But most of those don't offer long-term futures and you never feel quite settled. I've always had an interest in politics and working with the UN offers the best of both. But it's a pipe dream; jobs are so scarce and sought after, plus unfortunately, it seems to be about who you know when they do come about."

"Wow, well whatever you do, it sounds impressive. I imagine it's a job that could take you anywhere. And you should have a little faith in that pipe dream. They might be scarce but I'd defy anyone to turn you down." She smiled reassuringly and Lori appreciated the compliment.

"So how many languages do you speak?"

"Sechs."

Alex clearly recognising the language counted up on her fingers in German before holding up one open hand and a thumb. "Six!"

"Oui," she replied in French with a chuckle. "I speak all the official UN languages: French, Russian, Chinese, Arabic, and Spanish, and, of course, English, but I don't count that. I also speak German, which definitely comes in handy, and I get by in Italian. So, I guess that's six and a half."

"Now I know why you've no problem with my Scottish accent. You're a language genius."

Lori laughed, used to this reaction. "Yeah, I guess if you count a Scottish accent that makes it seven."

Alex looked at her in awe for a moment. "Well, Miss Hunter, you have thoroughly impressed me, and I don't impress easily."

"Ah, it's not so impressive. There are others out there who speak ten times as many as me. Some people's brains are wired for languages and I'm fortunate it was recognised at a young age and my family had the means to help me explore it." She shrugged. "Anyway, that's plenty about me. What do you do when you're not climbing mountains?" she asked, feeling her face go warm again from the attention.

The river had started to deepen and they both began scouting for a spot to set up. Frank was a dot in the distance, nose to the ground, taking advantage of his last hours of freedom before Alex put him back on his best behaviour. She had no worries about him out here. They were miles from any farmland and he was such a sweetheart, more likely to be chased by a cow or a sheep rather than the other way around. She used to worry about deer when he was younger, but it seemed Frank was in awe as much as she was when they passed through the Glen, stopping to watch them graze.

"Hmm, well as much as I hate to admit it, I'm a bit of a geek. Put me in front of a computer and you can lose me for days. But I'm also a fan of the outdoors, as you may have already guessed, so I have my hand in a couple of different things to try to strike a balance and keep things interesting."

"I'm intrigued, please do tell."

Alex pointed to a small clearing, down trodden where it had obviously been used as a fishing spot many times before. "Over there will be perfect." Once they reached it, Alex extended the pole, and baited the hook with one of a half dozen live worms she had in a small tub. Lori pulled out Frank's rolled up mattress, which had a waterproof base, and lay it on a low, flat rock for them both to sit on. After casting off, Alex joined her on the mat and propped the pole between her legs before continuing.

"Well, I did Computer Engineering at university without any real clue of what I wanted to get into when I finished. My best friend, Jess, is a social worker in Glasgow. Honestly she's the most unlikely social worker you'll ever meet. Anyway, she put me in touch with a police friend in the unit that investigates Internet crimes. It really grabbed my interest, the fact that I could make a difference in the world just with my computer. So now I consult with the police and National Crime Agency on a variety of operations, as well as freelancing for firms all over the world who develop cyber nanny programmes. There's a lot of work with social media sites, as you can imagine, and with that I've mostly been involved with child safety, but I've done a bit of work around human trafficking, stalking, cyber bullying, and fraud. Basically, anything illegal online."

"Now it's my turn to be impressed. That's sounds so rewarding. Do you get to see the results?"

"Aye, I have clearance to a certain level with the police and my contacts need to keep me in the loop on operations to help my work. When they've broken a ring or made a big bust, I'm always aware. And, of course, Jess gets involved when there are kids at risk who might be local to us so she tells me what she can. I play only a small part in something that is massive, but it helps a little at least."

"It must be hard, though, given the type of thing you're helping to investigate?"

"To be honest, I'm all about the technical side, following the electronic trail which can widen an investigation across countries with multiple authorities involved. These bastards know how to hide online, but, yeah, some of the stuff I come across and hear about is horrific. I couldn't deal with it day to day the way Jess does. In fact, I'm lucky that I get to work mainly from home, because I live out in the sticks and my other love is my home."

"Ah, this is the balance you talk about?"

"Yeah, I live on a small farm about thirty miles from Glasgow. I like to get my hands dirty so I keep a few animals and grow a variety of produce. It's just enough to keep myself and a couple of nearby village pubs stocked with seasonal vegetables for most of the year."

"That must take some work and I bet that fool over there is no help." Lori nodded in Frank's direction as he sniffed and yelped enthusiastically around a rabbit burrow.

"It's really not so bad. There's a couple who live a few miles away with a teenage son. He helps with the digging and deliveries for a few quid through the summer. Plus, two of my close friends aren't far and they keep any eye on the place if I want to head in to the city for a night. I also keep some chickens, and a goat that's daft as a brush and isn't averse to chasing Frank."

Lori laughed. "I wish you could see the image I have of Frank being licked all over by a goat."

"Oh, I've seen that for real. It's as funny as you're imagining, I'm sure."

"So you're a busy girl then?"

"You could say that, but I still manage the odd night out in the city. I've plenty of spare room so my friends escape out to the country with me some weekends to catch up over food and drinks. It's particularly fun on the one day of summer we get here in Scotland when we can get the barbeque out."

Lori laughed with her, recognising the perennial Scottish joke about the weather. "Have you been a farm girl for long or was it a wistful dream you made happen?"

"I've been on the farm all my life. It's been in the family for years. My mother loved horses and kept half a dozen in the stables. She ran a small riding school in the summer for local kids from the surrounding villages. She offered it cheap and they could ride, feed, and muck out until their hearts' content."

Lori smiled at the wistful look on her face as she remembered happy times.

"My dad preferred to be out in the field with the cows and sheep. We kept a healthy stock of noisy pigs, which were my favourite, especially as wee babies. I remember how distraught I was when a boy at school informed me the ham in my packed lunch was from pigs. I was so mad at him, and then at my parents."

"I can imagine you, red faced and indignant, arms crossed and stamping your feet."

"That's exactly how it went. I vowed never to eat pork again."

It was too much for Lori. "I can picture it now," she said and laughed. "How long did you last?"

"Well, I'm so pleased being fed Penelope the pig amuses you so much," she replied, lifting her chin in the air with indignation. "And I'll have you know I lasted a whole two weeks, until I realised pork was also bacon."

"Penelope? Are you serious? That's an amazing name for a pig."

"Aye, I named her after a bully of a girl in my primary two classes. It seemed fitting." She laughed along with Lori this time.

"My brother had a vegetarian stage in his dark, brooding teens, purely because it was cool. One day, my aunt Emily told him to hand over his leather jacket for the charity shop. If he wasn't going to eat animal meat, he wasn't allowed to wear its skin either. You should have seen the look of disgust on his face as he weighed up his choices. He was into motorbikes and never left the house without that jacket. The phase quickly passed."

"I'm surprised you city kids even knew what a cow looked like. I once met a girl, at University, from London who had never seen a sheep outside of a zoo. I honestly still don't think I'm over the shock of that."

"Cheeky." Lori nudged her with an elbow. "We did go to school in Switzerland for three years so I'm familiar with the odd farmyard animal."

Alex smirked. "Just checking."

"So if you live on the family farm, does that mean your family are still there too?"

The smile quickly slipped from Alex's face and she turned back to the water. Lori realised she'd asked the wrong question when Alex stood up without comment and absentmindedly reeled the line back in. She took her time to recast and avoided Lori's eye when she replied with a simple, "No."

It was clear this was a no-go area and Lori was certainly not going to pry, given her own past. If Alex wanted to share, she would. It was her story to tell when and with whom she wanted. Standing up next to her, Lori rested a hand on her shoulder and gave it a gentle squeeze in understanding. "No bites yet?" she asked, nodding toward the water.

"Thankfully not."

"I'm confused." Lori turned to her and raised an eyebrow. "I thought you were catching us lunch?"

"I'll be honest. I really just like the monotony of fishing. It's soothing and I do my best thinking just sitting, casting a line. In fact, I only really bother with worms so I don't look like a complete amateur if there are others around. I'm a big baby when I actually catch something."

Shaking her head, Lori chuckled. "So I guess we're having brown mush again for lunch then?"

CHAPTER 6

The old man woke with a cry. Drenched in sweat and breathing hard, panicking, while scanning the room. He felt the dimly lit room spin around him as the streetlight soaked through thin curtains.

He closed his eyes again, and furrowed his brow as the cloud moved quickly in. He chanced another look and realised it was a different room from the one he'd just been in. How did he get here so fast? Was the girl okay? He'd left before he had a chance to find out. He needed to know.

He called for his son, once, twice, but he didn't come. Perhaps he was still at the farm. He pushed himself up in the bed and tried to take in the unfamiliar surroundings blurred by poor vision.

Glasses. He needed his glasses. Sidling to the edge of the bed, he felt around for them on the nightstand while calling out again, louder, to his son. He jumped as his hand knocked something from the stand. It crashed loudly on the threadbare carpet, splashing him with its contents. Finally, laying his hands on his glasses he looked down at the spilt water. "Shit." His son would be mad.

He moved back in the bed when he heard heavy footsteps on the stairs. Finally, some help. The door swung open and the bare bulb in the hallway flicked on.

"For fuck's sake, old man, what mess are you making now?" His son pulled a towel from the hook on the back of the door and threw it onto the floor. Lazily treading on it to soak up the water.

"Sorry, I didn't have my glasses. I couldn't find them in this strange room. Where are we?"

His son's shoulders slumped. "For the last time, you stupid bugger. This is your room and has been for the last forty years."

The old man looked around again but the cloud wasn't clearing, save for the girl. "Is she all right? Did you bring her here?"

"Who are you on about now?" Picking up the fallen glass, he gave the towel a final rub across the burnt orange excuse for a carpet.

"The girl from the farm, of course. Did you bring her back here? She needed our help."

He watched as the glass flew across the room, smashing against the wall and bringing a picture down amongst the shards. In a flash, his son was over him. Eyes wide as he pushed his forehead against the old man's, forcing him back down into the pillow. He wrapped a hand around his throat and screamed, "What have I fucking told you about bringing up the girl? What have I fucking told you? Well?" Spittle flew from his son's mouth and splattered across his face.

He squirmed and tried to turn his head away whilst clawing at the large hand, but his head was pinned and his body paralysed with fear. "I...I..." He gasped and gulped for air, the pressure on his neck stopping any response.

The grip loosened and he managed to choke a breath before the hand swiped across his face, snapping his head to the side and his glasses to the floor.

Hot tears stung his eyes. He didn't understand. He just wanted to help.

"Jesus fucking Christ, are you going to cry?" His son picked up the glasses from the floor and threw them into his lap, shoulders sagging as he shook his head. "What the hell happened to my old man, eh?"

Shaking, the old man fumbled his glasses back on, determined not to put a hand to his cheek that was scorched with painful heat. "I'm sorry, son, I didn't know."

"That's right. You don't know anything and you don't ask any more questions. Got it?"

"Yes, yes, of course. If I could please just have some water?"

His son glanced at the damp patch on the carpet. "Get your own goddamn water. I'm going out."

He didn't move. Instead, he sat still and listened as his son moved around downstairs. He heard keys jangle and the front door close before a car finally pulled away.

He slid from his bed, then found slippers and a dressing gown.

He had to find the girl.

CHAPTER 7

After more coffee and the fish, thankfully, not biting, they packed up and continued the last few miles of their hike through the glen. Lori's mood was subdued and she could feel she wasn't the only one. Alex had gone quiet and she wondered if it was for the same reason. She was sorry it was Sunday, sorry that meant heading back to reality, and sorry they had to say good-bye so soon.

The track eventually brought them out onto a narrow country road which they crossed to a clearing in the woods that served as a small car park for climbers. Their cars were the only two there and Alex let out a low whistle when she saw Lori's BMW 3 Series convertible.

"Interpreting doesn't just pay the bills, I see."

It was an extravagance Lori indulged, telling herself that the time she saved in getting from London to Scotland on a regular basis by having such a fast car was worth the money.

"You can talk," she said, pointing to a nearly new Land Rover Defender.

"Hey, I own a farm. It's practically the law to own a Land Rover," Alex quipped while laughing.

They unloaded their rucksacks into the cars and Alex rounded Frank up, putting him in the back of the Land Rover. She cracked the window just enough for him to poke his nose out. She wandered over to the BMW where Lori was changing from chunky hiking boots to well-worn trainers more comfortable for the long journey.

Lori stood up out of the driver seat then leant back against the car, eyeing Alex who was looking distractedly at her feet. She didn't want this to be the last time she saw Alex. She had meant what she said about feeling like they would be good friends and she knew this wasn't meant to be good-bye.

She was about to speak when Alex looked up from her feet as if suddenly struck with inspiration. Tilting her head as if sizing Lori up, she looked her dead in the eye, and stroked her chin in the same mischievous way she had that morning.

"So, about that dark and naughty side of yours? I'm not quite sure I believe you have one."

Lori raised an eyebrow, playing along, "And what makes you think that?"

Alex looked at her knowingly, flashing that dimple again. "Your face is much too innocent and honest. I don't think you have it in you to take a risk."

"Oh, you don't think so."

"I don't. You're going to have to prove it."

"And how might you suggest I do that?" Lori replied, surprising herself with the hint of suggestion in her voice.

Alex stepped forward into her space, effectively pinning her against the car.

Lori felt her heartbeat pick up pace, taken aback at having Alex so close without warning. Yes, she'd admitted to herself that Alex was attractive and had enjoyed the friendly flirting, but Lori was straight and on the rebound, there couldn't be anything more than friendship between them.

Yet here they were and suddenly it wasn't so innocent.

"It's simple," Alex whispered, tilting her head up to stare into Lori's eyes again.

Lori couldn't tear her gaze away and realised she wasn't the only one feeling the effects of their closeness. She could feel the heat radiating off Alex, hear the quick, short breaths she took as her eyes searched Lori's. Was she searching for reassurance that this wasn't a one-sided thing?

Alex raised her hand, placing it lightly on Lori's chest. The smile that appeared told Lori she had found her answer in the form of her pounding heart.

"What's simple?" she whispered back. Glancing down at Alex's lips, she waited for a response. She realised how close they were to hers, plump and red from the cold.

"Don't let this be good-bye."

The intensity of the moment, and the emotion that came with it, overwhelmed Lori. She slid sideways against the car, moving away from Alex and breaking the spell. The look of disappointment on Alex's face was hard to miss. She quickly reached for one of her hands and tried for a reassuring smile.

"Are you sure you mean that? I mean, after the embarrassment of losing to me in a tickle fight, I thought you'd want to be well rid of me."

"Are you kidding? That's one of the reasons I want to see you again. I need an opportunity for payback." She looked at the ground again somewhat sheepishly. "Also I don't mind admitting, I'm strangely drawn to you and I'd like, in the very least, to call you a friend. I might have been tipsy, but my whisky-brain does remember you prophesising that last night." Her hand squeezed Lori's and it felt reassuring.

"Plus," she continued, "it's been a long time since I've met someone so interesting. Although chickens and goats aren't much competition."

"Oi!" Lori popped her on the arm. "Don't forget I can take your short arse down."

"So is that a yes?" replied Alex while rubbing her arm in mock hurt. "In the name of friendship, can I please have your number?"

Lori reached into the car and produced her mobile phone. "Sure. You can even have my e-mail too."

"Wow, aren't I privileged," Alex said with a giggle, then pulled her phone out of her pocket.

They swapped numbers and e-mail addresses, and both leaned back against the car and stared into the woods. Lori wasn't ready to part but was unsure what else to say.

She felt Alex's hand creep into hers again, linking their fingers together when they met no resistance.

Lori looked down at their hands. She couldn't remember the last time Andrew had offered such a simple show of affection. She wasn't quite sure how they'd gone from solo hikers sharing a bothy to holding hands in the space of a day. But she had a long drive ahead of her to think about it, so, for now, she just went with it.

As if reading her thoughts Alex broke the quiet. "I guess you better hit the road. You've a long journey ahead."

"Yeah, you're probably right. Early start tomorrow morning."

Alex stepped away from the car and turned to stand in front of her. She smiled and squeezed Lori's hand again before reluctantly releasing it. "So...I guess I'll speak to you soon?" she said, starting to walk backward to her own car.

"Wait." Lori reached out and grabbed her hand back. "Where I come from we hug our friends good-bye."

She didn't hesitate to envelop Alex in her arms, feeling hers slip around her waist and gently tighten. Lori took a deep breath to calm the butterflies going crazy again at the close contact, closed her eyes, and held on a little longer. Alex didn't seem to mind.

Finally, Lori pulled back, holding Alex at arm's length and she saw the same look of wonder in her face that she was sure had just crossed her own.

"As my dad always used to say, it's not good-bye, just see you later. Although I'm sure he stole that line from somewhere."

Alex smiled at that, both dimples appearing.

She got into her car without another word and, with a wave to Alex still standing in the same spot, turned out onto the road toward home.

CHAPTER 8

Alex jumped down from the Land Rover to open the gate that led to her farm. She let Frank out of the car, knowing he would enjoy running the last half mile home after four hours of being cooped up.

Normally, she would have had the music up, singing at the top of her voice while he yelped and howled along. Not today. She hadn't been much fun and he'd quickly gone to sleep.

She couldn't stop thinking about Lori. It was as simple as that. She kept glancing at her hand while it held the wheel and she would swear she could still feel Lori's thumb caressing the back of it.

She smacked the wheel and swore. Lori was straight and she was also straight out of a relationship. It might have been with a guy who, to be honest, sounded like an arrogant dick. But he was still a guy, and she had loved him. Alex was sure there would be a string of guys waiting to take his place.

Maybe being there for her at such an emotional time, just to listen and comfort her, had confused something for Lori. She'd heard her friends joke many a time after a break up that they wished they were lesbians because men were arseholes, only to call the next week telling her about the latest male love of their lives.

She chastised herself. Since when did she start assigning labels? Attraction can't be reasoned with or named. Besides, how well did she really know her? So what if she hadn't confessed to any previous Sapphic adventures. Maybe that meant she shouldn't assume.

She thought about Jess and how proud she'd be of her and what was going through her head right now. Rather than predicting future demise and running for the hills before anything even had a chance to begin, like she'd being doing ever since Rachel, she was talking herself into a potential mess.

What was it Jess always said? Break it down to its simplest form? Alex made a mental list of the positives that she knew about the situation.

She was single. So was Lori. They'd exchanged numbers. There was a definite connection which she knew they had both felt.

Alex thought about the intensity with which her body responded just being close to Lori, she hadn't wanted to let go, the urge to protect and be there for her was overwhelming. Add to that the undeniable fact she was beautiful. And ridiculously smart, and funny, and sensitive, and her touch made Alex's skin hum.

That was it. There was no way Alex could let this pass her by. She was a stronger person now, in charge of her own life and happiness. She could handle this.

Resolved to take control and make the first move, she let herself into the house, turned off the alarm, and pulled out her mobile phone.

A couple of hours from home, Lori saw her phone light up and vibrate on the passenger seat; Alex's name appeared across the screen. She glanced at the clock and smiled. Six hours. That's how long it had taken for Alex to call. She was impressed. Especially given she'd had a four-hour journey of her own to make.

She let it go to voicemail, not wanting their first phone call to be shouted through a terrible Bluetooth connection. The ping announcing a message shot a surprising wave of excitement through her. Such a small thing. Scary, but somehow full of possibility at the same time. She pressed her foot on the accelerator, the flashing message light propelling her home.

CHAPTER 9

Home at last, Lori threw her rucksack into a hallway cupboard. It could wait to be unpacked. The message light on her home phone was flashing so she hit the *play* button to listen whilst stripping off layers of clothing getting ready for a long overdue shower.

"You have eight new messages," the machine told her. Lori groaned because she knew who the majority would be from.

"Message one: Lori its Andrew. Listen I hate the way we left things last night. I know we both said some things we didn't mean. Let's talk about it. Please call me."

She sighed as she kicked off her trainers and when the option came, pressed delete. She'd meant every word and wasn't about to take anything back, including Andrew.

"Message two: Lori, me again. I don't know if you're away or not. I tried your mobile, but it seems to be off so I stopped by but you weren't home. I hope you aren't avoiding me. I just want to talk. Call me."

She had told him she was going away so this only confirmed her accusation that he never listened to her.

"Message three: Lori, please don't be like this. We're both adults here aren't we? I hit a crappy round on the course this afternoon, I was so distracted..."

Delete. Was he kidding?

"Message four: Lori, you need to..." Delete.

"Message five: Lori, why are you..." Delete.

The next two messages were also Andrew, getting more and more flustered that she hadn't called back. She was pretty certain he was drunk in them both. It was his own doing. If he'd paid attention he would have known she'd be unreachable this weekend, saving himself the childish tantrum he'd finally worked himself up to in his last message.

Well, he could stew. His barrage of messages and lack of thought that she might just need some time to think had well and truly nailed the coffin containing their relationship shut.

"Message eight: Hey, sweetie, it's Stella. I know you're away and won't get this until late tonight, but I just wanted to let you know I'm thinking about you and I hope that mountain air helped clear your head and give you some perspective. I've got court tomorrow afternoon, but it shouldn't take more than a couple of hours, so expect me on your doorstep around six. Make sure there's wine. Love you, bye."

Smiling at her best friend's presumptuousness, she was happy that at least one person listened to her. Well, two now if she included Alex.

Alex! She suddenly remembered the voicemail on her mobile and scrambled through the layers she'd just taken off to find her phone.

"You have one new message. Message one: Hey Lori. It's Alex. Um, so, I know you're still driving, at least I hope you are and not just ignoring my call." Lori chuckled hearing Alex's nervous laugh "Or maybe you gave me a fake number. Damn that would be disappointing, and a little embarrassing given how awkward I'm being right now. Anyway, I wanted to say again what a great weekend I had and I hope you get home safely. Maybe you could give me a call sometime in the week? Okay. So, hopefully speak to you soon. Bye."

Lori smiled all the way to the shower. Her thoughts of the weekend and Alex running through her head as the powerful spray pounded her tired muscles with hot water.

She wrapped thick towels around her head and body and then grabbed her mobile from the hall before falling exhausted onto her bed. It was after midnight, so probably too late to call and, besides, she was tired to the bone.

Deciding to save her first call to Alex until the following day and wanting to let Stella know she was home okay, she instead sent a couple of texts so neither would worry.

> Hey Alex, that's me home and mud free at last! Thought I'd put you out of your misery, you have the right number! Can't say I'm not disappointed you waited a whole 2 hours after you got home to call though...ha-ha! Anyway, I'll call you tomorrow. Sleep well. Lori x

> Stella, you're a sweetheart. Thanks for your message. It made up for the previous seven I got from Andrew. Anyway, we can dissect that tomorrow if you want, but I'd much rather tell you about my interesting weekend and the person I shared it with! Bring food x

She set her alarm and was about to put the phone on the nightstand when it pinged back at her twice in quick succession.

> Phew! Glad you're home safely and I didn't just leave that voicemail for Jim Smith in Manchester. Looking forward to chatting tomorrow. Sweet dreams, Alex x PS. You're right, two hours of dialling and hanging up again is clearly too long. I'll do my best not to disappoint you again! X

> Tease! I'm intrigued. Sod food, I'll bring extra wine. S x

Laughing at the pair of them, her mind started going over the events of the weekend again. Meeting Alex had been unexpected, but she couldn't deny it had made the trip better than she could have imagined. She thought of Andrew, the messages, his anger towards her. She tried imagining what he was doing right now and let her hand drift to his empty side of the bed.

She didn't need the light to see all the things surrounding her that held memories of their past seven years together. The photos of them, pink cheeked and excited, about to do their first black run together in the Alps. There was her favourite one of Andrew in the early days, windswept, tanned, and handsome, tugging at the jib line, and grinning her way on their sail around the Greek Islands. A small, carved box held shells and pieces of coral from every beach they'd ever been to. Even the lamp on her bedside table had come from an antique shop in Italy. She'd fallen in love with the lamp and he had gone back to get it for her as a surprise.

Feeling the loss in the pit of her stomach she knew she would miss him for a while to come. She didn't relish the idea of dealing with Andrew and the fallout of their relationship, but it had to be a priority until everything was sorted. Lori wasn't a cruel person and he was hurting. They shared a past and he deserved her time and understanding. Hopefully they could be grown up about it and maybe find a way to help each other move on, or at least not do anything to make things more difficult than they needed to be.

Trying to shake the sadness off, her mind drifted back to Alex. She had few people in her life to call important and certainly wasn't used to new people walking into her life and finding herself develop feelings for them. The feeling of warmth that spread through her as she pictured Alex's smiling face felt good, if a little confusing. What it meant, she couldn't comprehend right now. She was exhausted not just in body, but emotionally too. She held onto the feeling, pulling a spare pillow towards her and wrapping her arms around it for comfort, with Alex's face fixed in her mind, she let sleep claim her.

Sleep didn't come quickly to Alex so she gave up trying. She slipped out of bed and pulled on thick socks before padding through the farmhouse. Frank snored by the dying embers of the fire and didn't stir as she filled a glass with water.

The oven clock shone 2.03 am.

She glanced toward the shelf full of whisky, and considered it seriously. Not helpful. She sighed and ducked through the low archway that led to her music room before she could change her mind about the alcohol.

It hadn't always been only hers. A beautiful, smiling face looked out from a picture nearby on a shelf. It never failed to raise a smile, followed by a heavy heart.

She took the photo with her to the largest of the comfy chairs, curling up under a tartan throw she pulled from its back. She traced the smiling girl's face, a face she knew better than her own, before propping the picture on the small side table. Beth. Her talented, beautiful, and hilarious little sister.

Beth had spent countless nights sleeping in that very chair, a habit after practicing whatever instrument took her fancy that day or reading late into the night. It had become one more in a list of fateful choices that had led to her death.

Alex closed her eyes as memories overwhelmed her, bringing with them their inevitable conclusion. Emptiness, anger, tears. She wiped furiously at her eyes, frustrated at her inability to break the cycle, before gulping at the water until calmness returned.

Frank padded in. She would have normally kicked him out to his bed with Pedro in the barn, but he'd looked so cosy by the fire she didn't have the heart. He was obviously feeling safe about being allowed to stay inside now given the time of night.

Frank stretched out underneath her and she gently scratched around his ears. His gentle snoring started again, lulling her and dragging her thoughts back to Lori. She imagined Beth meeting Lori, instantly mimicking her accent and being secretly jealous she lived in 'the big city' that was London. She would insist that Lori listen to a Ryan sisters' duet, maybe even trying to impress her by singing in French.

She wondered what they would think of each other. Actually, she didn't have to wonder. She knew.

She squinted through her drooping lids and smiled again at Beth's picture. "Yeah I know, smart arse. Whatever's going on here, I'll try not to mess it up."

CHAPTER 10

He stood at the end of the street, looking back and forth. Each road looked identical with the same box houses on both sides and family cars in the driveways. Headlights came from the right and forced him to turn his back on them and head left. He was sure this was the way.

The rain had eased but it still soaked through his flimsy slippers. Ignoring this and pushing his hands deep into his dressing gown pockets he dropped his head against the chill. Cars sped both ways intermittently, their occupants seemingly oblivious to the old man walking the street in his pyjamas. Safe in their warm metal boxes, while he was merely a shadow on the pavement.

He reached another cross section and stopped. A gust blew him sideways and he jumped as a hedge caught his sleeve, sure it was someone grabbing him. He untangled himself and paused. It seemed late; dark and quiet on the roads. He felt his wrist and was irritated to find no watch. Closing his eyes he tried to picture where it might be. Should he go back for it?

A hooded figure approached from the opposite direction, head down against the wind. It was too short to be his son, but he hid anyway. He pinned himself against a garden gate, and peered around the edge of its fir lined garden watching until the figure turned away from him down an alley.

Something touched his leg. He instinctively kicked out, sorry to see it was only a cat. It hissed at him and his attention was drawn by its nametag glinting in the streetlight. His breath caught, a memory invaded his senses and from the corner of his eye, a hand was being raised, knife held firm in it. It swiftly plunged down silently until the dull thud of it meeting flesh vibrated in his ears. He cried out, raising his arm above his head as protection. The cat hissed again and he opened his eyes. There was no one else there. The knife was gone. He heard whimpering and it took him a moment to realise it was coming from him.

Beth. He needed to keep moving, needed to get to the farm to help her.

He reached a better lit area. The lights from a glass shop door illuminated its car park beyond, and beckoned him in. He looked left and right again, before crossing the road carefully, hopeful that someone inside could help with directions to the farm.

A young girl behind the counter glanced up from her magazine at the sound of the door beeping. Her eyebrows rose as she looked him up and down. He felt the cold set in as he became aware of what he was wearing. "You all right, love?"

He liked her smile. He was sure she would help. "I'm looking for the farm. I'm sure it's not far but I've lost my way."

She stood up and leaned over the counter towards him, he watched the smile slip and wondered if she knew what had happened. "And what farm is that? Got to be a load around these parts?"

He saw her reach for her phone and his own smile fell. She was calling his son. He knew it. He backed away, his feet barely reacting to his commands as he bumped into a shelf.

He rubbed his wrist where he wished his watch was. "You know what, its okay. I'm sure I'll find it. Thanks anyway."

Someone touched his shoulder, and he jumped, wheeling around to face them. "John?"

He retreated further, lashing out in panic, knocking a display over and losing a slipper. He needed to get away from the woman who had touched him, but the girl was on his side of the counter now, taking his elbow and shushing him. He glared at the woman who knew his name. It was that neighbour woman his son always had spy on him when he went on trips.

"John, what are you doing out here in your pyjamas?"

He hung his head. He knew he was getting no further tonight. "Please don't tell him. Please. He mustn't know I was out."

But she wasn't listening. She was already shepherding him out into the car park, into her car, pulling the seatbelt across his chest. He looked up as the shop girl watched through the window and he pleaded with his eyes to be saved.

His heart thumped as the buckle clunked in place. He'd been stupid to stop and now he would pay the consequences.

He felt like a naughty child being handed back to their parents after running away. His son kept his expression fixed, not allowing the neighbour woman to see past his mask to the anger John knew would be simmering.

John listened, head bowed as his son took the admonishment for letting him out of his sight. "He's not a well man, Mr Murray. You really should consider getting more help."

His son nodded but didn't speak, apart from a terse "Ta." once she'd said her piece.

As the door closed he shuffled back towards the stairs, pinned by his son's stare he dared not turn his back.

It took three strides before a meaty hand had a fistful of pyjamas and was pulling him up so only his tiptoes remained on the ground. His glasses steamed as his son breathed heavily in his face.

"What the fuck do you think you're playing at, old man?"

"I'm sorry. I'm sorry. I lost my watch. I went to find it." He could think of no other explanation.

The hand spun him into a tight head lock. Choking in surprise and clawing at his son's shoulder to no avail, he kicked out with his feet, trying to find some traction as his body was dragged up the stairs like a rag doll. He cried out as his hip caught the spindles of the banister, but it only made the grip around his neck tighten.

White spots appeared in his vision and he made a final gasp for air before feeling the wonderful release of his neck, leaving him on his knees inside his bedroom doorway.

Down on all fours, he greedily gulped at the air, willing his vision to clear but realising his glasses had been lost in the struggle.

He glanced up at the dark outline of his son's shadow in the doorway, willing it to be over.

"You and me are done, old man. Get in the fucking bed and don't move until I say you can."

He nodded and crawled toward his bed. He only dared to look up again as the door slammed shut.

CHAPTER 11

Monday flew by for Lori, who'd found herself surrounded by an avalanche of documents that needed to be translated for an upcoming conference. It meant a day hiding out in her office with plenty of scope for daydreaming.

No sooner had she closed her front door and kicked off her shoes when the bell rang to announce Stella's arrival.

"Sweetheart! Come here." Lori opened the door, and her friend enveloped her in a warm hug. Wine bottles clinked in her large handbag.

"I thought you were joking about the extra wine," she said while stepping back to let Stella pass into the hallway.

"When have I ever joked about wine?" She gave Lori one of her stern policewoman looks. "I plan on drinking the majority anyway because, honestly, Lori, this case is killing me."

"Well, maybe if you actually took a day off?" she scolded.

"You're the one joking now. I've forgotten what one of those holiday thingies is. I've at least allowed myself an extra hour in bed tomorrow to sleep the wine off, so it's not all bad I guess."

"Do you want to talk about it?"

"Not even a tiny bit. Now lead the way."

They moved through to the kitchen where Stella dumped her coat and bag before kicking off her shoes and getting comfortable on a stool at the large granite-topped island. Lori set about getting glasses and opening the first bottle of wine. She poured two large glasses and set them and the bottle down on the counter.

"Hungry?" she asked, opening her fridge to the sorry sight of jam, pickled onions, and some rather bendy sticks of celery.

"Don't panic, pizza's already on its way. I called from the taxi en route."

Lori chuckled as the bell rang again. "Speaking of which," she said and went to collect the pizza.

"How come the deal is you always order and I always pay?" she asked when she returned to the kitchen with a large, steaming box.

"Let's see," Stella said as she stroked her chin, "because you, my dear, are loaded whilst I only earn a paltry detective's salary. You must know by now, I'm only friends with you for your money." She winked, picking up both of their now full glasses. "C'mon, let's go get comfy on that oversized, expensive sofa of yours. I'm dying to hear all about your weekend."

Lori wasn't really sure where to begin once they were settled on the sofa. She'd tried to put Alex out of her head all day, immersing herself in document after document. But she'd failed miserably, finding herself on more than one occasion staring out of the window and wondering what Alex was doing, where she was, and who she was with.

It didn't help that she'd had two texts from her. Just a friendly good morning, hope you're not too sore after the weekend and, later, another to say she had to head into Glasgow and wouldn't be back until after ten o'clock that night, in case Lori was planning to call.

She'd been relieved at the second one, thinking talking things through with Stella might help before she got in any deeper. The picture of Alex's grinning face popped into her head.

"So come on." Stella snapped her fingers in front of Lori's face. "Let's get Andrew out of the way first. What on earth happened?"

Lori took a sip of wine before giving the simple answer, "I guess I just fell out of love with him. That's assuming I ever really loved him in the first place."

"Well that was obvious," Stella replied, eyebrows furrowed. "I mean, your relationship with Andrew seemed to suit you, however dull it was. But I have to say it's been a long time since it gave off the warm and fuzzy vibe."

Lori stretched out a leg and poked her in the ribs with a toe. "Oi! Don't be mean. Andrew is a good guy and ticked all the boxes, handsome, successful, committed, safe..."

"Self-centred, tedious, manipulative, jealous," Stella finished for her, feigning a yawn.

Lori shook her head but couldn't help but laugh. "Okay, yes, he was boring and possessive. Still there was a time I saw my future with him and now that's all up in the air and he's been constantly calling begging me to take him back."

Mid-gulp, Stella pretended to choke for effect. "Don't tell me you're considering going back to him?"

"No. Well, maybe." Stella glared at her. "Okay, no. You're right. He's just been such a big part of my life for so long. It's strange to imagine not having him around and I still remember the good times, I miss him. Even the self-obsessed, pretentious side of him."

Stella threw up her free hand and chuckled. "Finally, she sees it!"

Lori tutted. "Some friend you are. I mean, you could have told me sooner how he was. Saved me some time."

"Um, I think you'll find I told you at every opportunity. But no one likes their friends telling them their boyfriend is a miserable arse, so it's just taken you seven years to bloody listen." She gestured to the table. "And now I'm here with pizza and wine ready to help you pick up the pieces. I'm a fantastic friend." She got up to top up her glass, bringing the bottle back with her from the kitchen.

"So anyway, I'm bored even talking about Andrew and I'm not allowing you to wallow over it. Tell me about your weekend and this mysterious person."

Lori sighed, a smile automatically forming at the thought of Alex. "Well, firstly the climb was spectacular. I couldn't believe the views from the summit. Honestly, you need to come with me sometime."

"Never going to happen so stop teasing me, you can show me a picture. Who is he and how did you meet? At least give me a name."

"Alex," Lori replied, not quite ready to correct Stella on her assumption it was a man.

"And..." Her eyes widened expectantly; she wanted more.

"Okay, well I had planned on staying in this little bothy that the guide had mentioned was at the foot of the first mountain I climbed on the Saturday. It was empty when I got there, but by the time I got back down, Alex and Frank— Frank is the dog—had claimed the other bed so we ended up sharing it for the night." Lori smiled again, her thoughts drifting back to the previous couple of days.

Stella, obviously noticing the wistful look, exclaimed, "Oh my God! Something happened!"

Lori snapped back to it, "What? No! It was just a great weekend. We had a good laugh together, talked a lot, and I think we'll be friends. We've exchanged numbers and agreed to keep in touch, but I don't see how it can be anything more than that."

"And why is that?"

"Well, for a start, there's the distance. We live four hundred miles apart."

"That doesn't stop you when it comes to climbing a mountain. This is the age of technology and plenty of people make long-distance relationships work until they're in a position to settle together."

"We're just different, Stella. I live in the city, Alex lives on a farm in the country. I travel all over for work, Alex works from home. Alex has a ton of pets and animals and I don't even keep a goldfish."

"Wow, a farm in the country and a job working from home? That sounds amazing to me. Anyway, I thought you eventually wanted to get out of London? I thought that's why you escape to Scotland every chance you get for the quiet?" She gave a look that Lori was sure many of London's criminals had been on the receiving end of. "There's more to this. Come on, Lori, do you really think you can hide anything from me?" She said quirking a perfectly shaped eyebrow.

"I just think it's too soon after Andrew. I mean, I only ended it Thursday night. I need time to deal with him first." She looked down into her wine glass. "I'm not ready for this. I'm not prepared." She finished quietly.

She felt Stella's eyes on her and Lori knew she was wondering what the catch was. Why she was holding back.

"Please, Lori. You and Andrew have been over for a long time. He already knew it, which probably explains his jealous behaviour, checking your phone, the constant calls about nothing when you're out with anyone that isn't him. If he's honest he's been waiting for the day you'd leave him. It was just a matter of when you split up, not if. All jokes aside about him, because actually he's probably going to make someone else very happy, and you're right that he is a good bloke, just not the one for you. So forget him for now, this is about you."

Stella leant across to take her hand. "Lori, you deserve to be happy. You deserve to be safe and loved and taken care of and excited. If you've found someone you think there might be a chance of having that with, don't let what happened with Andrew get in the way. Don't make excuses as to why it can't work before you've even given it a chance. Sure the timing is off but I'm not suggesting you go jump into bed with the first guy you meet, only that you at least allow yourself to consider it."

"It's not that simple." Lori replied, getting up and pacing in front of the large fireplace. She chewed her lip in thought. She stopped her pacing to grab the bottle and top up her wine while deciding how much to admit. "I've never met anyone like Alex before, Stella. I can't explain the feeling I get inside just sitting close together, never mind touching. It was all so surreal."

"So there was touching," Stella said a knowing smirk on her face.

Lori glared down at her. "It wasn't like that."

"Okay, okay." She held her hands up in surrender. "Carry on, oh serious one."

"It's as if after all these years of being part of a couple with a clear direction and future, I've been set adrift. So many things are uncertain now. For the first time since I met Andrew, I'm not sure of myself or where I'm going."

"So someone finally gives you those butterfly feelings and you're not even going to give it a chance?" Stella sat forward on the sofa and emptied the last of the wine into her glass before choosing the largest slice of pizza.

"I'm scared, Stella." She hated showing her vulnerability, but if not to Stella, then who?

The pizza stopped in its tracks. Stella let it drop back in the box before smiling reassuringly. "I know you are, darling. It's a big, bad world out there. Believe me, I see it every day. None of us knows who or what is going to come along next. All I know is if I'm lucky enough to meet someone that has me speaking like you after one weekend, I'm going to grab on and never let go."

"But what if I'm wrong?"

"You can't think like that. What if you're right but you let it pass you by because you're too afraid of being wrong? Tell me more about Alex, have you had any contact since you got back?"

Lori smiled and sat on the arm of the chair opposite Stella, thinking about the voicemail and how cute Alex sounded when she was nervous. "Yeah, I had a voicemail waiting when I got home last night and a couple of texts since then."

"Wow, so he's keen. What else?"

"Yeah, I guess. Why do I feel like you're interrogating me?"

"This is what I do, sweetie. I need the facts before I can make an informed opinion." She put her wine down and formed a steeple with her fingers. "C'mon, tell Detective Roberts everything."

Lori took a large gulp of wine, wondering how to explain without giving away the fact that Alex was a woman. She didn't want that to be a consideration just yet in Stella's advice, besides she needed to figure out herself how she felt about that.

"Okay, well, I told you about the farm, growing vegetables and keeping chickens and a goat."

"So is that the job working from home? He's a farmer?"

"Computer engineer," Lori corrected. "For the police, specialising in Internet crimes, mostly the protection of children. The farming is more of a hobby and a way to keep sane, I think."

"Wow, so he's clever. That's a great way to use those kinds of skills. I work with people like him and they do a lot of good. But that's all immaterial. I'm interested in the touchy feely stuff, not his bank balance. Come on, there must be more to him to put that smile on your face."

Lori slid down into the armchair and thought for a moment. She had only spent twenty-four hours with Alex but had already got an insight into the kind of woman she was.

"Hmm, let's see. Alex is...genuine. There's no bullshit. Just an honest, compassionate person, who happens to be gorgeous, and have a wicked sense of humour. Oh and did I mention the outrageous flirting?" She laughed at Stella's raised eyebrows. "What?"

"Lori, the way you're talking about this guy, I really don't see the problem. In fact, I think I've had enough wine to be honest with you. Do you want me to tell you what I really think?" she challenged, sitting forward in her seat.

Lori glanced at Stella's already empty glass. "Go ahead and enlighten me." She sat back in her chair, crossing her arms, already defensive. She'd heard more than one of Stella's 'honest' proclamations after a few glasses of wine. Though to be fair, she was normally right.

"I think for too long you've hidden behind your tick boxes."

"My wha—"

"Shh!" Stella held a finger up to silence her. "You know what I'm talking about. They're superficial and meaningless and completely irrelevant when it comes to love. You've continued to lie to and undervalue yourself and pretend they are the things that matter."

She kept her finger raised, continuing. "You've been plodding along with Andrew and wasting your time. You're worried that if you have a list of real qualities you want in a partner, you might actually find someone who has them. And scarier still puts you first for a change. We both know what you're really scared of is getting too close to someone who matters because you think they'll eventually abandon you like your no-good father and brother." She took a deep breath and waited for the defensive onslaught, but Lori was quiet.

Stella took the opportunity to retrieve the second bottle of wine, leaving her to stew.

Lori chewed on the inside of her lip again and looked up as Stella came back into the room. "You're right."

"I'm sorry. Can you say that again?" Stella sighed with relief and moved to squeeze into the armchair beside her, putting an arm around her shoulders.

"You're right. I have an ingrained list of things my father always told me to expect from a partner. I might be old enough and ugly enough now to know he was a terrible father but when I was young, I'd take any little crumb of advice he offered. And what Andrew offered was basically someone the opposite of him. Safe. Dependable."

Stella stroked her hair. "Ah, my sweet Lori. So naive."

"I guess I found that quite quickly in Andrew and it has taken me this long to realise there was always something missing." She turned to look at Stella. "I guess it was real love."

"That old chestnut called love." Stella sighed again. "It sounds to me as if you may have at least found the beginnings of something worth exploring. It doesn't have to be your one great love, but don't let Andrew or your father or something as silly as geography get in the way of at least having some fun finding out."

"I know. I guess I have some things to figure out."

"Well, first things first, have you called him back?"

"No, the last text said to call after ten o'clock."

Stella glanced at her watch. "Brilliant. We've still got time for that second bottle of wine."

CHAPTER 12

Alex glanced at the dashboard clock for about the twentieth time, conscious as she bumped along the country road that it was nearing quarter past ten. She was hoping Lori would call and didn't want to miss it.

She'd tried to keep her text casual sounding, not wanting her to feel pressured into calling that night. If Lori had taken any feelings for her away from their weekend, then Alex knew she was probably feeling as confused as she was and the last thing she wanted was to rush things and scare her off. She was a little scared too, so slow and tentative worked for her.

She braked for the sharp corner, then glanced in her mirror at Frank who was sleeping spread out in the back seat. "A lot of bloody good you are to me tonight, dog."

It was dead on quarter past ten when she finally headed down her driveway. She juggled her phone and keys, not wanting to miss it if Lori called. The phone rang just as she unlocked the back door and reset the alarm.

She took a deep breath and smiled. "Hello, you," she said into the handset.

"Bonsoir," replied Lori, the happiness in her voice obvious.

"Show off," Alex laughed. "I'm glad you called. I thought maybe it would be too late."

"No, it's fine. My friend Stella's only just left. She polished off the better part of two bottles of wine and one large pizza.

All the while, laying into Andrew and grilling me about my weekend. It was fun."

Alex chuckled. "Sounds it." Then she realised Lori mentioned a grilling about the weekend. "So did you tell her you'd met a devastatingly pretty Scottish girl?" she asked, mischief in her voice.

It was Lori's turn to laugh. "Hmm, you may have come up. Though, I wasn't quite ready to share every detail with her."

"Like the small detail that I'm a woman?" Alex tried to keep her voice light to hide her slight disappointment.

Lori was quiet. "Yeah, well you know, your name works as a bloke's name and she assumed. I just didn't know what to say and there are so many things going round in my head right now. I don't want her judging me about something that might not be..."

"Whoa! Whoa! Lori, slow down. Take a breath, it's all right."

"It is? What is?" Her voice was small.

"Listen to me. Let's clear the air about this right now. I had a great time with you this weekend and I'd love to get to know you better. But let's not put pressure on ourselves. I understand there are huge changes going on in your life what with Andrew and all, that's a massive chapter coming to a close. The last thing I want to do is add to that. I'd rather be here for you as a friend. An unrelated outsider to the whole situation who promises not to say I told you so. I'll be in charge of fun and taking your mind off it and we'll see where it takes us. How does that sound?"

Lori was quiet so long that Alex would have thought she'd been cut off only for her quiet breathing. "That sounds perfect. Thank you."

"Hey, don't thank me. I'm being completely selfish here. I'll say anything to get you to come visit me again."

Lori laughed then, sounding more at ease. "Oh yeah, well, you know you do live where the mountains are. I guess I could swing by before my next climb."

"Swing by to pick me up?" Alex asked hopefully.

"Only if you bring Frank. I'm missing his kisses already."

Alex pictured Lori pinned on the floor by Frank not just once but twice. "I think that can be arranged. Although I have a bit of a different proposition for you that doesn't include mountains or a cold bothy if you're up for it?"

"I'm listening."

"My friend Susie is passing through this weekend on her way to Norway. She's my oldest friend from school and, despite being a pain in the arse sometimes, she's always kept in touch and I thought I'd have a little get together for her at the farm. Some of the guys are coming through from Glasgow to stay for the weekend and I thought you might enjoy it. We could maybe hit a hill on Sunday?"

Alex felt the nerves churn her stomach as she waited for Lori's response. Not only at the thought of seeing her again so soon, but also introducing her to her friends. "Yes. I'd love to!"

She was glad to hear the excitement in Lori's voice when she replied. "Really? Great, that's great. It'll be great."

Lori chuckled and Alex kicked herself for letting her nerves get the better of her again.

"Yes, I'm sure it'll be great," Lori reassured her. "So what's the plan? When do you want me?"

"It's entirely up to you. If you can get away early on Friday, you could come up then so you're rested for Saturday?

I've plenty of room. Otherwise, just be here by Saturday afternoon."

Alex hoped she'd take her up on the offer to arrive early when she realised the grin on her face was at the thought of seeing Lori as soon as Friday.

"I'll see what I can do about getting away Friday. Can I let you know later in the week?"

"Sure, of course." Alex relaxed a little. "Okay, well I guess I should let you get to bed, being a nine-to-five person and all."

"Rub it in, why don't you. Although, aren't farmers meant to be up with the sun?"

"Not this farmer. Why do you think I'm my own boss? I've trained Frank well enough to collect the eggs for my breakfast, then feed the other animals."

Lori laughed loudly. "You know I can actually imagine that. Does he wake you with the daily newspaper and breakfast in bed, as well?"

"What's so funny? I'm serious." Alex teased. "And you're only half right. I don't read the paper. It's too depressing."

"Wow. I need to get me a Frank. I don't remember the last time I was brought breakfast in bed."

"Score one for Frank. It's no wonder Andrew didn't make the grade." It slipped out before Alex could stop herself. "Sorry that was uncalled for, Lori. It's not for me to say things like that."

Lori chuckled.

Alex let out a breath of relief.

"Don't be sorry, Alex, you're right. Maybe if he'd taken a leaf out of Frank's book he'd still be around. Although, after the lecture I had from Stella tonight, I'm beginning to realise he probably could never have done enough for it to work."

"Phew." Alex let out a breath. "I'll remove my foot from my mouth, then. We can talk about that more when you get here, if you like."

"Sure, maybe. Anyway, I guess I had really better go before I talk myself into dreams of Frank bringing me breakfast in bed." She sighed at the thought. "Oh God, is that what my love life has been reduced to?"

Alex tutted. "Hey, don't diss the Frank. Trust me, there are worse dreams to have."

"Oh really? Like what?"

"Well, for one, I have this reccurring dream where I'm in that episode of Tom and Jerry when they're at a bowling alley..."

Lori cracked up. "You're a nut."

"It's been said once or twice."

"I'm going now."

"Okay, goodnight, Lori. Sleep well."

"Goodnight, Alex. Wish Frank goodnight, as well."

"I will. Oh and one other thing, Lori."

"Yes?"

"I'm excited about seeing you again," she said softly.

"Me too." She could sense Lori's smile.

"Sweet dreams, Alex."

Chapter 13

He could hear keys fumbling in the lock before the front door finally opened, crashing and bouncing violently against the hallway wall. Another bang told him it had been kicked shut with the heel of a heavy boot.

It was a pattern of noise that he recognised and was soon followed by the usual cursing as his son made his way along the corridor to the downstairs toilet. He flinched at every sound as he sat cowering in his bed.

His son was home. And he was drunk.

After switching off his bedside light, he slid down under the covers, hoping his bedroom door would remain locked.

Since he'd tried to find the girl again, but instead had been caught and brought home by a neighbour to his grateful son, he had lived upstairs. He was only allowed out when his son was home. The cloud passed often enough for him to realise his son was keeping him locked up. He didn't want him finding the girl, and didn't want nosey neighbours meddling.

He heard footsteps thumping up the stairs and braced himself for the onslaught. It was his fault for bringing her up. He should have forgotten her like everything else.

That's what his son would shout.

The footsteps paused and he held his breath. Watching as the shadow flickered under his door, he took his glasses off. It was better if he couldn't see his face.

The doorknob jostled as a clumsy hand gripped it. It didn't turn. Instead, a half-hearted thump rattled the door and the footsteps continued down the corridor.

He breathed again raggedly and lay shaking.

Closing his eyes, he listened to the riot of his son banging around in his room, and willed sleep to come.

He had a plan and needed to rest.

He needed to be able to remember.

Chapter 14

Lori had never wished time away so much in her life. Despite the nerves and trepidation, she was excited about the weekend and seeing Alex.

Andrew had called every day, each message pretty much the same.

"How can you treat me like this?"

"I can't believe you're doing this."

"You'll regret this, Lori."

There was no, "how are you?" No understanding or consideration that she might just need some time. It was still on his terms, him demanding answers because he needed them.

Well, Lori wasn't ready to answer his questions. She needed to answer her own first. Then maybe she could give him the explanation he wanted. She had tapped off a text asking him to stop, telling him she would be in touch when she was ready to talk and harassing her wouldn't hurry that moment up. He hadn't replied.

Alex had also been in touch every day, which she had welcomed. Lori had texted her on Tuesday to let her know she would leave at lunchtime Friday and should arrive by dinnertime. Her text response had been enthusiastic, making Lori smile.

Whoop! I'll get Frank to cook! X

Since then, they'd exchanged numerous texts and the odd cheeky e-mail at work. Alex had sent her a video of Pedro the goat chasing Frank, catching her by surprise and making her spray coffee all over her desk. Lori replied with a picture of the soaked stack of papers in front of her, thanking her for the light relief.

It was Thursday night and she had just crawled into bed after packing, unpacking, and repacking at least three times before settling on what to take. She'd shaken her head more than once, acknowledging that she wanted to look her best for Alex, and that was why something she did on an almost weekly basis was suddenly so hard.

Sleep had almost taken her when the shrill sound of her house phone broke the spell. She glanced at the caller I.D as she reached for the extension on her bedside table to answer it. A foreign dialling code flashed up. "Hey, dad, how are you?"

"Lori! I'm good thanks, sweetheart. Glad you answered. I know it must be late. How are you?"

She sighed, knowing exactly why he had called. "I'm fine dad, busy with work, the usual. Where are you?"

"Berlin. Just back from dinner, but, anyway, that's not important. Your relationship of seven years ends and you're fine?"

"Wow, you can't remember my birthday but you know how many years I was with Andrew? I smell a rat, Dad. Get to the point."

"Okay, okay. I won't pretend. You see right through me every time. Andrew called me. He's devastated, Lori. Says you won't even return his calls. What's going on?"

Lori silently fumed. She couldn't believe Andrew had the gall to phone her dad. In case of an emergency, she had given him her father's office number, which would redirect to his mobile phone wherever he was in the world. "I have nothing more to say to him at the moment. I've made my feelings perfectly clear and there's no use hashing over it all. He won't change my mind so what's the point? I'd just end up frustrated and say things I know would hurt him more. So I've asked for space in the hope he'll calm down in the meantime. Then we can talk, when I'm ready."

"So I'm assuming I can't change your mind either then? His parents have been on the phone to me as well; they're so upset. They love you and thought you were perfect together."

"Well, they're wrong and clearly none of you really know us. He was suffocating me, Dad, I had to end it. I know it's taken me a long time to realise he can't offer me what I want and I'm truly sorry about that. Sorry I wasted both our time."

She genuinely was. She felt as if she'd given the majority of her twenties over to her career and a relationship with no future. She wasn't about to continue that into her thirties and no amount of parentally induced guilt would change that.

"So what? Handsome and successful isn't enough for you? He's a good bloke and he can take care of you."

"That's what I used to think, but the Andrew I know now is a pretentious, self-centred arse and I already have one of those in my life. Besides, who says I need taking care of?

Her dad chuckled. "That's not a very nice thing to say about your brother. I'll tell him you said that."

"You know fine well who I'm talking about and you know it isn't him." She laughed with him then, the tension broken. He knew better than to push her.

Over the years he had tried to involve himself in her life, showing an interest in her career, friends, and relationship. Anytime he was passing through London, he made a point of having dinner with her and Andrew, or Stella when Andrew was busy.

But it was so sporadic it seemed he was always behind with her life, never quite managing to be there when it mattered. It meant he tried to play the caring father card but knew he had no authority. She respected him and understood he had done what he thought best for them when their mum had died, but he was also as selfish as they came and knew it.

"So when are you next in town?" she asked to change the subject. "I think we're due a dinner."

"So that's seriously it? You won't even entertain the thought of getting back with him?"

She took the same deadpan tone she always did when she was finished talking about something with him. "He wanted to name your potential first grandchild 'Kettle'."

That did it.

"Okay, moving on, then. I'm home in the next few weeks. I'll e-mail you to confirm when exactly. Don't even think about bringing that smart arse Stella with you though." He laughed.

"Ah, c'mon, you know you love her chat." She loved the abuse Stella gave him, getting in digs on Lori's behalf for his shoddy parenting skills.

"Wait a minute," he feigned shock. "Don't tell me she's finally got her claws into you? Is that why you split up with Andrew?"

"Dad. For the last time, Stella is not a lesbian."

He scoffed as he always did at that statement. It was a running joke with them, one she hadn't let Stella in on, knowing she would be relentless in making him pay for it. "All successful police women are lesbians, Lori. It doesn't matter what country you're in. Well, the ones I've met at least."

"Just because they're good enough detectives to see through your bullshit and, therefore, know better than to sleep with you, doesn't make them lesbians, Dad. You're crude and you're wrong and you know it. Anyway, what would be so wrong with it if she was?"

She suddenly thought of Alex, panicking slightly at how he might respond. Although being okay with Stella being a lesbian was one thing, your own daughter was another. Oh God, where was her mind going? She needed to move away from this subject and fast.

"Actually, don't answer that, I know you too well. You're bound to say something that'll make me cringe like 'it would be a waste because she's so attractive'."

"Lori, how little you must think of me."

She groaned, his laugh telling her that was exactly what he had been thinking.

"Anyway, I was in Scotland at the weekend, bagged myself another Munro."

"That's my girl, when's your next one planned?"

"Well, I'm actually heading up again this weekend. I met a girl in the bothy I stayed in. Her name's Alex and she's invited me up for a bit of a get together at her farm. We might hit a hill on Sunday." She tried to keep the excitement out of her voice, relaying it as if it was just a casual invite.

"You two must have hit it off for her to invite you to her house? Be great for you to have some friends up there. Climbing in a group is always fun."

"Oh, you know Scottish folk are always friendly. No big deal. You're right about having a group to climb with though. I do love the solitude but I'm not sure I'd like to be doing some of the more challenging mountains on my own."

"You'll be traversing the Cuillin Ridge in no time," he said, referring to the Black Cuillin mountains on the Isle of Skye. At twelve kilometres long, with eleven Munros and more than thirty summits requiring a technical climbing ability she hadn't quite reached, most considered it to be the most challenging mountaineering journey in the whole of Britain.

"One day, maybe we'll even get to do it together. But, for now, I'm tired thinking about it."

"Okay, sweetheart. I'll let you get to sleep. I miss you."

"Miss you too, Dad. Make sure you're behaving and be careful. Goodnight."

"I'm always careful, but behaving is for boring people. Goodnight."

And with that, he was gone. Lori rolled on her side, and stared out through the blinds of the rear facing window. The sky was orange with light pollution, not a star to be seen. She willed sleep to return but, instead, it was Alex who took over her thoughts.

The rest of the room faded around her as she imagined what the farm and her friends were like and wondered what she was doing right at that moment. The thoughts calmed her and with the daydream still in her head, she drifted off to sleep.

CHAPTER 15

Alex sipped her coffee while looking through a living room window as a red toy-like car sped down her driveway. She flinched each time the nose dipped, waiting for it to crumple under the impact, as it bumped and jolted with each pot hole it hit.

She laughed to herself as she saw the silhouette of her best friend, Jess, being thrown around inside the car like a ragdoll. No sooner had the car skidded to a stop in a cloud of dust when the door was thrown open and Jess was bounding around to the side door and into the kitchen.

"Alexandra Ryan, as I live and breathe!" She broke into a grin and threw her arms around Alex as if she hadn't seen her in years. It had only been three weeks.

"I swear you miss me more every time, Jess." She laughed while returning her best friend's squeeze.

"I do, I do. It's bad for my health, you know. In fact, if you were a real best friend, you would just let me move in, so I'd never have to miss you again." She looked at Alex expectantly, clearly doing her best to keep a straight face.

Alex took down a cup and poured her some of the freshly brewed coffee before eyeing her as if she was considering it. "Hmm, let me think about it."

Jess popped her on the shoulder. "I know you have no intention of thinking about it. Besides, as if I'd want to live all the way out here in the sticks. One of us has to have a social life to keep some excitement in our friendship."

"Ouch." Alex rubbed her shoulder "And I don't mean you beating me up."

"You know it's true, so don't pretend. Anyway, come on, which mountains have you been hiding up and why is this the first time I'm seeing you in three weeks?"

Alex shrugged. "Oh, you know, just a few of the usual and one I haven't been to in a while. But I'll tell you about that later. I want to know about this excitement you speak of. What's been happening in big, bad Glasgow city?"

Jess hopped around, as usual unable to contain whatever gossip she had brought with her. "Oh my God, Alex, you should have been with us at Mint last Saturday."

Mint was the main lesbian and gay club in the city and Alex was pretty sure she didn't want to be there. She'd done her time frequenting it, but for every half-decent date she'd been on, there had been ten absolutely terrible ones. She just didn't believe a bar was the place she would meet who she was looking for. Although she had to admit to only ever being half-hearted in looking and quickly dismissed anyone with potential, much to Jess's chagrin. "I highly doubt that. You know Mint and me spells disaster."

Jess rolled her eyes, then gulped back her coffee. "Oh, don't be so negative, you're just too picky."

Alex had always believed if she was meant to be with someone, it would happen; it didn't need to be forced. She thought of Lori then and nerves settled in her stomach at the thought of her arriving in less than eight hours. She couldn't believe she'd been so forward, inviting her up for the weekend already. But the invitation had felt natural, whatever it meant. Plus, Lori had been quick enough to say yes. Now she just had to tell Jess. "I know where this is going and I haven't changed my mind. You are not setting me up on any more dates."

Jess huffed and crossed her arms. "There was only that one really bad one and, I mean seriously, how could I have possibly known she was going to start waving her moon cup around the restaurant bathroom on a first date..." She trailed off, her face contorting.

The horrified look on Jess's face said it all. Alex was sure her own mirrored it. They cracked up. Not a date to forget in a hurry.

"Clearly 'bad' is set at different levels for us. What about the girl I lasted a week with who randomly said 'pants' and 'socks' all the time?"

"Please, that was only when she opened a drawer. It was endearing. You could have lived with that."

"Okay, then the one obsessed with being German, fake accent and all."

"Och, c'mon, it was a phase. She hadn't long come out and was having an identity crisis. You have to admit the accent was cute and she had good taste in music."

"Yeah, I suppose. Oh, wait, I've got it. What about the inventor? The one who kept suddenly inventing something new, and all through dinner she scribbled on napkins and then I'd have to tell her it already existed?"

"Yeah okay, she was odd. But she dressed well and that one drawing you showed me did look like a cool umbrella."

Alex shook her head and gave up. "Listen, you. Finding one good quality might justify sleeping with someone on the first date in your book, but you should know by now that's not me."

"Aye, I know. You're all about that chemistry crap. So I guess you're not interested in my latest potential then?"

Alex glanced at the clock. "No, I've had plenty of potential fun thanks. Just give me the gossip from your weekend but talk and work at the same time. We've a lot to get organised for tomorrow night." She topped up both their coffee mugs. "Let's go get set up outside."

CHAPTER 16

Lori almost missed the buzz of her phone as she tore along the motorway with the radio blaring. She hit the button for Bluetooth along with the radio volume, and there was a delay before her friend and colleague Adam's deep voice vibrated through the speakers.

"Lori? You there?" He shouted, making her wince.

She adjusted the volume once the connection was made. "Yeah, I'm here, Adam. Didn't you get my message? I'm on my way to Scotland."

"I got it but thought I'd try and catch you before you disappeared into the hills."

"Well, make it fast. I'm approaching the border and the signal normally goes around this point. Everything okay?"

"Everything is fine. In fact, it's more than fine. Guess what?"

She detected rarely heard excitement in his voice. Adam was as easygoing as they came. She often joked he was probably a surfer or maybe a sloth in a previous life. Nothing was done fast or above anything more than a mellow tempo. The only time she'd seen him break a sweat was the odd time he had dragged her to the gym. "I don't have time for guessing, and I told you the signal's about to go."

"Okay, well how about you slow down then and give me a chance because you really want to hear this."

She smiled that he knew her well enough to know she was more than likely sitting at the speed limit in her haste to get to the hills. He didn't need to know that's not what she was speeding towards this weekend.

She gave in and eased back on the accelerator. "Busted. I've taken it down to a Sunday driver's fifty for you. Now don't keep me in suspense."

He chuckled softly and Lori pictured him leaning back precariously on his desk chair with a bottle of some form of blended health drink in his hand. It was Friday and over the fifteen degrees he deemed hot enough to swap the office dress code for shorts, flip flops, and whatever T-shirt best showed off his abs. He got away with it because generally most people in the office, including the guys, liked checking him out, and a suit covered way too much.

"Wait, before I tell you, did I hear right that you and Andrew split up? Why didn't you tell me?"

She sighed. "Good news really does travel fast. How did you hear that? I haven't told you because I haven't seen you all week."

"Well, he came by the office when you were out yesterday, apparently had flowers but Jane on the desk refused to take them. She gave him some guff about security and receiving unexpected deliveries."

She smiled. "Remind me to bring Jane flowers. That girl has always got my back."

"So is it true? Is the lovely Lori Hunter finally on the market?"

She could picture his eyebrows waggling and knew what was coming next. "On the market, yes. Available, no."

"Aw, what. Don't spoil my fun!" He huffed down the phone at her. "When are you just going to admit you can't resist me and agree to let me take you out?"

She played along, putting on her best serious voice. "You're right Adam. All this time I've been wasting and there you were sitting across the room from me all along. I can't believe I didn't see it before."

"Are you serious? Wait, you're messing with me. Why must you tease me like this?"

"I'm not teasing. If you want to buy me dinner and a few cocktails, I won't complain."

"Really?"

"Really. Isn't that what friends do for each other when their hearts have been broken and they need cheering up?"

"Argh. The dreaded F word. Okay, you win. Call me when you're back and we'll have a tequila fuelled dancing date. But don't try pretending you're broken hearted. In fact, you sound particularly upbeat. Spill, Hunter. What's the scoop?"

"No scoop. I'm just getting out there and thinking of myself for a change." She smiled at herself in the rear view mirror. Yes, that's exactly what she was doing this weekend, and it made her happy.

"Well, keep that in mind for the next thing I have to tell you."

"Oh?"

"Are you ready? I think you might just love me after I tell you."

"C'mon, Ad, you're the one teasing now." She tapped the mouthpiece of the phone with a manicured nail. "Get on with it."

"Ouch. All right. My hearing is kind of important for my job you know."

"Adam," she said his name slow and deliberate. "Why did you call?" It was infuriating dragging things out of him sometimes.

"Okay, okay! Well, I just got a call from an old university buddy in New York."

Hearing New York, Lori's pulse quickened. "And?"

"And he says there's a couple of openings coming up that might be of interest to us."

She'd been telling the truth when she'd told Alex it was her dream to live in New York for a while and do some work with the UN. There had been plenty of regular translation jobs coming up but that's what she had already, and they tended to be one language specific. She wanted to move for something more challenging.

"What are they? And what do you mean by us?"

He laughed. "You're not the only one with aspirations, you know. He said they're looking for two chief of sections. A year secondment in Russian to cover sabbatical leave, and a full-time position in Spanish. What do you say we put our names in the hat? My buddy is more than happy to put us both forward as a recommendation. He's been chief of section in Arabic for three years with five years previous in Nairobi, so he's well thought of."

Lori's mind reeled. Normally, she would be squealing with enthusiasm. This was exactly what she had been hoping for and the potential to head there with one of her closest friends made it even better.

She crossed the border into Scotland. The large, blue "welcome" sign caught her attention. Remembering where she was heading and picturing Alex, she realised why her excitement was lacking. She mentally kicked herself.

Alex was a friend and nothing more. This was her chance. It couldn't be coincidence that the opportunity had come up only a few weeks after ending things with Andrew. This was her fresh start.

Or was Alex the fresh start?

The speaker crackled and Adam's voice came through in a stutter.

"Adam, the signal is going. I'll see you Monday and we can talk about it." She felt bad hanging up, but he would disappear in a mile or so anyway.

She spotted a lay-by and pulled over for a minute. Her concentration was shot, so the burger van at one end was a welcome sight, with its promise of coffee.

As she walked to it, her phone beeped with a text.

Are you far away? The beer is chilling and I have a chef for the evening ready to cook us a treat. And I don't mean Frank! X

She smiled and rubbed a thumb over the small picture of Alex next to the message before tapping back.

Just stopped for coffee. An hour or two, tops. Can't wait x

She pressed *send* and it beeped again, this time it was Adam,

Didn't catch your reply but I'm hoping you're as excited as me. This is it Hunter. You, me, and the big apple. The world is our lobster. It's gonna be amazing x

She laughed at lobster and, for some reason, she knew he was right. She could feel it.

Whatever happened next was going to be amazing.

CHAPTER 17

The sky was relatively clear with only a light breeze that promised to continue through the weekend. Alex decided to take the party outside, and Jess worked quickly alongside her. She was a veteran of helping to set up for their bi-monthly group get-togethers at the farm.

They chattered as they worked and Jess regaled her with stories from the previous weekend at Mint. Hook ups, break ups, and all the drama that went with them. Alex found herself rolling her eyes more than once.

The farmhouse was spread across one level. At its heart was a wide L-shaped kitchen/dining/living area that Alex had modernised a year after Rachel had left. It had helped to make the place feel like home again instead of a museum of memories. It was no longer the family home she grew up in, now it was just hers. It was with a heavy heart, that she had donated or placed antique family furniture and art in storage, then repainted, re-floored, and refurnished.

Original ceiling beams and stone work were exposed and she had kept the space traditional but stylish. Furnishing the living area at one end with worn leather sofas and chairs positioned sociably around a low scuffed coffee table. She softened the cold stone with cushions, throws, and rugs. Tall lamps lit dark corners.

A long dining table with high back chairs sat twelve people comfortably and shared its space in the corner of the 'L' with a custom-made bar that was always well-stocked.

The kitchen at the other end continued the traditional theme, with solid oak worktops, a breakfast island, seven burner stove, and deep Belfast sink.

All of it was designed around a wood burning fire, which stood proudly in the middle, pulling each spacious area together toward its warmth.

Double doors opened onto a large patio with the two inner walls of the 'L' providing some protection from the elements. Living in Scotland meant there were very few truly hot days, so she'd had a high wooden beamed roof erected over it, fitted with outdoor heaters and nets of fairy lights, which she connected to the main's power.

There was an area to the right, away from the house, that had become an unofficial bonfire pit with large rocks around the edge making it safe. Broken branches and fencing that had accumulated throughout the farm over the harsh winter were topped up with extra logs from the barn. When the night turned cooler, they would light it up and bask in the glow. She could watch a fire longer than any programme on television.

They dragged out an extra table and chairs she kept in the barn, positioning them under the roof to form a table large enough for everyone expected. Jess uncovered and checked over the gas barbeque. It had become her domain as chef while Alex's expertise lay in the bartending. She rolled a mini keg of her favourite local craft beer from the barn and sat it in place to settle under a table her neighbour had made especially for hooking up beer. It would be tapped and the rest of the bar inside set up the following morning with a variety of spirits and wines guaranteed to keep her friends happy.

Alex couldn't cook much more than an egg or soup with her home-grown veggies, so she'd shopped with the list Jess had e-mailed. She now sat back sipping a beer at the kitchen island watching Jess prepare the meat for the barbeque. Her friends would all contribute to the party with their favourite sides and desserts.

Jess loved to cook but didn't get much opportunity to do so in her cramped city centre apartment which she shared with two rather messy housemates. So she'd let Jess design the kitchen with a generous budget, in return for her continued services as chef whenever Alex had a party.

"Right, well, I've given you all my gossip," Jess said, massaging her famous spice blend into chicken legs. "Now it's your turn. Where've you been hiding?"

Alex sighed. "Don't give me that tone, Jess. I haven't been hiding, I've just been busy. I'm in the final stages of writing some new code and you know what I'm like after an obsessive stretch in front of the computer screen. I had to get away."

Jess smiled wryly. "Yeah, because it's so hectic living out here. I don't know how you get a minute's peace."

Alex rolled her eyes. "You think you're funny, but you're not. If you must know, I took your advice and went out to the bothy me and Rachel shared on our first climb together last weekend."

Jess's eyes widened in surprise. "Wow, three years and we finally have progress. I'm proud of you." She wiggled her spice covered fingers at Alex. "I'll hug you later."

Alex shook her head. "I've known you for ten years and I still can't tell if you're being sarcastic sometimes."

"On this occasion, I'm only being half-sarcastic."

Alex poked her tongue out.

Jess laughed. "I'm serious. I'm really proud of you. I know it must have been strange going out there on your own and spending the night, even if you did have Frank. But let's be honest, it's about bloody time. She spoilt enough for you."

Alex suddenly found the label of her beer bottle interesting, picking it around the edges. "Well, I wasn't actually on my own. I ended up sharing it with another climber."

"Oh really? I feel a story coming. Male or female?"

"Female."

"Good start. Please continue." She waved her hands expectantly.

"Well..." Alex continued to peel her label, unable to meet Jess's eyes.

"C'mon, Alex, don't leave me hanging. Was she good company? Did she snore? Have stinky feet? Did she say pants and socks a lot?" She laughed while packing the last of the marinated meat in airtight containers and stacking them in the fridge. As she washed her hands, she glanced over her shoulder to study a quiet Alex, before grabbing a beer and joining her.

The front label was off. After folding it into the tiniest square possible, Alex put it on the worktop before starting on the back of the bottle. "She was surprisingly good company. She didn't snore that I'm aware of. There were no embarrassing stinky feet situations or obsessive compulsive word play. In fact, we kind of hit it off."

Jess's eyebrows shot up. "Oh, please tell me I'm about to get a saucy bothy story?"

Alex finally looked up and laughed. "You wish. No, I don't mean like that. Well kind of like that. Oh, I don't know,

Jess." She sighed and slumped back in the stool. "She's just split up with her boyfriend so A, she's straight and B, she's on the rebound."

Jess shook her head and Alex watched her shoulders deflate. "Which in my experience always equals D for drama?"

"I know, I know. But..." Alex looked down at her bottle again, not sure how much to admit.

"She's really got to you hasn't she?"

Alex took a deep breath and looked her in the eye. She couldn't lie to her best friend. "Yes. I think there was something between us and I think she felt it too. I don't want to get myself too excited, but I haven't felt anything even close to this in such a long time, Jess. What if I've got it all wrong and make a fool of myself. Or worse I'm right, but the idiot in me either freaks out or stalls so much it passes me by? I don't want to let it pass me by."

"So don't let it. I mean apart from the being straight and on the rebound, what's your real problem here?"

Alex blew out her cheeks as the reality of Jess's glib comment tightened the nervous band around her chest. What was she thinking even considering the possibility of something more with Lori? "Oh, you know, the usual. A touch of paralysing fear that she'll reject me coupled with a little bit of worry for my face when she laughs in it."

Jess took her hand. "Is that all? Sounds like a typical Saturday night for me. It's character building, honest."

"Jess, I'm being serious." She drew a circle in the air around her face. "Note the panic face. You need to help me."

"Hey, c'mon okay. I'm sorry." She went to get them another beer from the fridge, forehead crinkling the way it did when on the odd occasion she tried to choose her words sensitively.

"Okay, I like that look. That's a sensible Jess look. Let me hear it."

Jess sat down and popped off their bottle tops. "Okay, well no situation can be ideal so I think you need to forget the ex/straight element. For you, what's going to work is to only concentrate on how you feel and, more importantly, try to get a sense of how she's feeling."

Alex rolled her eyes and took a sip. "Easier said than done, but you're right about the situation. I guess I can't change that."

"Exactly my point. I know what it took for you to get close to Rachel and then she goes and craps all over you so you're bound to be suspicious and well...I don't blame you for that either or for being scared but..." She sat back in her stool, blowing across the top of the beer bottle in thought.

"But what, Jess? C'mon spit it out. Don't pretend you're considering my feelings."

"Can I be honest?"

"I like how you say that as if it's a question."

She shrugged her shoulders. "It's polite to at least warn someone before saying something mean."

"Do they teach you that in one-night stand school for the morning after?"

"Hey, now who's being mean?"

Alex threw up her hands. "All right, I'm sorry. You know I only get mean when I'm about to become defensive. Out with it."

"Fine, well to be honest, I'm relieved you've finally met someone who might thaw out the ice queen we've been dealing with this past while. I mean, damn, you've been cold and distant and, frankly, a little miserable to be around. I thought we were through those dark times, Alex. I was beginning to worry that being out here all alone with only a dog and a goat for company was finally getting to you."

Alex took a long drink and rocked slightly on her stool. She could only nod and let her best friend's words sink in. "I hate it when you're mean but right. Although, don't forget the chickens."

They stared each other out a moment and then they both laughed. Alex felt a little relief. "So you don't think I'm crazy hoping for something to happen with a straight girl?"

"Are you sure she's straight?"

"Well, she didn't exactly have it branded on her, but she's been with her boyfriend for seven years."

"That means nothing, sweetheart. You should know better than to assume. But even if she has been up until this point, I defy her to not fall in love with you."

"Wait a minute," Alex held up a hand. "Firstly, easy with the L word there and secondly, I thought you'd be the first to warn me off this kind of potentially messy situation."

"Normally you'd be right. Maybe if you were some serial dater with a 'plenty more fish' attitude, I would. But as this is the first flutter you've felt since Rachel, and given the ice queen Alex I just told you about, I'm willing to hear you out before warning you off her." She winked and sat up straight, feigning a business-like manner. "So, I'm going to need the full facts if I'm to help you make an informed decision about how to move forward. Let's start with a name, occupation, location, and sexiness on a scale of one to ten."

Alex relaxed a bit. This is what she needed. To talk it out with someone who would give it to her straight, tell her she was crazy or give her the push she needed to go for it.

"Her name is Lori and she lives in London. She's an interpreter for parliament in Westminster and speaks, like, a million languages."

Jess gave a low whistle. "Wow, impressive. But you forgot the scale and you know that's all I'm really interested in."

"Too bad, I'm not. I will just assure you that she's outrageously gorgeous and funny, as well as smart."

"So, she's a ten on all counts. I'll say it again. Wow. And follow it with a, 'what's the catch'?"

"No catch. Well, not that I'm aware of anyway, if you take away the potential straightness and rebound issues. There's no arrogance about her, she just has this way...I don't know how to explain. It's like a kind of poise that you can't be taught. I only got to see her in hiking gear, which she totally pulls off by the way, but I also have this feeling she's one of those sophisticated city folk that look just as at home in a designer suit and killer heels. Oh, and she loved your brownies, by the way. I took a bag from the freezer."

Jess laughed. "Take a breath, my misty eyed friend. Are you sure she's real?"

Alex slapped Jess's thigh. "I know it's been a while but I'm not so desperate I have to make someone up."

"Okay, so this connection, what makes you think she felt it too?"

"Well, at first we just joked around a lot and Frank managed to get the better of her twice, which was hilarious."

Jess nodded knowingly. "We've all been there. I'm glad she survived."

"I know, what a way to break the ice." Alex chuckled at the memory. "Anyway, we sat up late talking and drinking whisky, and I kind of fell asleep on her shoulder..."

"Smooth." Jess nodded approvingly.

"It wasn't like that. I was exhausted after the climb. There was the whisky and despite my initial worry about going to the bothy, it calmed me having her there. Then Sunday, the weather wasn't great so we walked and fished and talked some more. It felt easy being with her."

Jess shrugged. "So maybe you made a new friend. I promise not to be too jealous."

"That's what I thought at first. I was determined not to read too much into it, but then it came time to say good-bye and I swear there was this look... As if for a split second, she wanted to kiss me."

"Did you?" Jess's eyes were wide.

"No, of course I didn't. I also saw another look that told me if she had been thinking about it, it had completely freaked her out. Besides, for all I know I imagined the entire thing and she's just a particularly tactile person."

"It's possible. But I think it's more possible she lost herself in those goddess-green eyes of yours."

Alex leant in bringing her eyes only inches from Jess's. "Well, they are magic, don't you know."

Jess fanned herself and leant back. "See, all this time we've known each other and they still work on me."

Alex shoved her shoulder. "Shut up, you idiot. I'm thinking it was more likely gratitude. We'd had a nice, chilled out day and she'd shared a lot about her ex and their break-up. We were both grateful in the end to have found someone there when we needed it."

"I'll pretend I'm not hurt that you didn't come find me. I'll merely say I'm not convinced by that explanation. No one gets under your skin like she clearly has."

"Jess, I'm sorry, I didn't mean that. It wasn't like that."

Jess waved her off. "I know. I'm over it already. Was there flirting?"

"Well, you know what I'm like sometimes and I don't even realise I'm doing it...I think I made her blush more than once, but that could have easily been from the embarrassment of my obviousness."

"Hmm... you're right. That will depend on how bad the flirting was. It's not pretty sometimes."

"Oi!" Alex slapped Jess's thigh again. "That's two strikes, Collins. You're meant to be serious right now."

"Sorry. Sorry. All right, what happened after the non-kiss?"

"We hugged and exchanged numbers, promised to stay in touch." She wasn't going to divulge the details of how she felt during the hug because, honestly, she couldn't quite explain it herself.

"And have you?"

"Aye, a few phone calls, some texts, and e-mails."

"Well, that's a good sign. Do you have plans to see her again?"

"Well...that's the thing..." She got up to get them another beer, sweeping her labels off the counter into the bin.

"Spit it out, Alex. What aren't you telling me?"

"She's on her way here," Alex mumbled.

"What? Alex, get your head out of the fridge and talk to me."

Alex grabbed two bottles, taking her time opening them before sitting back down opposite Jess. "She's on her way here to spend the weekend." She glanced at her watch. "In fact, she should be here any minute."

Jess shot up out of her stool. "What!" She ran to the window in the dining area, looking down the long drive. "I can't believe this. You're such a shithead not telling me that straight away. Oh, and clearly you have it worse than I thought if you're inviting her here already. Is that who you asked me to buy the wetsuit for?"

"Yeah, you're about the same height and build so I figured if it fitted you, it would fit her. I told her we would do a hill walk Sunday but thought a bit of a different adventure might be appealing." She smiled to herself, strangely pleased that she still had the ability to shock her old friend.

Jess plonked herself back down on the stool. "A bit of a different adventure...? Oh sweetheart, if that's the level of flirting there was, I think it might have been embarrassment on her part. Are you sure you know what you're doing? There's a good chance she's only coming out of pity."

"That's three strikes, Jess, and now I'm even more nervous. I have no idea what I'm doing and you're meant to be reassuring me."

"Oh crap, is that what I'm meant to be doing? I thought I was just meant to be judging and telling you if you're being an idiot?"

Alex hung her head, giving up. "I don't even know why you are my best friend right now. Please tell me there's no harm in it. Tell me I'm right to at least give myself a chance to find out if there's something there and the worst case is I've made a new friend."

Jess patted her on the head. "See, you knew the answer all along. You don't need me for advice. I'm better at general mockery and brutal honesty. That's why we're friends."

Alex shook her head, looking up and leaning in again, she pressed her forehead to Jess's. "I hate you. But you're all I've got."

"Bad luck for you. Now, come here, I owe you a hug."

Alex held on to the reassurance that came with the hug; she spoke into Jess's shoulder, "Do you think she's interested?"

Jess held her at arm's length. "Gorgeous, no one drives four hundred miles to see someone they've just met if they're not interested. The question is whether Lori's so called 'straight brain' knows it. And I don't want to see you hurt while she figures it out."

"So, this is where you warn me off? Or have you got my back?"

Jess blew out a worried breath. "How about I get to know her this weekend and then decide whether to warn you off?"

Alex smiled. "Deal."

CHAPTER 18

Lori took a right turn when prompted by her sat-nav. She drove slowly through an open five bar gate and onto the bumpy dirt road that led to the farm, taking in the views across the hills, along with some deep breaths to calm her nerves.

A whispered 'wow' escaped her lips as the farmhouse came into view. She'd had a vision of a quaint little stone cottage with wooden shutters and creeping ivy, not the sprawling beautiful home she'd come to a stop in front of. It seemed to stretch out before her on one level in every direction.

If she'd been nervous before, her stomach now churned at the sight of Alex rounding the corner from the side of the house with a striking stranger in tow. Slim with waves of blonde falling over her shoulders, she towered over Alex. Despite the early spring chill, her long legs stretched out of jean shorts into flip flops, and a light, zip-up peach hoodie brought out the colour in her cheeks. Alex herself was beautifully casual in dark red chinos rolled up to her calves and a fitted, navy T-shirt matched with sockless feet in well-worn, grey converse. Her hair was pulled back in a loose ponytail, tendrils curling around her ears, and, with hands tucked casually in her back pockets, she looked very much at home.

Lori extricated her stiff limbs from the car and returned the smile plastered on Alex's face. She inwardly kicked herself for not changing and now felt massively overdressed. "Bonjour."

"Hey, yourself." Alex stopped in front of her, clearly unsure whether to hug her or not.

The blonde stopped just behind her, quite obviously checking Lori out.

"I drive all this way and all I get is a 'Hey'?"

Alex laughed then, and stepped in for a hug. "How rude of me," she said, stepping back but keeping hold of her at arm's length. "Promise not to let it happen again."

The blonde feigned a small cough behind her. "Speaking of rude..."

Lori caught Alex's exaggerated eye roll as she stepped back to include the other woman. "Because she's suddenly such a shy little flower incapable of introducing herself, Lori, this is Jess. My most favourite human being and maker of the wonderful brownies."

Jess dug Alex in the ribs and then held out a hand. "Good to meet you, Lori. I love your accent." Lori felt her hand squeezed a little too tightly, but she held the eye contact, determined to pass whatever test this was.

"Good to meet you too." She gave Jess a warm smile. It felt important to get off on the right foot with Alex's best friend. The smile was returned, along with her hand, and seemed genuine. She relaxed a little at passing stage one.

She saw Alex look back and forth between her and Jess and shake her head, muttering under her breath. She had a moment of panic. Was Alex already regretting inviting her?

Jess draped her arm across Alex's shoulders in a protective move. She made to turn her towards the house. "C'mon, let's give the girl the grand tour."

Lori didn't miss the gesture and had to stop from laughing as she imagined Stella pulling the same move. "This place is grand all right. Knowing how behind the times you country folk are, I wasn't even sure there'd be an indoor toilet."

Alex stuck her tongue out. "You know your old friend Frank won't be long finding his way home to see who just arrived. Probably wet and covered in mud..." She looked Lori up and down, making her take a look down at herself and what she was wearing. She still wore her work clothes, one of her favourite suits, beautifully cut in all the right places and too expensive for Frank to cause havoc with.

Alex seemed to know what she was thinking. "If you get into trouble, I might not save you again."

"Oh, mature," Lori laughed. "You do realise I will have tamed that beast by the end of this weekend so you can never hold him over me again? I may even turn him against you all together."

"Do your worst. That mutt knows not to piss the master off."

Jess laughed at them both. "I don't know, Alex. I think I have faith the girl can do as she claims."

Lori took a second to grab her bag and another deep breath as Alex and Jess headed back toward the house. She needed to get a grip and willed her stomach to settle. The anticipation of seeing Alex had her jittery on the journey but now it was anticipation of the weekend to come getting to her.

It was real now. She was here. Alex was here. The farm wasn't a dream anymore and it was about to be filled with Alex's favourite people. Jess hadn't helped the nerves. She was clearly suspicious of Lori, and with good reason, given the short time Alex had known her.

Although the "I'm Alex's best friend, what are your intentions?" treatment felt a little over the top given they were only friends.

Friends.

Had she really taken an afternoon off work and driven four hundred miles to be friends?

She slammed the boot of the car shut, remembering their conversation earlier in the week as well as the call from Adam about the potential move to New York.

Yes. Friends, and fun. That's all this weekend needed to be about.

Catching up with Alex and Jess, she followed them through a side door into a porch where they kicked off their shoes. Padding along a short hall in her stocking feet, she was the last to enter the huge living space. "Wow, Alex, this is gorgeous."

Alex beamed. "Glad you like it. I redecorated a few years ago with a little help from this one over here." She nodded in Jess's direction.

"Aye, I got to do the kitchen since that's where she sticks me every time I'm here."

"Don't pretend you don't love it." She put a hand up to her face and spoke out of the side of her mouth toward Lori, "Jess still lives like a student, if it can't be microwaved her housemates don't eat it."

"Hey, that's not fair. Don't listen to her, Lori. I'm actually squirreling my pennies for the day I can finally ditch this one and head off on my great travel adventure." She poked her tongue in Alex's direction.

"Aye, right. You know you'll never leave me."

Lori watched the exchange with a smile. "Okay, break it up you two. I still need the tour, oh, and a beer if you'd be so kind. It's been a long week."

Alex laughed, shaking her head. "Damn, failing in my hostess duties already. Jess, my lovely kitchen maiden, please prepare us three cold beers and some of your finest nibbles on the double while I show our guest to her room."

Jess stood to attention in salute. "Yes, Mistress." She nodded in Lori's direction and put a thumb up. "Straight to the beer; I like you already."

Lori returned her smile before following Alex through the living area into another corridor much longer than the first.

Alex opened doors as they went. All but one. "All the bedrooms and bathrooms come off this corridor. That's the only room not in use." She pointed to the unopened door and Lori didn't question it. "There's a small library, study, and music room at the other end of the kitchen where we came in, I'll show you them later."

"This place is huge, Alex. Your friends must love spending time out here with you, away from it all."

"Yeah, Jess in particular. It's kind of a home away from home for her and gives her a real break from the city and her job. She kids on about living out here with me if I'd finally just ask her, but she couldn't leave the social life behind."

"I don't know. She seems pretty comfy here."

Alex turned a corner, passing two more doors before stopping outside one at the far end of the hall. "Trust me, our current arrangement works just fine. Anyway, this is you." She swung open the door, moving aside for Lori to enter first.

Lori wiggled her toes as her feet sunk into the plush carpet of another living room and stopped to survey the space. It was much smaller than the main room, furnished simply but cosily with a scent of vanilla in the air. A worn, oxblood red chesterfield faced the stone fireplace and a wood burner stacked high on both sides with logs. An oak bookcase rammed with paperbacks and board games ran the length of one wall while the opposite held two small paintings hung over an old steamer chest.

The breakfast bar separated the living room and the kitchen/dining area before the room led to French doors at the end and the view beyond. They opened outside on to a patio made for two, complete with gas heater, table, and chairs.

"Alex, this is stunning."

"Aye." Alex came up behind her and peered over her shoulder. "I had these doors and the patio put in when I discovered the views to be had from this end of the house. There's a larger patio space around the side, but you get the sun here early in the morning so it's a perfect spot for breakfast. C'mon, I'll show you your room."

Lori turned and noticed the door off the living room. "Through there?"

Alex nodded. "There's an en-suite so you won't have to fight with the others for the bathroom. The guys take ages so trust me, that's a good thing."

Lori was reminded of autumn as they entered the warm bedroom. "Okay, so who normally stays in what is clearly the best guest room in Scotland, and are they going to be upset when they find me here?"

Alex laughed. "You're right to worry, but don't. It's actually where Jess always stays, but she agreed you should have the star treatment this weekend as it's your first time."

"She agreed or you told her that's what was happening?"

"Okay, so I told her, then she agreed. It's mostly how our relationship works."

Shaking her head, Lori blew out a breath. "You realise I want your friends to like me right? This doesn't help that cause."

The dimples appeared with Alex's smile. "Trust me when I tell you Jess likes you already."

Inwardly, Lori punched the air. Outwardly, she attempted playing it cool. "Of course she does. I'm adorable. I wasn't worried for a moment."

"Sure you weren't. I mean, I wasn't nervous so why should you be?" Alex raised her eyebrows in mischief and they laughed together at the blatant lie.

Lori felt her stomach settle and her shoulders relaxed with relief. Of course she wasn't the only one who was going to be nervous and she had been daft to think otherwise. "Well, remind me to thank her later."

"Oh, you'd better. I only told her half an hour ago you were coming and kicked her out of here shortly after."

Lori laughed. "Well, I appreciate the thought. I'll try to think of someway sufficient to thank her."

Alex headed into the living area. "You'll find the essentials in the little kitchen but I'd recommend letting Jess cook you breakfast in the morning."

"This is great, Alex. Thanks."

"No problem at all. Take some time if you want to change and freshen up after the drive. I'll make sure that beer is waiting for you."

Alex wandered back through to the main part of the house, smiling but with a light headedness, as if all the blood had rushed from her head. Lori was in her house and staying for a whole weekend. She needed to get a grip.

"Well?" asked Jess as Alex sat in front of a beer at the kitchen island.

"She loves it and is eternally grateful to you for giving it up this weekend."

"So long as she knows it's only a one time deal?"

"Don't worry," she said, giving Jess what she hoped was her cheekiest wink. "If after this weekend she wants to come back to stay, hopefully it'll be in another room."

Jess sat down beside her, and lightly patted her head "Oh, Alex. Ten years and all we've been through, do you really think you can pull the wink and dimple bravado with me? You must know I can see right through you?"

"You're right. I'm a nervous wreck here. Do you like her? She's nice right?"

"She's beautiful. And you could have warned me about that whole sparkly-eye thing. How on earth am I meant to remain neutral when she's got that going on?"

Alex smiled despite herself; it had won her over in an instant too. "Tell me it's all going to be okay, Jess."

"Alex." She turned to face her, placing a beer in her hand before taking her by the shoulders. "It's going to be okay."

Chapter 19

Lori dropped her bag and plopped down on the end of the bed. She surveyed the room noting a few personal pictures and cosmetics that must be Jess's. It still felt surreal to be there, but her nerves had been eased, replaced with excitement and anticipation of the weekend to come.

She hadn't been wrong in her first impression of Alex. She had realised that as soon as she had stepped into her arms again.

It had also quickly become apparent how important it was to Alex and Jess that she felt comfortable and at home. This made Lori feel special and happy, that she had accepted the invite.

She stripped off her suit and then sauntered into the bathroom for a quick brush of her teeth and wash of her face. After removing the day's make up, she felt fresh and free. She pulled on a pair of worn skinny jeans and a loose fitting, dark green, wool jumper and then opened the wardrobe to find a hanger for her suit. There were more items that seemed to belong to Jess along with a brand new wetsuit. Given how far they were from the sea, she wondered what kind of sport Jess could be into.

She checked herself in the mirror once she'd brushed her hair back in a ponytail. "You look fine, Lori. Comfy, composed, and calm."

Next, she dug out some thick cosy socks and padded in them back along the corridor toward the kitchen. She found

Alex standing at the island watching Jess chop vegetables. "Something smells delicious."

Alex handed her a cold beer from the fridge. "It's Jess's famous chorizo and vegetable risotto. Told you she wanted to make a good impression this weekend." She winked Lori's way.

"Yeah, you see how this works, Lori. I do the work, Alex takes the glory."

"She's just earning her keep. I told you not to let her fool you, she loves the cooking."

"Well, maybe you can let me make you breakfast, Jess, to give you at least one shift off, and to thank you for giving up your room?" Lori said.

"Make me breakfast, eh? If Alex hadn't told me you're a straight girl, that kind of line would give me the wrong impression." She laughed, wiggling her eyebrows mischievously.

When Lori realised what she meant she felt heat crawling up her neck and cheeks and knew she'd turned crimson while Alex just glared at Jess.

Jess looked between the two of them. "What?" She raised her hands innocently and returned her attention to the saucepan.

"Ignore her, Lori. She's just cranky she has to share with Susie tomorrow night because none of the boys can cope with her snoring and she isn't trusted with any of the other girls."

"Oh no, is that a bad thing? I thought you and Susie were friends? Jess, you should just have the room you usually do. I don't mind sharing."

"It's fine, honestly," Jess pointed her wooden spoon. "Alex, untwist your knickers and don't be so mean. I'm just teasing her. Besides you really don't want to share with Susie. At least I know how to handle her."

"Sounds ominous," Lori said.

"Her bark is worse that her bite. Wait actually..."

Alex wagged a finger. "Now, Jess. Be nice."

"So sorry, Mistress. Please forgive me." Jess bowed and rolled her eyes in Lori's direction. "Seriously, it's fine. I'll just get her so drunk she passes out and I don't have to listen to her."

Lori was suddenly apprehensive again about the reception she was going to get from Alex's friends. "So long as you're sure, Jess?"

"I am, honestly. But I will take you up on breakfast. Now why don't you give her the rest of the tour, Alex, while I finish dinner?"

"Aye, good idea. Bring your beer."

They headed in the opposite direction from the bedrooms, back to the hallway where they'd first come in. "So you've seen the bedrooms at the other end of the house, there are six in total, including yours. One of them is mine which is en-suite as well, and then there's a family bathroom for the other rooms to share. All the rooms are doubles and a couple have sofa beds for when we have a houseful. There's one that's empty." She looked pensive for a moment and Lori was about to ask why when Alex answered before she had a chance. "I haven't decided what to do with that one yet."

"Is it a houseful this weekend?"

"Normally having a houseful means everyone has a boyfriend or girlfriend of some description that they bring. It can get interesting sometimes when there are a few new faces."

Lori forced a laugh. "So should I be preparing for it to get interesting?"

Alex smiled rubbing Lori's arm reassuringly. "Don't panic, you're the only new face this weekend so you'll be getting all the attention."

"Oh, great. Just what I wanted to hear."

"I'm kidding. Don't look so worried. They're a good bunch and Jess will have your back when it comes to Susie. It's their favourite pastime bitching at each other, so she'll relish it."

They headed down a few steps, and Lori had to duck under an archway that opened into a bright, airy room very different from the country feel of the rest of the house. The walls were painted white and hung with records, both old and new. Framed gig posters, set lists, and ticket stubs filled one wall, and an array of instruments and chairs of varying styles were littered around the edge of the room. A circular coffee table covered in books, magazines, playing cards, and poker chips filled the centre, surrounded by oversized cushions. "I'll say it again, wow. Do you play all these instruments?"

"I wish. I play guitar and drums quite badly and a little piano not half bad. My sister, Beth, was the real musician. She could pick up anything and give you a tune. She played violin, various guitars, and piano amazingly. She was five years younger than me but had surpassed me musically before she left primary school."

"You never mentioned you had a sister. Is she coming to the party?"

"I don't. I mean, I did, but not anymore. She passed away eight years ago. She was fourteen."

"Oh, Alex, that's terrible. I'm so sorry. What happened?"

"It's a long story for another time. That's her over there."
She pointed to a picture on a shelf.

"She's beautiful, Alex. She looks just like you."

A happy dimple appeared at her comment. "I guess I keep
this room set up for her. My friends get a kick out of it too. It
used to be mine and Beth's playroom when we were younger
and gradually became a music den. Dad didn't raise the
door height like the others, so we had a rule if you had to
duck down, you were too grown up to be in here."

She chuckled. "We had to banish a cousin one summer
after he hit puberty and had a growth spurt." She continued
around the room, pointing things out to Lori. "A few of the
guys play or like to try to play and everyone likes hanging
out in here." She pointed at the coffee table. "As you can
see, we mostly play poker."

Lori smiled and imagined the scene. Content that Alex
would talk about Beth if and when she wanted, she chose
not to pry any further. She picked up a set of cards and
gave them a fancy shuffle. "Good job I can play poker then,
because I couldn't play a single chord if you paid me."

"That makes us a perfect team then because I can't bluff
to save my life. You can help me fleece the others later.
C'mon, I'll show you the library."

"Does this house ever end?"

Alex laughed. "This is the last room, apart from my
office. I'll give you the outdoor tour in the morning before
the others arrive." She pulled open a heavy wooden door
that looked original to the house, and held it open for Lori
to enter first.

"Okay, so this is definitely my favourite room." Lori turned in a circle, taking in the floor to ceiling stacks. "Have you read all these?"

"Most of them. The piles over there are top of the list of those I haven't."

Lori picked up a copy of Sarah Waters novel from the pile. "I've never read any of hers, but I saw the BBC made some into shows for the telly. Are they any good?"

"Oh yes, they're great. Wonderful lively stories, and guaranteed to give a straight girl like you an education."

"Education?"

"Don't give me that innocent look. Here." Alex pulled out one of her books from a shelf. Smirking, she held it out to Lori. "Give this one a try."

"Why do I feel as if you're setting me up here?"

"Maybe because I am. Just read it and let me know what you think."

"And also why the presumption about my straightness?" Lori hid her own smirk at the mild surprise that washed over Alex's face. Lori might not have a clue what was going on herself, but there was no harm in calling Alex out on something Lori had never confirmed.

"Sorry, I didn't mean to do that. I assumed, what with Andrew and...I'm sorry. I'm only having some fun with you."

Alex seemed genuinely sorry, and a little annoyed with herself. Lori wagged a finger her way playfully. "Never assume Alex, you might miss out on something." Lori turned away but not before she caught Alex's eyes widen at her comment.

She continued to circle the room, surprised at her own bravery in the moment. But something about both Alex and Jess commenting on her straightness had niggled at her.

She turned back to Alex who'd been quiet, leaning back against one of the stacks clearly deep in thought. Lori interrupted her thoughts, taking the book from her hand. "Okay, I don't trust you but I'm intrigued. I can save it for a couple of trips away with work that I have coming up."

Alex stood upright and nodded, the smile returning to her face. "Perfect. Now let's head back through for dinner before Jess gets grumpy."

CHAPTER 20

Lori slumped back in her dining chair. "Jess, that was truly delicious. I'm so stuffed. Thank you."

"You're welcome. I'm glad someone around here appreciates me," she said, looking pointedly at Alex.

"What? You know I love your cooking. I even bought you a new kitchen so you'd cook for me. What more do you want?"

Jess put a finger to her chin, considering her options. "What do you reckon, Lori? Should she clear the table and do the dishes while we go finish the wine?"

"I think that's a perfect idea." She looked at Alex.

"Hey, I thought you came to see me?" Alex protested.

"I did, but I can't pass up an opportunity to find out some of your dirty little secrets from your best friend." She winked at Jess.

Alex stood, pretending to huff. "Fine, fine. I know when I'm not wanted." She collected the plates and then leant close to Jess, kissing the top of her head before whispering just loudly enough for Lori to hear, "Be nice about me."

Jess stood and laughed, picking up her glass and the half bottle of wine still left on the table. "C'mon, Lori, let's head outside where she can't hear us." Alex's eyes bored into her and she turned to poke her tongue out before heading out on to the patio.

"So, I take it this is where the fun happens tomorrow night?" Lori looked around her, taking in the seating arrangements and barbeque.

"It sure is. Get yourself comfy." Jess pointed to one of the outdoor sofas before pushing a button that turned on the fairy lights and heaters above them.

"I see you're all set up. This is fantastic."

"Aye, Alex sure knows how to throw a party and keep her friends happy. She put a lot of work into this house with all of us in mind."

"She enjoys being the hostess then?"

"To be honest, it's not really like that. Once everything is set up we all muck in and see to ourselves. It's a close group and we all feel at home here. She's not really a centre of attention girl. I think she likes having the company every now and again and enjoys seeing the place filled. Alex likes making people happy."

"I guess it must get a bit lonely out here. It's a big place for one person."

"It is and, even after everything that happened here, she'll never leave it."

"What do you mean?" Lori wondered if she was talking about Beth.

Jess waved the comment off. "Believe me, Alex wouldn't have it any other way hiding out here on her own. She'll be glad to see the back of us Sunday."

Lori clearly wasn't getting anymore from Jess and chose not to press the issue. As she looked around at the beautiful home Alex had made, she wasn't sure anything could get her to leave either.

"So..." Jess interrupted her thoughts. "Alex tells me you're an interpreter?"

"Oui." She smiled. "Sorry, I can't help it sometimes."

"No, please, I love hearing accents. I can't wait to travel: Europe, Asia, and South America..."

"Oh yeah, you mentioned that earlier. When does the big adventure begin?"

"I'm not sure. I actually have the money saved and my work is willing to agree a yearlong sabbatical. They're so desperate for social workers they're just happy I want to come back."

"So what's the problem?"

Jess glanced toward the kitchen then looked back at her, seemingly debating how much she should say. Taking a sip of wine, she seemed to make a decision. "I can't leave Alex."

"Oh." Lori wasn't sure what to say. She didn't know anything about their friendship, or even if it had only ever been a friendship. Her conversation with Adam echoed at the back of Lori's mind. About getting out there and doing things for herself and her happiness. "Surely Alex wants you to do what makes you happy though, and has been expecting you to go eventually?"

"I don't know. I've been talking about this for so long, I think she thinks that's all it is, talk. I don't think she believes I'll ever do it."

"Have you talked to her? I mean, Alex is a big girl and it's only a year. I'm sure she'll cope—"

"Listen, you hardly know Alex, so you don't know what she's been through. The longest I've gone without seeing her is three weeks in over ten years. And that was just this past three weeks."

"Okay, I'm sorry." Lori held her hands up in surrender, worried about upsetting the person so obviously closest to Alex. "You're right, I don't know her. I don't know what you've been through together. I didn't mean to be flippant."

Jess took a breath and slumped back in the sofa. "No, I'm sorry. I'm being unfair. If I'm honest, it's not all about her. I guess it will be hard for me too. I'll miss her. I tried to get her to come with me, but she won't leave the farm for that long."

"Jess, are you and Alex... I mean, have you and Alex..."

"Oh no. Me and Alex have never...you know... It's not like that. Apart from a couple of drunken disco kisses in our teens, but then who hasn't kissed their best friend when drunk eh?" She laughed.

Lori thought of Stella. "Um, well—"

"Seriously? Wow." She whispered conspiratorially, "Is your best friend ugly? It's okay, you can tell me."

Lori laughed out loud then. "Actually, she's gorgeous, but I guess I was with Andrew almost the whole time I've known her and I've never really thought of girls like that so..."

"Gorgeous you say?"

"Yes. And straight, I'm afraid."

"Hey, you know what they say?"

"No, enlighten me. What do they say?"

"You're only straight until you're not." Jess winked then, a knowing look on her face.

Lori took a gulp of wine, feeling her face heat. "Why do I think that's a dig at me?"

It was Jess's turn to hold her hands up. "Hey, it's just a saying. Anyway, does that mean you've only ever been with guys then?"

Feeling slightly uncomfortable with the way this conversation was going, Lori filled their glasses, buying herself some time. "Actually, just guy."

"No. Way." Jess's eyes widened. "You've only been with one guy?" She practically squealed in disbelief.

"Shh. Yes. I mean, I dated other guys before Andrew but nothing ever clicked and I studied hard at uni so there wasn't much time for relationships. I guess I wasn't really interested."

"Wait a minute." Jess leaned forward towards her making sure she had Lori's full attention. "Answer me this. How old were you when you lost your virginity?"

"Jeez, you really aren't shy are you? Has Alex put you up to this?"

"No, cross my heart. C'mon spill. I promise it won't leave this patio."

Lori coughed into her hand. "Twenty-three," before gulping half her wine back.

"Twenty-three! Holy shit, Lori!"

Lori couldn't help but laugh then. "I know, I know. It's tragic. What can I say?"

"Wow. I don't think I've ever met anyone who made it through university without at least one night to regret. Or half a dozen, in my case."

Alex stepped out on to the patio then, wine glass in hand, just as the pair of them burst into a fit of giggles together. "I hope that's not at my expense?"

"Please, sweetie pie, we've more interesting things to be talking about than you." Jess winked Lori's way.

"Okay, so what did I miss?"

"I was just about to give Lori the low down on who else is coming tomorrow night."

"Ah, yes. Jess loves a good gossip about her friends."

"Hey, you said you were trustworthy," Lori protested.

"Don't you worry, my innocent little English rose. I prefer to do it behind your back so you'll never know."

"Oh, I feel so much better. Okay, so prepare me for tomorrow, then. Who is coming and what do I need to know? I need back stories plus dos and don'ts. I have big feet I regularly find myself chewing on."

Alex and Jess exchanged glances then Alex blew out a breath and got up and headed back inside, calling over her shoulder, "I think we're going to need another bottle of wine for this."

Chapter 21

All the food, wine, and chat, knocked Lori out and she slept like a log with Frank warming her feet on the end of the bed. He had arrived at the patio door with kisses for her and, despite Alex's protests that he was an outdoor dog, who had a cosy home in the barn with Pedro, she had sneaked him in with her for company at bedtime.

She heard the faint sound of music and slipped out of bed. Pulling on a large hoodie over her pyjama vest she headed in the direction of the kitchen with Frank in tow.

Jess was humming to the radio by the cooker, expertly flipping a pancake.

"Hey, I was meant to make you breakfast this morning."

Jess jumped at her voice and leant over to turn the radio down. "Well, if you weren't such a sleepy head my stomach wouldn't have forced me into it."

"Sorry, I guess between the journey and the wine, I needed that sleep. I'll make it up to you. Promise."

"Oh, don't worry. Tomorrow morning when everyone is hungover, demanding bacon and eggs, you shall be my kitchen slave."

"You've got a deal. Where's Alex?"

"Out in the barn. It's feeding time. She shouldn't be long."

Right on cue, the porch door slammed and Alex appeared in the kitchen doorway. Lori took in the skinny jeans, wellington boots, and long, wool jumper underneath a racing green Barbour coat. She looked every bit the modern farm girl, casual and relaxed with a pinkness in her cheeks. It suited her and Lori had to admit she looked adorable.

"What are you smiling at? What's Jess been telling you about me now?"

Realising Alex was talking to her, Lori started. "What? Oh, nothing. Just you in your farm girl get up. I was just thinking it suits you."

"Hmm...okay. I'll believe you." She pulled off her wellies, shrugged out of the big coat, and left them by a chair at the kitchen door before joining Lori at the island. "What's for breakfast, chef?"

She took in Alex's side profile as she leant across the island towards the pan Jess was working. Lori could feel the chill of the outdoors come off her along with the fresh scent of hay and washing powder.

"Pancakes, square sausage, and scrambled eggs. That should set you up before your ride this morning."

That was enough to snap Lori's attention back to the room. "Ride? Wait, when you said you were giving me the outdoor tour you said nothing about horses?"

"It's okay, don't panic." Alex smiled reassuringly. "I don't have the time to keep horses anymore. How does a quad bike sound?"

Lori grinned, relieved. "Much more up my street. It's safe to say I'm not a horse person."

Alex rubbed her hands together. "No horses. Got it. Let's eat and get going. The others will start arriving soon."

Alex was glad to see that Lori had taken her advice and dressed warmly for the quad ride. She'd borrowed long socks and wellies from Jess who shared her shoe size. She headed out to the barn, Frank following on behind, hoping to get in on the action.

"You let him sleep in your room, didn't you?"

"Maybe. How did you guess?"

"The fact he's following you like a lapdog rather than jumping all over you. He's obviously hoping for more of the same tonight."

"I said I'd have him tamed, didn't I?"

Alex laughed. "You don't play fair, but one for you, I think." She licked her finger and scored the air.

"Yup." Lori nodded. "About time I got one back."

"Okay, okay, don't gloat. Let's see if we can lose this puppy."

Alex wheeled the quad bike out and handed Lori a helmet before tugging on her own. "I'll drive us out to the top field, let you get your bearings, then you can bring it back in if you want?"

"Sounds good. Let's go."

Lori slid onto the back and Alex turned the engine over, giving it some revs to warm up before turning around to check Lori was set. She shook her head at Lori who was holding the handles at the rear of the bike. Instead she took Lori's arms and pulled them tight around her own waist. "Safer," she called back, happy when she felt Lori move in closer and tighten her grip.

With a wheel spin they set off, heading for a small patch of woodland and the hills beyond. Alex knew the woodland tracks well and pushed the quad tight around the corners and over humps, enjoying the thrill of the speed coupled with the gorgeous girl hanging on tight behind her.

The cold wind made her eyes water, but Alex didn't slow
down until they came out the other side of the woods, into
a field high above the farm. She slowly took them up to the
crest, allowing Lori time to take in the views around them.

They came to a stop, and Alex killed the engine. She was
sorry to feel Lori's arms slip from her waist as she got off
the bike.

Both women removed their helmets and were silent for
a few minutes. Alex could make out only some of the farm
visible beyond the trees below as they stood side by side,
looking out across the hills. She felt Lori slip her cold hand
into hers and turned toward her. "Thank you for inviting me
here. I think it might just be perfect."

Alex returned her smile and, keeping hold of her hand,
tugged her in the direction of a crumbling wall farther up the
hill. "C'mon. It's even better up here." They reached the wall,
and Alex hopped up as she'd done a hundred times or more.

She reached down for Lori's hand again. She didn't let go
after pulling Lori up beside her and blowing out her breath
from the short hike, she smiled and waved her arm at the
view.

The only sounds she could hear were birds and the rustle
of leaves as branches swayed in the breeze. Wind turbines
on the brow of a nearby hill turned in a steady beat as what
appeared to be toy-sized cars drove silently along the road
Lori had travelled the day before.

"See? I told you." She watched Lori scan the vista before
turning to Alex. Her smile was gone and, as Alex held her
gaze, she wasn't sure what to say or do. There was sadness
in Lori's eyes and she didn't know where it had come from
or what she was thinking. She lifted Lori's arm and tucked

herself underneath it, slipping an arm around her waist and pulling her in closer.

Lori didn't object and Alex couldn't help drawing her into a full hug. Tucking her head under Lori's chin, they gazed out across the landscape, content in the moment. She'd tried not to read too much into Lori's little comments when they'd chatted on the phone, was she flirting, or did Alex just want to hope she was? It had been so long since she'd wanted attention from someone. So long since she had craved a touch or a glance from one person. That alone was enough to convince her that this connection wasn't all in her imagination. And now here they were, with their arms wrapped around each other. Alex held on to the moment, and realised it was the most peaceful she had felt in a very long time.

"Thank you for coming, Lori. I think it might just be perfect having you here." She glanced up and saw Lori smile at that, felt her squeeze a little tighter before pulling away and jumping down from the wall.

She moved toward the bike then stopped and turned to face Alex, hand held out. "Hand them over. It's my turn to play," she said, referring to the keys.

"You sure you can handle one of these bad boys?"

"Don't underestimate this city girl. I did grow up with a brother in the Swiss mountains, remember? You don't have to be scared."

"Aye, okay, hot shot. I don't scare that easily. They're still in the ignition."

They swapped places on the bike, Alex needing no invite before wrapping her arms around Lori's waist. "Let's go then, driver. Show me what you got."

CHAPTER 22

Once back in the warmth of the farm, they both changed out of their mud spattered clothes while Jess finished with the food prep. As she headed toward the kitchen, Lori could hear an unfamiliar voice. She guessed it was Susie as the rest of the guests weren't due until later in the afternoon. After the stories she'd heard the night before, mainly from Jess, she was determined to be on guard and not rise to any bait Susie might throw.

Alex had assured her that Susie's heart was in the right place, but Lori thought she knew her type. The type of girl who was your best friend until you got in the way of something they wanted. She'd met many Susies at boarding school.

Putting on what she hoped was her warmest smile she moved into the main room and found the three other girls lounging on the sofas. Her nerves must have been showing as Alex quickly stood and came to her side, smiling reassuringly. "Lori, this is Susie."

Lori held out a hand, keeping her smile fixed. "Great to meet you, I've heard a lot about you."

Susie glanced in annoyance in Jess's direction before leaning up from the sofa to shake her hand. "I've no doubt you have."

Jess looked away guiltily, jumping up from her spot on the sofa where she'd been sitting next to Alex. "Here, Lori, have my seat. Let me get you something to drink."

"Oh sure, thanks, Jess." She caught Alex's eye and fought not to laugh at Jess's hasty retreat from trouble. She turned to straighten out the cushions and her face, before sitting down with Alex.

"So, Lori, Alex tells me you're an interpreter who speaks like a gazillion languages? Her words, not mine."

The way she said it sounded like an accusation rather than a question. "Yeah, that's right, although not quite a gazillion. I learnt at a young age, so, you know, it's easier. Not such a big deal."

Lori had expected someone stern and professional looking, maybe a little older than them from Jess's description. Someone tall and too skinny, with pointy features and a severe fringe to go with bobbed hair. Okay, so maybe her imagination had created a modern day witch of sorts, but the girl before her was more pixie than witch. She looked to be around Alex's age and height, but with a physique more like a teenage boy, and blonde hair cropped short with a shaggy texture. She had a pretty, petite face and a clear complexion interrupted with nose and lip piercings that gave her a hard edge. She was dressed in baggy, boyfriend jeans with a checked shirt open over a Blondie T-shirt. Lori guessed this was what Jess meant by the term 'baby butch,' although she seemed a little old for the look.

"Ah, so you went to some posh school? I should have known from your accent. Let me guess..." She put on a mock English accent and sat up prim and proper. "The boys preferred a good game of ruggers rather than that ghastly game, football, and you were on the tennis and lacrosse team?" She laughed derisively.

Lori attempted to laugh with her, trying to hide her annoyance. Deciding to play the game she plumbed up her own voice. "Yes, daaahling...guilty as charged." She tilted her head in challenge. "I also shared my chamber with a princess, my correct title is Lady Hunter. I had a maid to dress me in the morning and we only dined off solid silverware. Oh, and one mustn't forget summers at the yacht club."

Alex burst out laughing, choking on her beer while Jess roared from the kitchen, "Lady Hunter. That's brilliant."

Even Susie couldn't help but laugh now. But Lori didn't get the joke which now seemed to be at her expense.

Susie rolled her eyes. "As in a girl who hunts for ladies? A lesbian?"

"Oh!" Embarrassed, she squirmed at the statement and was clearly getting no help from Alex who was mopping up her beer. "Funny. I get it." She needed to get this conversation back on safer ground. "So you know Alex from school? She says you travel a lot with work. Do you speak any languages?"

"Aye, we've known each other since primary school, and no, I never saw the point of languages at school. It's not as if we could afford to go abroad anywhere. Now, I can probably say 'beer' and 'cheers' in about ten languages. That's all you need to get by these days anyway, isn't it?"

Lori didn't bite, deciding a lecture on the value of learning languages wasn't going to be the way to get on Susie's good side.

She caught Jess rolling her eyes as she came back from the kitchen loaded with more drinks. "Okay, Susie, enough. You've been here five minutes. At least have a few more drinks before you get your bitch on. That way you can at least use the alcohol as an excuse in the morning."

"What?" Susie was indignant. "I'm just getting to know Alex's new 'friend' here."

Lori didn't miss the emphasis on the word friend and watched as Susie sat back in her chair smugly, seemingly pleased that Jess's admonishment must mean she had scored a hit.

"Here." Jess shoved another beer into her hand. "Drink that and give it a rest, eh? I know you struggle with those two personalities of yours, but we'd really prefer a visit from your good twin for the one night you're here." She winked over at Lori in solidarity.

"Oh, you're as funny as ever, Jess, really. I've missed you so much."

"All right you two, that's enough." Alex held up her hands. "Behave or I'm kicking you out. Tonight is for relaxing, enjoying the one night we are all here together, and welcoming Lori to the farm. Clear?" She looked back and forth between the two of them.

"Crystal," they mumbled in unison.

"Okay then, who's for getting the barbeque started? The boys just texted that they'll be here in an hour and the girls won't be far behind."

"Aye, okay, I get the hint." Jess got back up again, pulled on some trainers, and headed for the patio doors.

"What a good little wife you've got, Alex. You realise that's your competition, Lori?" Susie smirked.

Alex just glared back. "I said enough. Go get some meat out of the fridge and take it out to her."

Susie huffed but got up, and Alex followed suit. Alex put an arm around her shoulder and gave her a peck on the cheek. "C'mon, play nice, Susie."

Susie looked guilty then and a tinge of pink came into her cheeks. "Aye. Okay, sorry."

Alex looked back at Lori and mouthed a silent "sorry" before nodding in the direction of the bar. "Want to help me set up the bar?"

Lori smiled, letting out the breath she'd found herself holding while Alex and Susie had been talking. "Only if I can drink while we work."

Alex laughed then, flinging an arm up around her neck and pulling her down for a quick peck to her cheek as well. "Anything you want for being such a good sport."

The boys soon arrived in a flurry of hugs, kisses, introductions, and good spirits. They were happy to see treats already being cooked up on the barbeque and the bar ready to go.

Neal and Mike quickly emptied the car of bags and booze before grabbing beers and giving their manly opinions to Jess and Susie on how the steaks should be cooked.

It was tradition for Alex to serve them their first drink at the bar, but then they were on their own. "Fancy helping me with a round of cocktails?"

"Sure. I love a cocktail." Lori stepped behind the short bar with her as Chris and Danny appeared, perching on the two stools opposite.

"So how do you guys all know each other? I lost track of all the links when Jess tried explaining it last night." Lori started muddling limes in glasses, adding sugar syrup as instructed by Alex.

"Well, these two are my fellow computer geek friends from university. We've spent many an all-nighter together, and not in the fun way."

Chris laughed. "Hey, we had a few party nights. And don't forget our all-night Red Bull and cheese puff binges when assignments were due. They were pretty epic."

Danny chimed in, "Don't let them fool you, Lori. We partied with the best of them when the notion took. Besides, I'd say we've more than compensated for all those sensible nights by now."

"Red Bull and cheese puff binges?" Lori raised an eyebrow in Alex's direction.

"Hey, don't knock it until you've tried it. All that caffeine and preservatives were the main source of our imaginative power."

"I bet. I'd be on the ceiling." Lori finished with the last of the lime and sugar, wiped her hands, and took down a bottle of Havana rum, handing it to Alex.

"What about Neal and Mike?"

"Neal and Mike are twins, non-identical, obviously," Chris answered while appraising them both through the patio doors. "Neal is my better half but they are pretty much inseparable so if one is around, you're almost guaranteed to find the other."

Lori eyed them both. "Nice catch, Chris. He's very handsome. Mike isn't bad either. Does he have a better half?"

Alex looked up sharply at her comment, spilling the rum she was measuring.

Lori didn't seem to notice but unfortunately Danny caught it and decided to have some fun as he answered for Chris. "Oh, he's very much single and would be a great catch to the right girl." He winked at Lori.

Alex watched her blush. Had she been checking Mike out? She had stopped mid-pour and gave a start when she realised Lori was looking at her, still blushing as she backtracked and directed her words at Alex. "Oh! I didn't mean for me, not that there's anything wrong with Mike. I'm sure plenty of girls would be lucky to have him but, you know, I just broke up with my boyfriend and—"

Danny held up his hands in surrender. "Hey, Lori, sorry. I'm just teasing."

Chris didn't seem convinced as he said, "I thought maybe Alex had invited you up here with Mike in mind?"

Alex felt Lori's suspicious eyes on her. She smiled, ignored the look, and carried on with the cocktails. Satisfied Lori wasn't actually checking out Mike, she decided to have some fun of her own. "Well, you know, he is a great guy: handsome, smart, and funny—" She smirked at her teasingly.

Lori bumped her shoulder. "Enough. And the same goes for you." She playfully scowled at Danny.

"Am I missing something here?" Chris looked from one to the other.

"Ah, Chris, slow as ever." Danny put an arm across his shoulders. "How about we go thrash on the drums for a bit before Mike gets to them?"

Just then, Neal appeared scooping up one of the Caipirinha cocktails Alex had finished adding crushed ice to. "Sounds like a great idea. He's currently lecturing Susie on the importance of a pension."

"I'm up for it." Chris agreed, taking a cocktail of his own and looking Neal up and down. "But only if you take your shirt off while you play."

Danny groaned. "You know what? I'm just going to stay here. You guys go for it."

Giggling, Chris and Neal headed off like naughty school boys to the music room.

Lori filled a tray with four of the Brazilian cocktails. "I'll take these out to the others and say hello. Give you two some time to catch up."

Before Alex could protest she was already heading out onto the patio, leaving her and Danny at the bar. She walked around and took Chris's vacated stool, sliding the last two cocktails toward them.

"C'mon, then. I know you're itching to grill me about what just happened."

"What did just happen? Is something going on with you two? I thought she was just a new climbing buddy. And what was that about a break up? With a guy I might add."

"There isn't. She is. She has. She was. But I still think there's something there, Danny."

"Oh, there's definitely something there, but whether she knows it, is another matter."

"I know, I know. We're friends and I'm happy if that's all it is. We've talked a bit already on the phone. She got the wrong idea about me inviting her here. Well, actually she got the right idea but, ultimately, I'd rather she was here as a friend than not at all, so I put her at ease."

"And are you really happy if that's all it is?"

Alex took a sip of her drink, giving herself a second to think. Danny was the most honest person she had ever known. He was an all-round good guy who she had never hesitated to tell the truth. He had a way of listening and giving it to you straight that had helped her through some very dark moments in the past. Since then, she had never skirted a question from him.

She took another sip and looked past his floppy brown hair to eyes hooded with thick brows and a concerned forehead. It was also impossible to lie to him. "No, I don't think I am. I think she's amazing, Danny. She's beautiful and smart. We talk really easily and she's so funny and genuine. I feel comfortable around her and have this urge to be near her all the time, to touch her, to protect her. We've probably spent a total of three days together and she's got me hooked already. What I don't know is if it's just an infatuation? I mean, look at her."

Danny looked out at the patio, watching Lori laugh with Jess. "I can't deny it, she is stunning, and seems pretty genuine like you said. What does Jess say?"

"She's worried she's straight and on the rebound, looking for a bit of excitement after a seven-year snore-fest."

"Seven years. Wow. She could be right."

Alex's shoulders slumped. "I know, but, I mean, it's not as if she's tried anything. Surely, if it was just a fling she was looking for, she'd have maybe tried something at the bothy and we never would have had to see each other again. We had a bit to drink and it's safe to say my guard was down."

"I guess. Or maybe it's just because she's straight and she sees you as nothing more than a friend."

Alex rested her face in her hands, thinking back to Lori's comment in the library she wondered if it was only meant innocently. It had surprised her at first, given her hope maybe. She didn't know. Scrubbing her face she looked up, dejected. "You're probably right. Who am I kidding? Do you think that's all it is?"

Danny shrugged. "Listen, all I know, Alex, is I haven't heard you speak like this about anyone in a long while, in fact, not even about Rachel. And the way Lori got all, I don't know, flustered maybe, when I suggested she was eyeing up Mike says she feels something too. It's maybe just not computing yet and she'll need time."

"Or maybe it's just all in my head and I've inflated the entire thing. I'm worried it's been so long since I felt anything like this, I'm letting all the good things cloud my judgement without seeing past them to the bad."

"Why do you always do that?" Danny's face was suddenly stern, his eyes boring into her.

"Do what?" She sat back, away from him, not used to the look being pointed in her direction.

"Why are you always looking for the bad? It's as if you're determined never to be happy. Jess is right when she says you sabotage any potential for a relationship."

"What? I do not sabotage. I just don't waste my time, that's all."

"You barely give anything time. And if you go in with the attitude of already seeing it end, it'll never get started."

"My point is, I'm not seeing it starting. I don't even know if she's thinking this way, never mind if she's ready to dive straight into something new right now."

Danny's face softened and he squeezed her shoulder with his big hand. "Well, you know it doesn't all have to be up to you. How about trying something new for you and don't worry so much. Let things take their natural course."

"You think I should wait? Let her make the first move if she wants more?"

"Well, it's that or try talking to the woman."

"What...but...I can't..."

Danny laughed. "You look like a goldfish."

"Bastard."

He squeezed her shoulder again and smothered his laughter. "You love me anyway."

"Don't know why."

"Because I give you the best advice."

"Which is what?"

"Continue to be your charming, lovely, beautiful self, and she will quickly see what the rest of us do and not be able to resist."

Her cheeks burned. "Thanks, Danny. I can always count on you for an ego boost. That's why you're my favourite."

He laughed at that, leaning in for a hug. "Don't let Jess hear you say that or she'll have me on the barbeque. Now come on, let's go party."

CHAPTER 23

The rest of the day flew by for Lori, with everyone taking their turn to grill her on everything from boarding school and politicians to her favourite Elton John song, *Crystal*.

There were comparisons with Mike and Neal about being a twin, laughter at her love of all things Lady Gaga, approval that her favourite eggs were poached, but also dismay that she'd never done a Sambuca shot or stayed out in a casino until breakfast time. Both of which seemed to have been a regular occurrence for Jess and Alex at university.

A couple more friends from uni, Lola and Gail, had arrived in time for steaks and the second round of cocktails.

Jules and Katy, a local couple, arrived soon after. Alex told her it was them who kept an eye on the farm when she was away. They told her about their own farm a few miles down the road. There they had built yurts and cabins on their land, renting them out as holiday accommodations, mostly to walkers, but also young couples looking to escape the city for a weekend.

While inside getting more drinks, Lori had watched them wobble down the bumpy lane on a tandem bicycle and had quickly called the others inside to witness the funniest thing she had seen in a long time. That was, until Chris and Neal attempted to ride it around the garden.

Curled up on one of the outdoor sofas, her glass and plate were never empty as she was regaled with many a funny story, starting with the first time Lola and Alex had met.

Jess had challenged them to play a game of shot chess which Alex had spectacularly lost before promptly disappearing to bed in a cloud of tequila. It had apparently endeared her to Lola though, who asked her out on a date the next day.

Lori looked between Lola and Alex, trying to picture them as a couple. She felt a pang of jealously at a look that had passed between them as the story was being told. It was one of knowing what had gone before and having secrets kept only by them. She wondered how long they had been together and if any residual feelings remained.

A game of 'Who can tell Lori the funniest or most embarrassing story about Alex' then ensued, despite protests from Alex. She heard tales of partying all night and sleeping in bouncy castles for entire weekends. There were numerous anecdotes of music festival mischief, as well as all the times Alex had managed to get herself thrown out of gigs. She didn't know whether to crack up or feel bad when Neal told her how Alex and Danny had accidentally crashed a wake in a gay bar.

Their fancy dress nights sounded epic and she couldn't help but wish she had been to them. She laughed hearing about their embarrassing failures at a French surf camp, along with ill-fated dinghy adventures on Loch Tay. There was of course also a round of who had kissed who in the group over the many years of partying together.

It was clear everyone adored Alex and loved spending time in her home. They were a tight group who'd experienced it all together and it warmed Lori that she had met someone so obviously special to a lot of people and been invited in to join the group. She had been made to feel as if she belonged, even if it was just for one weekend.

The food was amazing. Jess had truly outdone herself and Chris had kept the cocktails coming, giving each one a progressively filthier name until his final one had resembled mud, and he'd called it a night after naming it as such.

He was definitely the joker of the group, along with Jess. They had come to her rescue on more than one occasion where Susie was concerned, as she seemed careful not to try to bait Lori when Alex was around. In a group with ten of Alex's friends, she could handle one nippy person.

They'd hung out in the music room where it turned out that behind Mike's sensible accountant exterior, was a rocker bursting to get out. He and Neal had thrashed a few tracks out, tearing off their shirts to finish, much to everyone's amusement and Chris's delight.

Danny had plucked out a few chilled tracks on the guitar accompanied by Jules on the piano. She managed to lull them momentarily quiet as she sang *Caledonia*, while the rest of them listened and played poker. True to her word, Lori fleeced them all for Alex.

As the evening came in and the air chilled, they were drawn out to the patio with leftovers, wine, and a roaring bonfire. Frank had spent most of his day out having adventures on the farm but once the bonfire was lit, he curled himself contently at Lori's feet and she cemented his new found loyalty to her by sneaking him pieces of sausage.

The boys had overindulged and, once the fire had died down, it wasn't long before they headed to bed. Lori hadn't managed any time on her own with Alex since their quad ride that morning so she had planned to be the last one standing with her at the end of the night.

But after Jess and the other girls had followed the boys to bed, Susie was unsurprisingly reluctant to leave. Despite her head periodically bobbing as her eyes closed in drunken exhaustion, she just sunk lower in the chair, getting comfortable and seemed to have no plan to allow them time alone.

It hadn't taken long for Lori to realise that Susie's problem with not only her but Jess as well, was that Susie clearly had long standing feelings for Alex and simply didn't like her having other women in her life. Lori consoled herself with the information that Susie worked offshore as an engineer so spent the majority of her time on oil rigs. That meant if Lori and Alex remained friends, at least she would only have to deal with her once or twice a year.

The night became still and the three women quiet with it. Lori looked from Susie to Alex, who sipped her red wine, as she stared from the dying embers of the bonfire up to the starry sky. Lori rested her chin in her hand and leaned an elbow on the arm of the chair, she felt content, serene even.

She looked away from the fire and caught Alex staring her way, she held her gaze. "I love it here, Alex."

Alex smiled lazily back at her. "I love having you here."

Lori felt the warmth of the smile and the statement from the tips of her ears to her toes.

Susie's head bobbed again and Alex was blunt. "Susie, don't feel you have to stay up to help tidy. Lori and I will clear the empties and the rest can be left for the morning."

Coming to, Susie shook her head to protest but thankfully clocked the brush off and realised she had no choice but to take the hint. She made a point of giving Alex a long hug before huffing inside with only a nod in Lori's direction.

Alex sighed and Lori took it as relief. "Stuff the empties. I need more wine and a comfy chair. How about you? Going to stay up a bit longer with me?"

Lori smiled, happy Alex wanted some time just the two of them as well. "After all of today's excitement, I could use a bit of quiet time before bed."

They took their glasses into the living area and Alex headed for the large, curved love seat. Handing her glass to Lori, she pulled a small lever on the side of the seat. "Check this out." Gently, she spun it around until it faced the middle of the room and the wood burner whose embers were barely hanging on.

"Once again, I'm impressed. You really have thought of everything with this place."

Alex beamed. "I'm so pleased you're enjoying being on the farm." She added another log to the burner and opened a vent to get it going before curling up on the chair next to Lori. "So you survived my friends okay then? No one gave you any more trouble? And by that, I mean Susie?"

"Nothing I couldn't handle. It's easy to see that they all love you very much and want to make sure I'm not here to corrupt you."

"Did you get the best friend lecture from Jess last night?"

"She went surprisingly easy on me, but there was definitely a hint of warning from her. I'd expected it anyway and you haven't met Stella yet remember. I guarantee you'll get pretty much the same from her."

"Interrogated by a female Police Detective? That could be kind of hot."

"Oi," Lori slapped her arm. "I'm going to tell her to be extra hard on you for that!"

"Oh, please do," Alex teased.

"That's enough of that chat," Lori scowled at her. "I mean it, you're not funny."

"Ah, see you know that's not true, but okay, I'm sorry. Forgive me?"

"I suppose this once. As long as you promise not to try it on with my best friend when you meet her."

"So, you want me to meet your friends, eh? I must be doing something right."

"Don't get smug. I'm a posh bird who went to boarding school with a princess remember. I'm just being polite and returning the invitation to visit. Feel free to be polite also and gracefully decline."

Alex laughed at that and Lori joined in. "Well played, point to you."

"I think that point puts me ahead, you know."

"You also know the weekend isn't over. There's time."

"True. I'll save my smugness." Lori took a sip of wine and decided on directness. "So can I ask what Susie's problem is anyway? I can't say she went as easy on me as Jess did."

"Ah, Susie is a long story. Like I told you, we have some history that goes all the way back to high school that she can't seem to let drop. We were both confused and vulnerable, not realising yet we were gay, or what it was going to mean for us being different from our friends. All we knew was we were the same and so stuck together. When we were fourteen, I made the mistake of kissing her and she developed a crush that didn't materialise into anything. We've been friends so long now, I can't just cut her out, and besides, underneath she has a good heart."

"Well, obviously you know her best but are you sure about that? People change. Things happen that change them."

Alex shrugged. "Aye I know. She takes an instant disliking to anyone new, particularly women. You should have seen her when I started seeing Lola back in uni, and then with Rachel... Bitch doesn't even cover it. But I know the other side of her so you'll just have to trust me and not pay any attention to her."

"I have to say I was a little relieved to see her treat Jess, and then Lola, the same. At least then I knew it wasn't just me."

"Oh, don't worry, it's not just you. I mean, me and Lola were eighteen years old and it only lasted a year, but Susie acted as if we were about to get married or something. At the time I said yes to Lola, I'd just turned Susie down again, saying I was too busy with study to get involved with someone. I was trying to let her down gently but then I met Lola and she was raging. She's never quite gotten over it."

"But she must realise by now that it's never going to happen with you two."

"Yeah, of course she does. One day she'll finally settle and get a job onshore and meet the girl that will change it all."

"I hope you're right."

"I am. And until then, she's around so little it's not worth worrying about. But I'm sorry about her, and Jess too, if she was a little in your face."

"Honestly, Jess was fine. She's quite intense when it comes to you but, like I said, I expected that from a best friend. She's actually been a sweetheart and made me feel very welcome."

"Aye, she is a sweetheart, and she has kind of assigned herself as my protector ever since, well, ever since stuff happened a long time ago and I found myself needing someone."

"Are you talking about Beth? Or other family stuff? Is what happened to her why they aren't around?"

"Let's just say Jess stuck it out with me through the worst time of my life. I owe her a lot."

Lori saw the same shadow cross Alex's face as she'd seen in the bothy. She decided to at least offer an opening this time. "Want to talk about it?"

Alex turned away from the fire and looked intently into Lori's eyes.

Lori wasn't sure what she was looking for, but she hoped whatever it was, Alex would find it. She wanted her to open up, to trust her.

Instead Alex found Lori's hand and linked their fingers. "Another time?"

Lori squeezed her hand in understanding and smiled. "Sure."

"So, tell me more about your dad. Do you see him often?"

"Not really. He tries to get home a few times a year but even then the most I normally get is a dinner. It's okay though, that's how it's always been and I've made peace with it."

"Still it must have been hard, especially not having your Mum around?"

Lori let out a long sigh. "I guess, but once my aunt Emily took over, we were well taken care of. And I always had Scott."

"I'm sorry, Lori. Way to change the subject. We don't have to talk about this."

"No, no. Like I said, I've made my peace. I don't mind."

Alex got up and headed to the bar. "Whisky?"

"I guess if I'm about to spill my guts then yes, please. A large one."

Alex chuckled. "Two large whiskies coming up."

"Oh, wait. Aren't we climbing a hill tomorrow? I hate climbing hungover."

"Um, not exactly. I had something else in mind. It's more water based. I promise it will clear your head along with whatever hangover you have."

"Would that explain the wetsuit hanging in my room?"

"Ah, you saw that did you? I got Jess to pick it up for you. I figured you were around the same height and build."

"Now I really am intrigued, as well as happy I can have more whisky. Go ahead and make it a large one."

Alex handed her the drink with a smile before getting comfortable again, curling up to face her.

Lori studied her profile in the orange glow from the fire and had the sudden urge to trace a finger down her cheek. She mentally shook herself, then took a gulp of the whisky, letting it burn its trail to her stomach before she was able to speak.

Alex beat her to it. "So how did you end up in boarding school?"

"You want the long story or short?"

"Long. There's more whisky if we need it."

"Good to know." She stared in to the fire again, thinking back to those lonely years and wondering where to start. "Scott and I got passed around for a while after Mum died. My dad's solution, was to disappear and drink in as many different countries as possible. We didn't understand at first. We thought he was gone forever, the same as Mum."

Alex didn't say anything, just took Lori's hand again.

"Our aunt, Emily, reassured us, told us he would be back once he'd 'gotten better and got some sense.' I don't think he wanted us to see him so broken. He didn't want to tarnish our image of him as our big, strong, adventurous dad who travelled to far off lands in search of magical stories and exotic gifts for us."

"So instead, he deserted you?"

"I know, I know. It took a year, but he finally sobered up enough to get some sense, remember he had two kids, and come home. But he was never the same. I think he saw too much of our mum in us, and it reminded him every day of what he'd lost."

"So his answer was to lose his kids, as well?"

"Yeah, that still doesn't make sense to me, and I'm not sure he could explain it even now. He was still young and selfish, and didn't think he was any good for us without our mum. He said she made him a father and he couldn't do it on his own."

"Then he packed you off to boarding school?"

"Not straightaway. He came home to claim us eventually. There was a run of unsuccessful nannies who weren't prepared for him disappearing for days at a time on binges. Then we went back to our aunt Emily's until we were eleven and in his mind old enough to go to boarding school."

"Didn't your aunt protest?"

"Of course, but she was actually my mum's aunt, retired with her own family already grown up. Despite her protests, she knew she would struggle with two teenagers in the house again and besides, my dad was the one paying our way so he had the final say."

"I guess at least you had Scott with you."

"That definitely helped, although it was weird going into dorms and not having him in the next room at night. But when I got homesick or needed advice, Emily was only a call away. I guess she became my touchstone in life. Unfortunately, she passed away two years ago. I think that's when I started realising the problems Andrew and I had. It always seemed to be Scott or Stella there when I needed to talk about it, not him."

"You definitely find out who really gives a crap when you go through something like that."

"Speaking from experience?"

"Aye." Alex swallowed the last of her whisky and got up to refill their glasses. "So you don't have much of a relationship with your dad then?"

"No. I know he loves me and I love him. We're family so it's unconditional. But he doesn't know me."

He had at least provided well and they had never wanted for anything. James Hunter was from serious money, although you wouldn't think it given his lifestyle, drifting from country to country, depending on the story. His motto was 'if it didn't fit in a carryon bag, it wasn't a necessity.' Seems that motto applied to his kids, as well.

She and Scott both had healthy bank accounts and money in trust, courtesy of their wealthy grandparents. Their properties in London were bought outright and there were no student loans to be paid. It afforded them independence and freedom, at least given their lack of family ties.

"Anyway, I think that's plenty of my sombre life stories for one night. Can we just sit and watch the fire die out with the last of the whisky?"

"Sure." Alex smiled, reaching out to brush some hair behind Lori's ear. "I'm glad you can talk to me."

Lori placed her hand over Alex's and held it against her cheek and closed her eyes. With one small, tender gesture, Alex had soothed the pain away and she wanted to savour the moment.

"Oh, I didn't realise you guys were still up." Jess stood in the doorway, breaking the spell. "Sorry to interrupt. I just needed some water."

Alex quickly dropped her hand and moved back in the seat. "No problem, the fire's nearly dead. We were just about to call it a night." She got up, collected their glasses, and brought them to the sink where Jess stood filling her glass.

The moment passed, and Lori didn't know if it was the whisky or the 'Alex effect', but she suddenly felt lightheaded and thought bed was probably for the best. "Good idea. I think that last whisky did a number on me."

"Aye." Jess smirked. "I'm sure it was the whisky."

Lori saw Jess take an elbow to the ribs as she stood next to Alex at the sink before Alex smiled her way. "C'mon, I want to make sure Frank hasn't snuck in and set up camp in your room again."

She followed Lori down the long corridor and into the living area of the annex apartment, sticking her head through the bedroom door, she checked the bed. "No sign of him. Looks as if you've got the place to yourself."

"You do realise I actually let him in last night, don't you?"

Alex looked down guiltily. "Busted. I guess I wanted an excuse to avoid an interrogation from Jess and also maybe walk you to your room."

Lori smiled at the gesture. "I had a brilliant time today, Alex. Your friends are great and I can see why you love this place so much."

Alex grinned, her dimples coming out in full force, which always pleased Lori. "Well, it's not over yet, adventures tomorrow remember."

"I can't wait," Lori held her gaze, momentarily unsure what to do next. A glance down and she knew. Leaning in she softly kissed her left dimple, before moving to her ear to whisper, "Bonne nuit et dors bien, Alex."

Alex stood rooted to the spot a few moments after the bedroom door had closed. Every fibre in her body hummed and begged her to knock on the door, not let Lori off so easily with only a peck on the cheek.

Instead she took some deep breaths and focused on one of the landscape paintings opposite, allowing her heart rate to settle. She heard Danny's voice of reason in her head, telling her to go with the flow, don't rush it, and let Lori lead the way. If she wanted more, she would let her know.

She quietly closed the annex door behind her and wandered dazed along the corridor, meeting Susie on her way to the bathroom.

Susie nodded in the direction of Lori's bedroom. "Been given your marching orders have you?"

"Ah, Susie, don't look so pleased. I know everything I need to know."

CHAPTER 24

Sean ground another cigarette under his boot, then leaned back further into the shadows as an upstairs light in the house opposite came on. A figure he knew well pulled the curtains, blocking his view with rocket ships and astronauts.

His eyes shifted to the living room window where another figure stood, sipping from a mug, surveying the street. This one was less familiar and he immediately stood taller, jaw working to control the roar building inside.

"Bitch," he muttered under his breath as he pulled another cigarette from the battered pack. It was the third night that week he'd watched the family scene play out. Her return from the school run, a glimpse of his sons bounding into the house, lights appearing, the flicker of the television. His return from work in his fancy car, a kiss at the front door, and no doubt a cosy dinner with banal chat about their boring days. Then his youngest son's bedroom light would appear, along with the imposter at the living room window.

Sean wondered if the man could see him, or maybe just sense his presence. He was sure the man knew he didn't belong in that house. He was only playing a character. He could never be their father.

The rocket ships and astronauts disappeared as the bedroom light went out. Only the faint glow in a corner of the window told him his son still slept with a nightlight. This annoyed him. He was ten, for fuck's sake.

A moment later, he watched as she slipped her arms around the waist of the imposter at the window. This hadn't happened before. Apart from a peck at the door, he hadn't seen them together. The wave of rage that ran through him at the sight almost propelled him across the road to wipe the smile off both their smug faces.

He pulled on the cigarette and imagined doing it instead. He envisioned their terrified faces as he busted through the door, and made the arrogant prick in the window watch as he sliced the smile from his lying, cheating, ex-wife's face, before bashing him over the fucking head with the mug.

That calmed him. All in good time, he thought. One day, he'd have his revenge.

He glanced upward at the glow in the window and thought about what kept him from realising his fantasy, of ending the woman who had cast him aside so easily when he needed her the most. The woman who had stolen his sons, and, with them, his life.

He made the trip south every few months. Winter was always best because he could get closer in the darkness and didn't have to rely on hiding in a car. It drizzled around him and he turned his collar up against the wind rushing through the alley at his back.

Breaking their embrace, the imposter moved away as she reached to draw the curtains. Sean watched her pause for a moment, looking both ways down the street as if searching. His legs almost engaged, oh how he wanted to step out from the shadow. To see the shock on her face when she realised that what she was sensing was there. He wanted to make her feel the fear he knew he could instil in her, even after all these years. But his feet wouldn't move. It wasn't time.

So long as his sons were in that house, she was safe. He wondered if she knew that was all that was keeping her alive.

Another second's pause, and she was gone. His family shut away from him for another night.

The rush of the fantasy was still there. Coursing through him and he could feel himself harden at the thought. Taking a breath, he allowed one last glance at the house before turning down the alleyway. Tonight was the night. There was no satisfaction in watching, but until the time was right, he'd have to make do with some other whore out there asking for it.

The urge was becoming more regular. Every night he stood across from the house built it further until it was beyond his control. He had to allow himself the release. He needed it.

Time was ticking away, and he felt a surge of impatience at the situation. But he was smart, and he'd been trained well, there would be no impulsive mistakes. He just needed some calm, if only for a night.

His mind was set. Someone would pay for what she had done. He'd probably be doing some other poor bastard a favour. Head down, he stalked towards his car. He'd have his fun tonight and be gone before his sons sat down to their breakfast in the morning.

CHAPTER 25

By Sunday lunchtime, Alex's Defender was packed and the girls were heading off on their water adventure. After breakfast, Jules and Katy had headed home to feed their own animals and all four guys had passed, citing that they'd done it before. The truth was they were heading back to bed to nurse their hangovers.

Lori had watched with Frank at her side, while Alex packed wetsuits, towels, life jackets, and helmets, but she had still refused to tell her where they were heading.

If it was possible, Susie had been even frostier with her, barely mumbling a good morning at breakfast before leaving the kitchen to get ready, and not appearing again until they were about to leave.

As the smallest, Susie had been forced to sit in the childlike seat in the boot, which only deepened her dark mood. She only spoke when an opportunity arose to get a dig in at Lori or Jess. If Alex noticed, she didn't say anything.

They were on foot now, Alex led them over fences and across a sheep-filled field that gradually declined downhill to a wide, shallow river. It was crystal clear and barely ankle deep so Lori was unsure exactly what water adventures they were going to have.

Stepping out onto a couple of stones, she voiced her uncertainty, "Are you sure wetsuits are really necessary? I mean, where exactly are we heading?"

"All in good time, Lori." Alex held out her gear. "You'll just have to trust me."

Realising she would have to change in front of Alex, she grabbed her gear, and bagged a bit of privacy behind a large tree, much to Jess's amusement.

"I can't believe you went to boarding school and are still shy getting changed around the ladies."

Lori stuck her head around the tree. "Well, you see my problem is that after last night, unfortunately, I now know you lot aren't ladies."

Everyone but Susie laughed along with Jess.

"What. You mean because we're all lesbians, you think we're going to perv on you? Please. Get over yourself," Susie said with a sneer.

Gail raised a hand. "Um, how many times do I need to remind you all? Straight girl here too."

Lori pulled her wetsuit up over her torso and stepped out from behind the tree, determined not to bite. "Actually, it was only Jess I was worried couldn't resist, but come to think of it..." She winked at Jess before turning her back to Gail. "Straight girl, could you zip me up please? It seems to be stuck and I'm not sure I want any of these lesbians near me half-naked."

Everyone broke into giggles apart from Susie. She looked between them all, snatched up her own wetsuit, and stomped behind the tree without another word, leaving them to stifle their laughter for the sake of peace.

Lori took her wetsuit boots and lifejacket and headed to a rock by the water to put them on. Turning her back, she gave the others privacy to change. After the incident in the bothy that had left her blushing scarlet, she didn't want to risk a peek at Alex and give Susie any ammunition.

"Okay, so what's this grand adventure? Because I can't see very much water?"

Alex stepped gingerly into the frigid river, sucking in her breath. "Follow me."

The cold was a shock at first, but the neoprene boots made it bearable. The women moved slowly and took care over the rocks in the shallow water. The banks on either side of them soon heightened and created a narrow path upstream.

Alex led the way as the water rose to knee height, she stopped at two large rocks that seemed to act as a kind of doorway, blocking their view ahead.

Lori didn't know what lay beyond, but she had a feeling it was special.

"Welcome to the Devil's Pool Pit," Alex declared as Susie brought up the rear.

"No way." Lori was delighted. She had heard of this place but never ventured out to find it, always short of time or eager to hit the road after a climb.

"Yes way. I take it you've heard of it?"

"Of course. I've seen it mentioned on websites but never thought I'd get to check it out. This is so cool. Are there really waterfalls?"

Alex looked pleased at Lori's excitement. "Aye, they're at the end. We haven't had much rain so the water should be low enough for us to make it through okay. We've all been before so should find our way easily enough."

"Cool," Lori grinned. "Well what are we standing around for? Let's go."

Her enthusiasm seemed to be infectious and, even though the others had been there before, they seemed just as excited as she was.

Susie visibly shivered. "I can't believe you've dragged me out here again."

Jess gave her a playful shove. "No one dragged you, Susie. In fact, why don't you just head back to the car if you're going to keep that face on you the whole time?"

She pulled a face and pushed past them all. "C'mon, let's just get there already."

They slalomed through the rocks either side, and the water turned almost black the deeper it got, only the dark red colour of the smooth rock ledges below the surface was visible, forming their path. The water quickly rose to waist height on Lori and Jess, chest height for rest.

Lori felt her way carefully, conscious of slipping. She didn't fancy a full on dunk under, no matter how hungover she was. Periodically, they stopped to clench and unclench their cold, stiff fingers, which were unprotected in the icy water, while Jess took pictures with a compact, waterproof camera.

Eventually, the deeper water gave way as they approached a natural dam. The foliage scaling the cliffs of the gorge became thicker and hung all around them. It had the effect of insulating the gorge to create the kind of muffled quiet you would find at the top of a mountain.

Lori took a breath and joined the others as they sat along one of the larger logs in the dam. She was in awe, taking it all in, while Lola and Gail acted out the log scene from Dirty Dancing to Jess's coaching and everyone else's amusement.

Alex pointed to a jagged path cut up through the cliff. "That's a stairway of sorts. We'll carry on from here through to the waterfalls, but on the way back, we'll climb up there and follow the path back to where we started to get the view from above."

"Sounds like a plan." Jess hopped off the log, back into the water. "Shall we make a move?"

"Sure." Alex jumped down after her, holding out a hand to help Lori.

Lori couldn't help but note Susie's dramatic sigh at Alex's gesture and, petty though it might be, she kept hold of Alex's hand and allowed her to lead her back into the deeper water.

Alex smiled back at Lori, obviously happy she hadn't let go of her hand. As they travelled further upstream Lori's excitement at seeing the waterfalls built. She glanced back at the others, Jess was beaming and gave her a wink, but one look at Susie soured the moment.

Suddenly her leg was knocked out from under her and she shrieked before falling under the water, letting go of Alex's hand.

Her life jacket quickly forced her back to the surface but, wincing with pain as she tried to stand, she lost her footing again and went back under. The icy cold water stabbed at her face and she gasped for air as someone grabbed the front of her life jacket and pulled her back up.

It was Alex, and she attempted to keep her on her feet while wiping the water from her face. "Shush you're okay. I've got you."

The others splashed their way over to her, apart from Susie who Lori noticed made no move to help. She simply leaned against the gorge wall watching the commotion.

"What happened, are you all right?" Alex placed an arm around her waist to help her stand, letting Lori's arm drape across her shoulders for support. Gail took her other hand.

"I don't know." She winced again trying to put weight on her left foot. "Something caught my ankle and then my other foot slipped and kicked out against a rock. Even with the cold it hurts. Is there shallower water soon so I can check it out?"

"We should probably just head back, take a look at the dam quickly and then get you up the steps and back to the car."

"No, no," Lori protested. "I really want to see the waterfalls. I can make it." She tried to take a step, but her face must have said it all.

"Oh no you don't. Whatever damage you've done, you're not making it worse. The only direction we are going is back. We'll come see the waterfalls next time."

Lori smiled down at her. "Next time? You mean, I'm getting a return invite?"

"Sure, I spoke to Frank last night. He's allowing it."

Jess chuckled. "C'mon you two. Let's get going before we all freeze and are good for nothing." She looked pointedly at Susie, who was still showing no signs of concern or intent to help.

Lori saw her shoot Jess a filthy look before huffing out a breath and turning back.

Lori couldn't help the smile stuck on her face at the thought of another weekend at the farm with Alex and Frank despite her disappointment of not making it to the waterfalls and the pain in her foot.

She gritted her teeth against the pain and with an arm around both Alex and Gail, they started the slow journey back to the car.

Chapter 26

John pushed his dinner away as the front door slammed closed. Why was the mashed potato always cold? The neighbour who had put it in front of him was friendly enough, but he didn't trust her. She only appeared when his son was away, and he was sure she only meant to spy on him. Besides, she'd gotten him in trouble before; he knew she wouldn't hesitate to do it again.

At least she was gone now and he was free in the house. His son didn't give her the key to his room, instead only a warning came his way to behave or there would be consequences. He'd made the mistake of asking if his son was leaving to help the girl. A backhanded crack had been his answer. Now every time he looked in the mirror, he saw the livid bruise, and remembered never to speak of her again. Every time he opened his mouth, his jaw ached, and he remembered he needed to do it himself. He needed to help her. To make sure she was all right.

He slipped a piece of paper from his dressing gown pocket and glanced at the kitchen clock. He listened to it tick and noted the time next to the others he had. He read the line along the top.

My name is John Murray. I have to
help the girl named Beth.

He knew the neighbour wouldn't be back. The times for the past few days matched the ones he had written that day. He was on his own now and had hours to find her. He left the table and put his plate next to the sink like the neighbour had told him. He collected his glass and poured more water as he'd watched her do earlier. He sipped it and looked out across the unkempt garden, remembering a time when his wife had kept it pristine with lush green grass and colours galore.

The radio played a familiar song and he took a moment to enjoy the memory that went with it. He was sitting out on a chair with the radio balanced on the kitchen windowsill, a toddler at his feet in a sand bucket. Sean had been such a content child, occupying himself for hours, he went wherever his mother was.

John held a newspaper but didn't read it. Instead, he watched as his wife pruned and weeded, the sun beating down on the top of her head, making her blonde hair glow like a halo. He'd been happy then, content. But only a few short years later, it would all be ripped away from him.

He had bonded with Sean when the same had happened to him. Drinking away their pain together, travelling, working, and hunting; they'd survived. But whereas John had eventually accepted his situation, the darkness had got hold of Sean. He could see it in his son's eyes from the first time at the farm and it had never quite disappeared. John wondered again where Sean went on his trips.

The farm.

He glanced down at his slippers and listened as rain battered the grim streaked kitchen window, washing the happy memory away. No, his slippers wouldn't do. He needed real clothes and shoes. He headed for the stairs feeling confident that this was the night. He felt clear in what he needed to do.

One misstep and the confidence crashed out of him as his chin connected with the stairs. He tasted blood in his mouth as his body crumpled onto the cold tile of the hallway floor. Pain shot through his left arm and he whimpered at it and his own foolishness. He fought the stars swimming in his head but it was no use, the darkness took him.

He woke with a start, the dull ache in his arm kept him momentarily still on the floor. His neck ached and he slowly turned his head to the side, testing it for injury. A streetlight cast its glow through the small window in the front door and he noticed a slipper lying next to a small fold of paper. He wiped at his mouth, the dried blood cracked over his lips and his tongue throbbed against the damaged cheek. Under his chin he found more dried blood that brought with it the memory of cracking it on the stair.

He used his good arm to push up against the hallway wall, stealing himself against the pain, he clawed the piece of paper towards him. He knew it was important. Opening it, he looked around for a clock, listened for the ticking. He had no idea how long he lay there but guessed there wasn't much time to waste. He looked up the stairs, daunted by the climb, then back to the front door. He unfolded the note and read the top line.

My name is John Murray. I have to
help the girl named Beth.

He had to go. He'd figure it out along the way. He braced himself and stretched out his arm, the pain radiated down his side but was bearable. He was sure it was no more than bruised. He steadied himself on the banister and tucked his foot back inside the rogue slipper.

With the note safely back in his pocket, he thought of the poor girl. She needed help more than he did. With that in his mind, he was through the front door and on his way.

Chapter 27

A few hours after their waterfall adventure, Lori was packed and ready to leave. The guys had already headed off with Lola and Gail, leaving Jess and Susie to begin the tidy-up after their late lunch, while Alex fussed over her. Lori had tried to help, but hobbling around with a big toe turning all sorts of black and purple had been difficult, and Alex had soon ushered her back to the sofa to rest.

She limped to the car, and with darkness fast approaching, she felt a heaviness on her shoulders at the thought of the long drive home to her lonely apartment.

"Lori, it was brilliant to meet you," Jess said as she pulled her into a tight squeeze. "I'm sure we'll see you back here soon, but don't forget my invite down to the big smoke."

Susie stood off to one side and Lori caught her eye roll. "Aye, I'll be sure and not look out for mine."

Jess swatted her arm. "You just can't help yourself, can you?" She grabbed Susie's shoulders and spun her on the spot before nudging her back toward the house. "C'mon, it's time we got ourselves packed and out of here too."

Alex shook her head and smiled Lori's way. "So how did you like your first visit to the crazy farm?"

The events of the weekend ran through Lori's mind and she couldn't help but smile back. "It was wonderful, Alex. I haven't enjoyed myself so much in a very long time."

Alex grinned. "So you think you might come back then?"

"I don't think I'll take much persuading. But how about you? Think the country girl could survive down in the big city for a weekend?"

"Oh, I think I'd manage with Lady Hunter looking out for me."

"Oi," Lori swatted her arm. "That was not funny."

"You're right. It was hilarious."

Lori pouted. "Okay, okay. I've had enough abuse from Susie. Don't make me leave in a huff with you."

Alex's smile fell at her words. "You sure you should be driving with your toe in that state? I mean, surely your work would understand if you took a day off, and you're welcome to stay another night."

Lori smiled and took her hands. "I wish I didn't have to leave yet either."

Alex glanced back at the house, just in time to see Jess and Susie quickly duck out of view. "It seems we have an audience." She nodded toward the dining room window.

They both laughed, breaking the tension. "Okay, well, we can't stand here all night, I guess." Alex pulled her in for a tight hug and Lori felt an instant pull in her stomach as she stepped into Alex's arms. She closed her eyes and allowed her body to meld to the other woman as she breathed in the scent of coconut shampoo.

It's just a hug, an innocent show of affection between friends. But the heat building inside betrayed her thoughts. This wasn't just a hug.

She heard a small sigh escape Alex's lips and as the heat travelled down to her toes, all the questions she had about what was happening between them left her mind. She still didn't have all the answers but, in this moment, she knew she didn't want to let Alex go, and that fact was going to change her life.

Her arm prickled with goose bumps as Alex's hand slid up her spine to the back of her neck, her thumb stroking gently behind her ear. She felt her face flush, and knowing the thump in her chest was about to give her away, Lori gave her a final squeeze before stepping away.

Staring at one another, no words were needed. Something had just passed between them and it wasn't just heat.

With a smile, Alex reached up and brushed a stray lock of hair back from Lori's face. "See you later."

Lori climbed into her car, lowered the window, and reached out to give Alex's hand one last squeeze. "Adiós, Alex."

CHAPTER 28

His slippers were cumbersome and heavy with rain. They scuffed the uneven surface of the country lane as John charged on, determined to find the farm. The wind whipped across the fields, but he didn't feel it anymore. His head was down and he jumped as brambles clawed at him from the side of the road.

Branches swayed all around him and he expected one of them to grab him any minute now. A shadow moved to his left, and he swerved from its reach, picking up the pace when a creature darted out from the darkness, skittering into the hedge opposite.

As he rounded a corner, headlights blinded him and he stood still, hoping not to be seen. The car slowed but passed him by and he took off again, pleased there was no one to stop him this time. His son was away on another one of his trips. He normally came back from them in a good mood but John couldn't remember the last good mood, only the key turning in the lock of his bedroom door, and the sting of his cheek from another beating. He didn't forget those.

He heard the car turn and froze for a moment but didn't look back. "Damn it." He pushed on, ignored the slow approach of the car and focused on the next corner. He knew it had to be close. The farm was nearby; he was sure of it.

The car cruised alongside him, but he blanked it, even when a girl's voice called out to him. She wasn't going to stop him.

"Sir, are you okay?"

He kept walking, not daring to look towards the window. The wind howled louder and with it, the rain began again, quickly soaking through his thin bathrobe and pyjamas. He heard her swear, before calling out to him again.

"Sir, do you need my help? I'm a police officer."

He stopped at that. Maybe she could help. He reached for the piece of paper in his pocket but it was sodden. Looking around, he tried to think what direction he had come from, was the farm just around that corner?

"What's your name, sir? Where are you going?" The girl called out again.

He looked down at the pulp in his hand. The answer was within reach, on the tip of his tongue. He hung his head, defeated. He had lost again.

He bent to the window and saw the concern on the girl's face. "Do you know the way to the farm? I was out there yesterday, but I can't remember how to get back."

"What farm is that, sir? There are quite a few out this way around the villages, which one do you live on?"

He rubbed the bristles on his face and plucked at his hair irritably. "Please, you have to help me find it."

The sun had long set and the lane was dark, the moon hidden behind clouds bursting with rain. He felt her study him and he avoided her eyes.

"It's okay, like I said, I'm a police officer." He watched as she removed her ID from her bag and held it up to him. "Would you like to get in the car and maybe I can help you find it?"

His shoulders sagged and he scanned all around in exasperation before looking at her properly for the first time. He believed her when she said she could help. She was young with a gentle look about her. Bright blonde hair and rosy cheeks, just like his sister when they were teenagers. He looked down at his bedraggled appearance, noticing for the first time his bathrobe was hung open and his skin had taken on a blue tinge. He didn't recognise himself, his body. It didn't belong to the man he knew. "I don't know where I am."

The girl jumped out of the car and jogged around to the passenger side, opening the door. He felt a gentle hand on his shoulder and didn't fight it as she guided him into the car. "Let me help you find out."

He got in, fidgeting with the belt of his robe while the policewoman pulled the seatbelt across him and draped a blanket from the back seat around his shoulders.

"My name is Hannah, PC Hannah Wallace. I'm just going to make a call to my police friends, see if they can help too. Is that okay?"

He continued to fidget, not looking her way and pulling the blanket tighter. "Please don't get me in trouble. He'll be very mad."

She stopped dialling. "Why would you be in trouble? Who with? Have you done something wrong?"

He tried to unclick the belt, but she covered his hand with her own.

"You can talk to me. Tell me what's wrong. What have you done?"

He started rocking, pulling at his hair again. He was a fool to trust her. She was going to take him back to his son. Oh, he would pay for it this time. He'd been away so long; he was sure this time the door would be locked forever. "I don't know. I don't remember. He told me I shouldn't remember, but I have to help. I know I have to help. Please don't take me back, please."

"Okay, okay. Calm down, sir." She rubbed a soothing hand up and down his back. "I'm going to call my friend and then we're going to go somewhere where they can help. Is that all right with you?"

He sank back into the seat, resigned. Tears filled his eyes and he looked at her again. "Please help her. You have to help her."

"Help who? Who's in trouble? Is someone hurt?"

"You just need to find the farm. We can help if we can find the farm."

He heard her sigh, muttering under her breath about a hot bath and a glass of wine. She picked up her phone again and he didn't object, waiting for his son's voice. Instead, it was one he didn't recognise although muffled by her ear.

"That was just the control room," she said, and he believed her. He liked her smile.

She turned the car around and he hung onto the door handle. Why was she going this way? He looked across at her and she smiled again. He felt himself relax and she patted his arm.

"Don't worry, sir. I'm here to help."

CHAPTER 29

"Who was that?"

Stella placed the phone back in its cradle as strong arms wrapped around her waist from behind, and eager lips began pulling at her earlobe. She squirmed at the whiskers tickling her neck, then spun herself around in the embrace, stealing a kiss before answering.

"Lori. She's asked me to meet her for dinner Friday night."

"Well, I hope you said no because you already have a hot date."

She looked up into mischievous brown eyes and wished she could lock the doors and hide in her apartment all weekend, getting up to all kinds of badness in the bedroom. But no matter how tempting the offer in front of her was, she had her priorities straight.

"Sorry love, you might be a Hunter but your sister will always be my number one."

Scott dropped his shoulders and poked his bottom lip out. "I fly thousands of miles with only you on my mind and you ditch me for my sister? That's just flipping charming." He stomped to the living room, throwing himself on the sofa like a five-year-old. "You can see Lori anytime. Couldn't you put her off a couple of days?"

Stella followed him to the sofa, climbed on, and straddled his lap. "You know very well how much I've been looking forward to you being here this weekend, but she said it was important and she sounded kind of nervous, jittery almost.

I haven't seen her in nearly two weeks. In fact, I think she's been avoiding me, and considering everything that's just happened with Andrew, and then there's this new guy Alex who's appeared from nowhere—"

"Alex? You didn't mention she'd met someone else." Scott leant forward in a move to get up, clearly annoyed he'd been kept in the dark.

Stella pinned him back, wrapping her arms around his neck and pecking his lips. "She hasn't. At least not in that way. Well actually maybe it is in that way and that's why she's been avoiding me. I'm not sure what's going on, only that she seemed excited and was talking all stardust and unicorns about him the last time I saw her."

"And you didn't think this was information I might like? All the calls I've been getting from Andrew and she's already moving on?"

She frowned down at him, leaning back. "I didn't say she was moving on. I said there was a guy and she was showing an interest. If you were a better brother and called her once in a while, maybe she'd have told you about him herself."

He huffed again. "I call, but it's hard on the road. Time differences, signal—"

Stella held a hand up. "Stop. I'm not asking for your excuses because I know they're bullshit. I'm just saying she needs more than me in her life right now, so some extra effort on your part wouldn't go amiss."

He sank back into the sofa and conceded her point. "I know, you're right. I should let her know I'm in town and try to arrange a catch up. But I will remind you that it's your decision to keep our steamy romance a secret from her. Otherwise I could be going to dinner with you both."

Stella sighed. "Scott, we agreed. Until we figure out what we're doing, why involve others and complicate the situation? Do you really think I like keeping this from Lori?"

"No, of course not, and I hate it as well." He wrapped his hands around her waist, pulling her closer.

"So while we're on the subject, what exactly are we doing, Scott? Apart from having all the sex."

"You mean the hot, passionate, earth shattering sex."

"Hmm... The adjectives are debatable, but I'll agree we are having sex."

He tickled her side. "You're cruel."

"And you're avoiding the question."

He threw up his hands. "Stella, what can I say? You know me. You know my job and you know my lifestyle.You knew it before we got involved."

She moved off him, putting distance between them on the sofa. "Yes, 'before' we got involved. Now we are involved, Scott. Doesn't that make you want to change any of those things? Or am I just sex to you?"

"You forgot hot, passionate, and earth shattering." He tried a cheeky grin.

She glared at him.

He moved to close the gap. "I'm sorry. Of course not, sweetheart. After all the years I've known you, do you really think you mean so little to me?"

"That's the problem, Scott. I don't know what I mean to you at all."

He gave her the same look Lori did when she was in the bad books. Damn, it always worked for her, as well. She could feel herself thawing but didn't want to let him off so easy.

"Stella, I think you are wonderful and funny and beautiful and the thought of seeing you has dragged my sorry ass back to London more times this past six months than the previous six years combined." He stroked some loose curls gently from her face and held her gaze. "But I've been stuck in my carefree ways for a very long time and I'm just asking for a little more time to figure things out."

She pressed her cheek into his palm, closing her eyes to consider his words. It had been six months since they'd had a drunken fumble after one too many cocktails. Scott had offered to get her home and in return she'd offered him her sofa.

He'd been gone in the morning and she'd resolved to forget about it, as he so clearly wanted to. But three weeks later, he appeared at her door as he'd now done another half a dozen or more times since then.

They hadn't put a label on their time together, only agreeing that Lori didn't need to know until they had. It wasn't just Scott keeping his cards close to his chest, Stella had her own career and independence that she wasn't going to give up for just anyone. She had to be sure Scott meant business.

She was reluctant to waste the precious time they had arguing, so took him at his word that he only needed time and this wasn't just a meaningless fling. He'd done nothing to make her mistrust him.

She moved closer again and smiled before planting a soft kiss on his lips. "I guess you're not so bad yourself, but I'm still ditching you for your sister Friday night."

"Damn it." But he was smiling. "Okay, well I plan on waiting up for you so don't hit the wine too hard." He got up and headed to the fridge for a couple of beers. Plonking back down on the sofa, he handed her one. "Now, tell me all you know about this Alex."

Chapter 30

Female voices broke through the fog and John thought he recognised one of them. Was that his sister? He opened his eyes and tried to move but a sharp pain up his side caught his breath, forcing him to remain still until it passed.

He pulled open the white gown and ran a hand over the tight bandages around his ribcage, outlining the purple and green bruising that spread out from them. A flashback came then. His son dragging him, kicking him, the sound of the key in the lock of his bedroom door.

The door to his room was partway open and he heard the voices again. He closed his eyes, trying to concentrate, remember how he'd gotten here. It was obvious he was in a hospital bed and had been taken care of. He remembered being cold, so cold. There was a young girl who looked so familiar. Had she been a copper? That was the voice he could hear? Yes, it was her, not his sister.

The voices became louder and a male voice joined them, moving closer to his door. He flinched for a moment, expecting his son but it was deeper, mellow, and sounded concerned.

"I thought I might find you here."

The girl's voice returned. "Evening Sergeant, just thought I'd check on him."

"Given I know you're meant to be off duty, and it's after midnight, let's forget formalities."

John heard her laugh. "Does that mean I can get a hug off my favourite uncle then, because it's been a bitch of a day?"

There was quiet for a moment and John assumed the girl was getting her hug. "Ah, Hannah, why on earth did I ever let you get involved in the police, eh?"

"I wonder that myself every day."

John smiled to himself. Hannah. That was her name. He remembered her putting a blanket around him and promising to help. He remembered now. She was going to find the farm.

"So any change in his condition? Has he woken up?"

He heard her sigh and wanted to call out, he was here, he was awake, but they continued before he could and he realised his voice was failing him, dry and raw with thirst. He moved slowly, reaching for the cup of water on his bedside, continuing to listen to them talk.

"Not that I'm aware. I'm just waiting for the nurse to come and check his vitals before I head off, but he was asleep when I left the room earlier and I haven't seen him awake what with all the pain medication he's on."

"Anything on missing persons?"

"I checked this afternoon again, but still nothing matching his description. It's been days now so he either lived alone and there's no family around, or they aren't sorry he's missing. It makes me sad."

"Well, if there is family, I'd be asking questions about that bruising. Someone physically assaulted that old man and, out in the cold the way he was, you could have easily come across a corpse."

"I know. It makes me furious to see him in that state. I keep thinking of granddad."

John felt warm at the kindness in her voice. It had been so long since someone had cared. He knew then this was the girl to help him find the farm. She would help and she wouldn't call his son.

"I don't want to wake him tonight so I'll pop back tomorrow before my shift. In the meantime, I've been trying to piece together all the little things he does say when he has moments of lucidity, I asked the nurses to note them down."

"Like what?"

"Well, they've run some scans and unfortunately the doctor found multiple tumours on his brain. We'll need to wait for the specialist tomorrow to confirm a diagnosis, but she said it would explain his confusion, it may be he's jumping from the present to the past, having dreams that feel real, and it would also account for memory loss. The farm and girl he keeps talking about is more than likely something from his past. He keeps saying he needs to help her. Maybe there was an incident long ago that's stuck with him? He still thinks he can help fix it? Like maybe a daughter or granddaughter?"

"That makes sense and might be worth looking into, but I don't want you spending too much time on it. You have other duties, you know."

"Yeah, I know, but I don't want to abandon the old guy. Plus, my gut says there's more to this and we should stick around until we at least identify him."

A nurse came in then to check his vital signs and the door stayed open. He pointed to the water, and she produced a straw to help him drink. He called out for the girl. "Hannah?"

Hannah appeared in the doorway, and the nurse left. She smiled at him, and asked if she could come in. He recognised his sister in her once again.

He gestured her over to the bed, and another figure filled the doorway, a bear of a man with a friendly smile of his own.

"Good to see you awake." She sat on the edge of the bed, and took his hand. "Can you tell me your name, sir?"

He patted her hand. "You can call me John, young lady. Now when are we going to help Beth?"

CHAPTER 31

Lori was nervous.

She was also forty-five minutes early getting ready which meant more time to think about how nervous she was. There was only one thing for it. Wine.

She headed to the fridge and shakily poured a glass of white, forcing herself to sit at the kitchen island and take a breath.

Okay, pep talk time. She spoke to her reflection in the darkened kitchen window, "She's your best friend, Lori, she loves you, she will support you, she will not hate you, she is an open-minded, caring person, and she will not judge you."

Right, much better.

Oh, God, but what if she does?

She groaned, gulped back the wine, and began pacing. The beep of her phone drew her into the living room.

Alex.

Even the anticipation of opening a text from Alex made her giddy.

She smiled as she opened the message.

What are you wearing? x

She laughed at the cheesy line. It had become almost a competition who could come up with the worst. Much to her own surprise and Alex's amusement, it turned out Lori was an outrageous flirt too. They'd exchanged numerous texts, calls, e-mails, and a couple of Skypes in what had felt like the longest two weeks of Lori's life.

Of course, she hadn't yet admitted that fact to Alex.

Each time they spoke, it was easy going and light, well, at least, it was until the moment that it wasn't.

She could never quite pinpoint when the conversation would turn, but suddenly being four hundred miles apart felt like a distance some words shouldn't have to travel.

She tapped back a response, feeling the Alex-effect calm her.

> A red, tartan onesie and Christmas socks with candy canes on them x

The doorbell rang and she glanced at her watch, Stella wasn't due for another half an hour. She'd obviously had a bad week and wanted to get started on the wine early.

Lori headed to the hall pressing *send* on her phone as she pulled open the large front door. Instead of Stella, she was looking down at green eyes and dimples.

Alex.

"Liar." She held up her phone and laughed before throwing her arms around Lori with an excited giggle.

Lori pulled away and held her at arm's length, she couldn't take it in. Alex was here in her doorway, in London, and she looked stunning.

Gone was the woolly jumper and boots, instead, a gorgeous woman stood before her dressed for a night on the town in slate grey, skinny-fit trousers, leather boots that gave her an extra few inches, and a simple, black scoop neck top with a jacket to match the boots. She'd finished the sophisticated look subtly with a delicate silver pendant and diamond stud earrings and had let her hair fall softly in waves onto her shoulders.

Lori stepped aside and ushered her in. "What are you doing here?"

Alex dropped her bag in the hall, grinning from ear to ear. "For a Lady your manners are somewhat lacking. Don't I even get a hello?"

"Sorry, I'm just so shocked. Let's try again," she smiled widely. "Hey, Alex."

"Hey, Lori," she smirked. "Much better."

"Okay, now formalities are out of the way. What are you doing here?"

Alex looked her up and down then, giving a low whistle under her breath. "If I didn't know any better, I'd say you're all dressed up for a date?" She quirked an eyebrow inquisitively, waiting for an answer, and still not giving one to Lori's question.

"No, no date." She glanced down at her watch anxiously.

She silently started to panic and Alex must have caught the look on her face. "Oh crap, I'm sorry, Lori. Have I busted in on a date?"

She looked crestfallen and Lori was shaking her head, trying to reassure her, but Alex continued, flustered, "When we spoke last night you said you didn't have anything special planned for tonight. Then my reason for not being able to visit this weekend didn't exist anymore, so I thought I'd surprise you and let you take me to dinner. We'd have this whole sophisticated night in the city and—"

"Alex." Lori placed reassuring hands on both her shoulders, stopping her worried rant. "Please, don't be sorry for coming. It's an amazing surprise. You're an amazing surprise and I would love nothing more than to take you to dinner. But right now, it's me that's about to freak out because my best friend will be here in approximately twenty-five minutes and she still thinks you're a bloke."

Alex's eyes widened and Lori hated that she felt anything but happy to be here with her. "Exactly. This is not how I envisaged introducing you and I'm not sure how happy she'll be getting ambushed. I really want her to like you, Alex."

Her face took on a pensive look. "Can I ask why it's so important that Stella likes me? And why she still thinks I'm a bloke? I mean we're just friends aren't we? Not all friends have to get on with each other."

Lori held her eye, she hadn't expected this moment so soon. This question. But Alex stood before her asking and she couldn't lie. "Is friends all you want?"

"Oh no." Alex shook her head. "That's no fair. You can't turn it back on me."

Lori shrugged, trying her best at nonchalance. "Worth a try."

Alex took her hand and tugged her closer. "Same question back at you. Is friends all you want, Lori?"

Lori held her gaze, the space between them palpable with energy. She felt her throat constrict and ran her tongue over now dry lips. It was a one word answer. That's all the question needed. One word. Her life was about to change. "No."

Alex's smile was slow, but quickly spread to her eyes. "Good answer."

She stepped away suddenly, breaking the moment. Lori felt the air fill her lungs again as the room around her rematerialised.

Alex was still smiling. "Okay then, what should I do? Tell me what to do. Should I leave? Hide in the cupboard? Crawl under the bed? What?"

Lori laughed as Alex crouched down and darted her eyes around comically looking for her best form of escape.

The panic left her then as she realised she had absolutely nothing to worry about when it came to introducing Stella to Alex. She didn't like side swiping Stella like this but, bar sending Alex on her way, she had no choice. "How about you follow me to the kitchen so I can pour us both a large wine?"

Alex looked up to the heavens. "Oh Lord, thank you for the French and all their wine. Lead the way, Lady Hunter."

The buzzer sounded again just as they settled on the sofa. Lori's eyes widened anxiously and she took a deep breath. "Okay, here goes." She pulled a face at Alex before heading to answer the door.

They'd agreed she would steer Stella into the kitchen and get a wine in her hand, allowing a couple of minutes to give Stella some kind of explanation before meeting Alex. As she did just that, she noticed Alex's jacket draped over the back of a stool. Mistake.

"Wow, nice jacket," Stella exclaimed holding it up, feeling the soft leather. "I never had you down as a leather girl. Does Alex like his girls a little bit naughty?" She winked suggestively in Lori's direction, causing her to cringe and blush all at the same time.

Conscious that Alex could hear every word, she cleared her throat noisily and headed for the fridge. "Seriously, Stella, try to allow more than that one subject to cross your mind occasionally." She heard the edginess in her tone and was immediately sorry for speaking to her in that way.

"Hey you, look at me. What's up? And why have you been avoiding me?"

"I haven't. I've just been busy at work preparing for a big conference. And nothing's up, as such. It's just, well, I got a bit of a surprise earlier."

"Okay, good or bad?" Stella was still examining the plush leather coat curiously, as if something wasn't right.

"Good, in fact, very good." She glanced in the direction of the living room, not sure how to do this, and very aware of Alex listening in. "Okay, I was going to tell you about this at dinner tonight, but there's been a slight change of plan so I'm just going to tell you now and hope you understand why I kept it from you."

Stella nodded distractedly, trying to shrug into the jacket but it was much too short. "Lori, this can't possibly fit you. Whose jacket is this?"

"That's what I'm trying to tell you. Stella, will you put that down and listen, please. I didn't tell you to begin with because I wasn't really sure what I was thinking and, to be honest, I was a little freaked out, and I didn't want you to freak out. I just needed some advice without any judgement and you're my best friend and I know you wouldn't judge really but—"

Stella held up a hand, she was confused and Lori was babbling. "Lori. Whose jacket is this?"

At the sound of a gentle cough, Stella spun around to the doorway.

"Hi." Alex stepped toward Stella extending her hand. "I'm, Alex, and that's my jacket."

Lori watched Stella's eyes widen as she looked back and forth between them. It took a lot to shock her best friend and a little bit of her didn't want to hide the involuntary giggle she felt bubbling. This was going either one of two ways and she hoped she wasn't wrong in her earlier pep talk. Until she'd opened the door to Alex, she hadn't realised just how important she'd become in her life and knew tonight was another step in acknowledging that fact. She willed Stella to stop staring and break the silence.

Looking down at Alex's hand, Stella visibly shook herself before reaching out to take it. "Hi, I'm Stella. And I think I'll have that wine now."

CHAPTER 32

As she finished her dessert, Lori glanced back and forth between Alex and Stella, a happy smile playing on her lips. It had been a different story earlier in the evening when, after quickly downing half her glass of wine, Stella had set about grilling them both as only a detective could.

"So I'm going to give you the benefit of the doubt and assume you didn't purposefully lie to me about the fact your Alex is a woman?"

Lori had been coy. "Of course I didn't. I'd planned on telling you straightaway but then you assumed and I just ran with it." They'd stared each other out until Stella had nodded, seemingly satisfied the lie wasn't intentional.

Alex cleared her throat. "Listen I can go. I turned up unannounced and I don't want to get in the way of this."

When she'd made to head for her coat, Stella had caught her by the arm. "Oh no you don't, young lady. I have some questions I need answering. Sit."

Lori had tried not to smile at the worried look on Alex's face as she took a stool at the kitchen island but Stella caught it.

"I don't know what you're smiling at. Take a seat, Hunter."

She'd felt like a kid in the headmaster's office, swinging her legs and looking anywhere but at Stella.

"So, Alex, you're a woman."

"Aye." Alex had glanced Lori's way in disbelief.

Lori gave her a slight shake of her head and pleaded with her eyes for her to go with it.

"And you're Scottish?"

"Yes, your honour." She tried to hide the smile but failed and Stella was having none of it.

"Oh, so you're a joker? I think given your position right now we should save the smart mouth and just answer the questions. Agreed?"

Alex had nodded, again sliding a sideways glance towards Lori.

"Lori tells me you live on a farm but work computer stuff, in particular for the police?"

"That is correct." Alex kept a straight face this time.

"Is it also correct you keep chickens and goats and an enthusiastic dog named Frank?"

"Aye, that is also correct."

Lori watched as Stella did her finger steeple thing, pressing the tips together and tapping them against her lips in thought. Lori knew that's when she was getting serious.

"And you're single?"

"Yes."

"Are you a lesbian?"

"Yes."

"And you like my best friend Lori here?"

"Yes. Well, I mean we're friends, isn't that right, Lori?" She winked Lori's way.

"Don't look at her. You're talking to me. And don't give me that 'friends' crap. I see right through the pair of you."

Stella was stern, but Lori caught the twitch of her upper lip. She felt herself relax. Stella was just playing with Alex, and Lori was interested to see what else she could get out of her.

"What about family? Tell me about the Ryan Clan."

Lori noisily coughed, thinking of Beth. Stella glanced her way but didn't get the hint to move on. She continued. "Well? Do they live with you? Nearby?"

Alex seemed to shift uncomfortably. She sat on her hands and cleared her throat a few times before answering. "My friends are my family."

Stella raised an eyebrow in Lori's direction and she could only shrug in response. Apart from admitting that Beth had died, their talk about Rachel in the bothy, and some college stories from her friends, that's as far as she'd gotten with Alex's past. Something she was just realising.

But she could see Alex was uncomfortable and Stella had had her fun. She intervened before Stella could take it any further. "Stella, c'mon. Let's go to dinner and chat like normal people."

"What? I'm just getting to know your new friend here. This is how I chat."

"Yes, but how you chat and how normal humans chat are very different things. We haven't all got four years as a detective on our resume."

Stella threw up her hands. "Fine. Spoil my fun." She turned to Alex. "Seriously though, Alex, I'm sorry, I'm just playing. You'll get used to me."

Alex smiled, grabbing her glass and taking a gulp before speaking. "It's okay, Stella. Lori, don't worry. I'm used to answering this question and Stella wasn't to know." Alex rubbed her palms down her thighs and took a deep breath. "My parents and my younger sister died. So it's just me left."

Lori spun towards her as Stella's arms dropped to her sides. Alex didn't look at either of them, instead she continued rubbing her palms across her thighs, chewing the inside of her lip.

"Alex, I'm so sorry." Lori slid a hand across her back, getting her attention. "Stella, you're an ass, you always go too far."

At Lori's words, Alex reassured them again. "Lori, it's okay. Don't be mad with her. It was an honest question that's normally simple and anyway, I should have told you that already, especially after you told me about your mum."

Stella looked genuinely upset with herself. "No, Alex, I'm so sorry. I was just playing with you. It's my thing, you know, the whole interrogation bit. Here." Stella topped up her glass of wine and handed it to her. "Get this down you."

Alex did as instructed with the wine. She didn't want to get into the rest of the story so knocked back the rest of it and stood, nodding in Lori's direction. "I'm starving. You going to take a girl to dinner or what?"

That had put an end to the questioning. Lori was happy Alex hadn't held the cop routine against Stella but it nagged in her mind that, despite Lori confiding about her own mum passing, Alex hadn't admitted the same at the bothy. She had clearly wanted to avoid further questioning from Stella on the details and Lori continued to wonder what had happened.

Now, three hours later, Lori looked between the two of them as they laughed like old friends. She had shaken off the unease after Stella's questioning and focused on the happy feelings seeing Alex hitting it off so well with her best friend.

She knew she wasn't off the hook that easy and Stella would begin the real grilling once she got Lori alone, but the evening would go some ways to making that easier on her.

Their waiter appeared, cleared the table, and offered coffee.

"I have a better idea," Stella declared. "How about we head down the street to a little cocktail place I know? Get our coffee with a shot of vodka?"

Lori raised her eyebrows. "Espresso martini? I know only one other person who would finish dinner with one of those."

"Really? Who?" Stella asked.

Lori visibly deflated. "My poor excuse for a brother. Do you know he hasn't called in nearly three months?"

"Seriously?" Alex's voice was incredulous. "How do you have a sister and not call her in three months?"

Lori could understand why Alex might not understand the situation, given she had lost her sister. "I guess that's how it works with us, with his travelling and work. Although this is the longest I can ever remember." She felt Alex place a comforting hand on her knee under the table and give it a gentle squeeze.

Stella was having none of her excuses for him. "I'll kick his arse for you the next time I see him. He's a degenerate, so let's not waste any time wondering."

Stella seemed antsy and ready to move on. Lori was surprised given one of her favourite pastimes was cussing her brother and dad and letting Lori know she was too easy on them.

As she made to voice this, Stella continued, "So let's speak no more about him and go get us one of those yummy cocktails."

Lori stood, shaking off the disappointment in her brother. "What are we waiting for, let's do it. I will not let someone who isn't even here ruin our night."

Alex followed suit, helping Lori into her jacket. Lori smiled at the sweet gesture and the tension left her as Alex bowed slightly, stepping to the side with a giggle and a wink in Stella's direction. "After you, ladies."

Two cocktails in and Alex realised she'd gotten off easy with Stella's earlier questioning who was now relentless and sailing close to dangerous waters again.

"So what happens to make a young, pretty thing like you hide away in the country on a farm?"

Alex bought some time taking a sip of the French martini they'd now moved on to. "I'm not hiding. I grew up there and its home."

"So it's your family farm? It must be hard being there without them?"

She saw Lori give Stella an unsubtle jab in the ribs. "I thought we were through with Alex's interrogation?"

Stella raised her hands innocently. "What? I thought we were friends now. Friends ask these kinds of questions, especially after a few drinks."

Alex appreciated the smile Stella gave her, she was up to mischief that's all, but Alex knew she couldn't avoid the questions much longer. They couldn't possibly be imagining anything close to the real story. When others had pried in the past, they'd assumed some tragic car accident, or a run of unfortunate illnesses. Alex was skilled in letting people believe what they wanted. The truth was too hard to tell, and the pity she saw, too hard to take.

"I think it would be harder to leave. That's where all my memories are. Good or bad, it's the last link to my family so I'd never give it up."

Stella stared her out for a few seconds, her left eye squinting in a moment of what Alex imagined was suspicion. "Something tells me you've avoided this line of questioning before and become quite good at it. If you're not giving anything else away, at least confirm I'm right about that."

Alex laughed then. "Yes ma'am."

Lori laughed with her. "Well played, Alex. I think you just eluded the great Detective Roberts."

"Hmm..." Stella eyed her again. "For now, I guess, but only because I like you. You should know I don't give up that easy though."

Alex was an open book about most things but realised quickly that Stella was definitely a pro. However, she wasn't about to discuss things that not even Lori knew about yet.

She decided offense was the best form of defence, and asked a question she knew would buy some time to catch her breath.

"I just realised you two never told me how you met? Have you been friends for long?"

"Oh, let's see, how long is it now, Lori? Eight years?"

"Yes, you know fine well it is." She glared at Stella.

"Hey, what's that look for?"

"You bloody well know what for. Please don't tell the story!"

"Oh yes. I love it when there's a story," Alex exclaimed, clapping her hands. "Please tell it, Stella. I'll be your new best friend if she disowns you."

Lori groaned and gestured to the barman for another round. "Whisky all round please. Doubles."

Stella chuckled. "It's not that embarrassing."

Alex feigned impatience. "C'mon, get on with it."

"Okay," Stella said, getting comfy. "Well, I know my very English accent betrays me but my dad is actually Scottish and I went to university in Edinburgh."

The barman put the whisky down, and they all clinked and took a warming sip.

"After university, I joined the force in Scotland and on my first night shift I get called out to a flat after a complaint of loud music."

"It wasn't loud," Lori protested, but was quickly shushed by Stella.

"Well, maybe it was more your singing that got the complaint. Are you going to keep interrupting?"

Lori pouted into her whisky. "Fine, carry on."

Stella nodded. "So, we arrived at this flat and the music actually isn't that loud and we find there are only a dozen or so people in the house having a Eurovision Song Contest party."

"A what?"

"A Eurovision party. Basically this one here," she said, gesturing to Lori, "was there to watch The Eurovision Song Contest with a bunch of friends and when we got 'nil poi' it turned into some kind of Karaoke party. We found them all in a rather silly state, drinking who knows what out of pineapples."

"That's amazing. I can't believe I've never thought of having a Eurovision party!"

Lori laughed. "See? I told you it was a thing."

Stella waved her off. "Yeah, well, whatever. You still looked ridiculous in your costume and, no matter what was in that pineapple, it was no excuse for cracking onto me."

"Wait, what?" Alex inhaled her sip of whisky. Wide eyed, she let the coughing subside. "You, Lori Hunter, tried it on with a police officer at a Eurovision party?"

Lori looked strangely pleased with herself. "I'm glad in my old age I still have the ability to shock. Yes, I did. My friend who was desperate for a girlfriend thought she was cute but was too shy, so I thought I'd show her how it's done."

Stella laughed. "She failed miserably."

Alex held her stomach. "I can't even imagine it. Although what would you have done if she'd said yes?"

"I'd probably have locked myself and a pineapple in the bathroom until she was gone."

They all cracked up then. Alex wiped away a tear and caught her breath. "So if you turned her down, how did you end up friends?" She looked between them.

"Ah, well, I left thinking I just had a funny story to tell, but then on the Monday, I got assigned to patrol around the cobbled streets of the Royal Mile, right down to the Scottish Parliament building. Anyway, I see this woman rooted to the spot, and she's frantically looking around, bashing at her phone, clearly panicked."

Alex laughed. "Lori panicked? I can't ever imagine that." She smirked at Lori's blush, knowing she was referring to her state before Stella's arrival.

"Believe it. She saw me coming in my uniform and went beetroot red. I asked if she needed help and she rather haughtily told me she was fine and was just having a problem with her phone."

"Haughtily? Is that your polite way of telling me she acted like a stuck-up bitch?"

"Exactly. I like this girl, Lori. She's definitely got your number."

"Hey, that's enough of the bashing. Just tell the bloody story."

"Okay, okay. So I'm about to walk away and leave the posh princess to it, when it suddenly clicks and I realise who she is. I turn around to make a joke about pineapples, but she had obviously remembered who I was too and, in her haste to get away, she kind of lost her balance and started falling. I caught her but, as she fell, her foot comes out of her shoe and I find out the problem..."

"Oh no..." Realisation dawned on Alex. "Did a little thing like a stiletto stuck between cobbles bring down Lori Hunter?"

The look on Lori's face said it all, and they couldn't help but laugh again at her expense. Eventually, Lori joined in. "I have to say it was a terrible day until Stella promised me a large glass of wine and company for the evening as consolation for missing my flight back to London."

"Wait, you missed a flight? How long were you stood there?"

"Almost an hour. I'd been heading for a taxi to collect my bags from the hotel."

This started a renewed round of giggles at the absurdity of the situation.

"Couldn't you just leave the shoe?"

"Are you kidding?" Lori was incredulous. "Those shoes cost more than my flight."

Once the laughter had died down again, they ordered one more for the road. Stella regaled Alex with party stories from when Lori visited and on the beat in Edinburgh, before she decided to transfer back to London for the detective fast track.

Alex noticed her dismissing a couple of calls on her phone before eventually sighing at the fourth attempt and heading outside to take it, mouthing, "Work."

She glanced at Lori who watched Stella through the bar window, her conversation seemed animated and angry, and Lori seemed suspicious.

"Isn't she off tonight or does she get called in a lot?"

She watched Lori peer thoughtfully at Stella. "She doesn't normally drink if she's on call and that's her personal phone, not her work one. I wonder what's going on."

"You look worried."

Lori turned away from the window and smiled. "I'm fine, sweetheart. I'm just being nosey. What do you say we call it a night? I think I'm still at the point where a hangover shouldn't get in the way of me showing you some sights tomorrow."

Alex liked how "sweetheart" sounded coming from Lori's lips. "I thought you'd never ask." She held out her hand. "Take me home."

CHAPTER 33

They pulled up in the taxi and Lori saw the familiar outline of someone she knew sitting on her front steps. Andrew.

Lori sighed and Alex, following her gaze as she paid the driver, made a calculated guess as to who it was waiting for them and asked, "Is that Andrew?"

"Unfortunately, yes. Don't worry though. I'll get rid of him."

He straightened up when he saw Lori get out of the taxi, and she saw his eyes narrow as Alex got out after her. She watched him square his shoulders and guessed it wasn't going to be that easy to send him on his way.

"What are you doing here, Andrew?" Lori fumbled for her keys, wanting to get inside and away from him as quickly as possible. She'd had a great night and was determined not to make a scene and spoil it.

"Seven years together and I don't even get a 'Hello'?"

She rolled her eyes at him. "Hello, Andrew. Now, what are you doing here?"

He glanced Alex's way, clearly unhappy at being treated like this in front of a stranger. "Who's your friend?"

Lori blew out a breath, exasperated at being ambushed like this. "Alex, this is Andrew. My ex." She noted his grimace at her emphasis on the word ex but realised she should give him no illusions he was anything else. "Alex is a friend of mine visiting from Scotland."

Alex reached up to shake his proffered hand with a small nod, before taking Lori's keys from her with a reassuring smile and climbing past Andrew up the steps to the front door. Lori watched her open it and was relieved when she stood back politely in the threshold to wait, but didn't leave her alone.

"So, I'm already being referred to as the 'ex' then?" He spat the word ex, moving down a step closer to Lori where he still towered over her.

She'd never before felt threatened by Andrew, but looking up at him now, jaw muscles twitching as he strained to keep his obvious anger in check, eyes dark and shining from the alcohol he'd clearly consumed, she realised she didn't know how to deal with this side of him.

Lori moved up to the same step as him, trepidation and the smell of whisky made her keep her space. She softened her tone in a bid to keep things calm, giving him a small smile. "Andrew, it's late and we've both been drinking. I know you want to talk but would you agree this probably isn't the best time?"

He visibly deflated. She could tell he was spoiling for a fight, but she was resolute he wasn't going to get one. "Well, when would you say is the best time? I've been calling you for weeks. I've stopped by your office, but that bitch Jane wouldn't let me speak to you. You're never at home or at least you don't answer my calls. I called your brother—"

"Wait." Lori held up her hand, her resolve to be nice rapidly disappearing. "You called my brother? It was bad enough that you went to my office and you called my dad. Just who the hell do you think you are, Andrew?" She closed the gap between them, her voice rising in frustration. "Actually, let me answer that for you. I know who you are. You are my ex-boyfriend. *Ex*, as in past tense, as in no longer, as in not anymore. Do you understand? If this is your way of winning me back, I can tell you, you've got it wrong."

He glared down at her, his chest heaving with anger but seemingly unsure what to say.

She took his silence as understanding, and with nothing more to say, she brushed past him and started up the steps to the door that Alex held open. There was no warning as she was suddenly spun back around, pain shooting through her wrist as he gripped it and yanked her back down the steps to him.

Alex was down the steps and between them in a flash. With one arm protectively across Lori, she shoved Andrew hard in the chest with the other, causing him to release his grip on Lori's wrist before stumbling backward down the last two steps.

Lori's heart had quickened at the unexpected confrontation, and she stood breathless behind Alex, who'd reached back to hold her hand. She could only glare down at Andrew, at a loss for words. Tears sprung in her eyes at the sorry sight of him swaying in the street, swiping pavement dust off his trousers before looking up and glaring right back at her.

"This is how you treat me? After all the time we spent together, I don't even get an explanation."

Alex spoke up for her. "I think it's time you left."

He turned his glare on Alex then, pointing a finger, he hissed through gritted teeth, "Who the hell are you to tell me to leave? This has nothing to do with you."

They watched as he steadied himself against a car parked at the curb, the fall had clearly rattled his alcohol-addled brain, and Lori could tell he had to concentrate hard on focusing. She felt sorry for him. He was clearly hurting, and this was completely out of character. But she wasn't taking any chances and just wanted to be inside and safe with Alex.

Alex took a slow step down toward him.

Lori tugged at her hand, worried at what she was doing and how Andrew might react.

Alex squeezed it and kept hold but didn't look back. "You're right, Andrew." She held up her other hand in acquiescence. "This doesn't have anything to do with me, apart from the fact that I care about Lori and hate to see her upset. I'm sure you don't like her being upset either." She was appealing to the side of him that clearly still loved Lori.

He leaned back against the car, nodding more to himself than her. Lori could see the glisten of tears in his eyes before he scrubbed at his face with his hands and took a few breaths.

"Can you call me a taxi?" He didn't look at them, but Lori could see the shame on his face. A face she knew so well and didn't want to hate. This wasn't him and he'd realise what a mistake this was in the morning.

"Aye, of course, but you'll need to wait out here for it."

He simply nodded before moving to sit on the bottom step with his back to them.

Alex turned back to her and smiled as Lori mouthed a silent thank you. Never letting go of her hand, she fished her phone out and handed it to Lori to make the call. She then led her up the steps into the safety of the building.

It wasn't until they were inside the apartment with her back to the locked door that Alex closed her eyes in relief and blew out the breath she'd been holding. She had always avoided confrontation but seeing Andrew put his hands on Lori had sobered her instantly and flipped a switch. She was between them before her brain had a chance to engage. The urge to protect Lori overrode any fear of putting herself in the firing line.

She didn't think Andrew would have gone any further, it was a moment of frustration at the situation, not helped by the alcohol. He seemed genuinely sorry, and she felt sorry for him. He had lost Lori and, the more she got to know her, she realised what a hard knock that would be to take.

Alex took another deep breath, and the syrupy, sweet scent she had come to associate with Lori washed over her. She opened her eyes, jumping at Lori's proximity.

"Hey. Are you okay?" She took Lori's hand and rubbed it reassuringly.

Lori nodded, but the bottom lip caught between her teeth told Alex she was struggling.

"Listen, he's drunk and didn't know what he was doing. In the morning, he's going to wake up with the mother of all hangovers and a bag full of remorse. I guarantee it."

"It's not that... I..." She stepped in closer, holding Alex's gaze.

Alex searched her eyes. "Lori, what is it? You look scared. Honestly, I don't think you have to worry about Andrew again. If he does come back, well, you've got me here to protect you." She puffed up her chest and gave her a smile.

A small laugh escaped Lori. "You truly were very brave. My very own honest to goodness heroine." She leant in a planted a peck on Alex's cheek. "In fact, I'm not sure anyone has ever stepped in like that for me before. He could have hurt you." Her expression grew serious again.

"Hey, don't talk like that. He wouldn't have. You said underneath he's a good bloke and I believe that. He's just upset and doesn't know how to deal with it. Anyway, it's over. He didn't hurt me, and we're fine."

"I know. It's just... I guess it scared me, that's all."

"I take it he's never been like that before?"

"No, I don't mean Andrew scared me. Well, yeah okay, he did scare me a little. I thought I knew him and then, when you stepped in and I thought he was going to hurt you, that scared me more."

"Of course it did, sweetheart. Anyone in that situation would feel the same if one of their friends—" Alex stopped at the word friends thinking of their earlier conversation. This was Lori's opportunity to take it back.

"No, Alex, let me finish. It was more than that. You're more than that..."

Alex shut up and held her breath, letting Lori continue.

"I meant what I said earlier. It's just, well, this is all so new to me and so soon after Andrew. I'm not sure..." Her voice was barely a whisper.

Lori looked down at her hand in Alex's, and Alex did the same. She picked a freckle to stroke reassuringly, giving Lori time to find her words.

Either time had stopped or Lori had lost the ability to speak. She remained silent, her head still bent, and Alex couldn't wait any longer. She hooked a finger under Lori's chin, raising her eyes back up to meet her own. Brushing the hair back off her face, she whispered back, "I'm sure."

Those two small words were all the reassurance Lori needed. She wasn't thinking any more. The rush that came with the realisation of what those words meant, melted her doubts in a second. Her body took over for her until she was closing the gap between their lips, finally covering Alex's with her own.

She sank into it, into Alex. A small groan escaping as the kiss deepened, and Alex's tongue made the faintest of contact with hers. It was all she needed, her body reacted hungrily, and she wanted more. Her own tongue explored and found its target, eliciting a moan from Alex that shot straight to her core, pulling her in tighter.

Alex pulled away suddenly. "Honey lip balm. That's what's been driving me crazy all these weeks." She was breathless and smiled. "You taste like honey."

"Taste it again." Lori never wanted Alex to stop kissing her.

A hot tingle followed Alex's fingertips as they traced a line up Lori's spine and threaded through her hair. Urgent lips traced her jaw line, nipping their way down her neck, along her collarbone, to her earlobe.

One word whispered in Lori's ear, and she was close to being lost.

"Bed."

It wasn't a question.

She held on tight, unwilling to allow their bodies to part, as she backed them through the hallway into the bedroom.

Then it was Lori's turn to pull away as they reached the bed and her brain began intruding, the fear kicking in. She'd been with one person in her entire life, a man. Now here she was, in her bedroom, with a woman. She felt anxious, almost giddy at what would come next. Was this really about to happen? "Wait, wait." Her body cried out as she pulled away, but her mind needed the reassurance. "Alex, I'm sorry, I..." She burst out laughing then, and Alex looked perplexed. "I have absolutely no idea what I'm doing."

Alex pulled her back in, wrapping arms around her waist and planting a light kiss on her lips before murmuring against them. "Well, you know, I like to think I do, so maybe we can start there and see what happens."

Lori returned the kiss, couldn't help herself as it deepened. She was kissing Alex, and it felt as if it was the only place in the world she was meant to be at that moment. She wanted her. She trusted her.

"But this doesn't have to happen tonight." Alex pressed her forehead to Lori's, staring intently into her eyes. "I understand what a big deal this is."

Lori ran her fingers through the long hair, stroking her fingertips across her cheek, outlining her beautiful lips. "I want this." She whispered it, but meant it no less than if she'd shouted.

"Are you sure?" Alex murmured.

Lori responded with a kiss that she hoped left no doubt she was sure. Her head was lost and all she felt was every touch Alex lay upon her. They took it slow and the anticipation as each layer of clothing was peeled away only heightened her need to have Alex be a part of her.

Her goose bumps rapidly disappeared as she lay down and Alex slid between her legs. Their bodies melded together with heat, overwhelming every one of Lori's senses as each caress left her wanting more.

Alex pulled her into a sitting position and then sat in her lap, wrapping arms around her neck and silky legs around her waist. Lori broke away from her lips and leaned back, taking Alex in. Her expression in the glow of the streetlights was open and trusting. This woman, this night, was going to change her life. Of that, she was sure.

She ran a hand through Alex's hair, following it down her back, tracing fingertips up her side, taking her own time to explore the gorgeous female body before her. Alex's breath caught more than once as she discovered sensitive spots and committed them to memory, wanting to follow her fingers to them with her lips later.

Lori cupped Alex's face in both hands as they sank into a slow, languid kiss, before Alex took over, lowering her back onto the bed, exploring and finding places with her lips that left Lori desperate for more.

She clawed at Alex's back, pulling her back up for a kiss. "How are you doing this to me?" She was breathless now as Alex's weight pressed into all the right places, making her gasp, craving everything Alex had to offer. She needed it now and told her so. "Please, don't make me wait any longer."

Alex took her hand somewhere it had never been before. "This is what you're doing to me," she whispered in Lori's ear as Lori felt the truth of the words.

The blood rushed from Lori's head at the realisation, overwhelming her. She groaned against Alex's lips and felt Alex respond to her touch before moving away, continuing to explore every inch of Lori's body, frustrating and exciting her all at the same time.

Everything was new to her. Every caress, kiss, and stroke ignited her body more as it responded with relish, squirming with urgency and anticipation. Then Alex was part of her, and Lori lost any control she had left. She gave it over to

Alex. This was intimacy, this was what she'd been missing all these years. Alex was showing her the way.

She opened her eyes but saw only stars punctuating the darkness. As her mind cleared of everything, the rush coursed through her without warning and it kept going as Alex took everything she had to give.

Breathless, she closed her eyes, covering them with an arm and shaking her head in disbelief that how she now felt was possible. Her body felt limp but deliciously satiated, and she reached her other hand out to pull Alex up, until she was laid the length of her, head on her beating chest.

"I changed my mind." Alex's head shot up at her words, and Lori laughed.

"Why are you laughing?" Her eyebrows were knitted in confusion.

"Don't look so worried. I'm just not sure I was ready for that after all."

Alex smiled then, clearly pleased with herself. "You're a rotten tease." She shimmied up and planted a kiss on Lori's lips. "But you're beautiful."

CHAPTER 34

Stella awoke disorientated. It took a few moments for the alcohol-induced fog in her brain to clear enough for her to, firstly, be sure she was in her own bed, and, secondly, recognise Scott's raised voice in the next room.

She winced with pain as she tried to lift her head. She rolled over and groaned into the pillow, willing Scott to be quiet.

Reaching for the bottle of water she hoped was on her bedside table, she tried sitting up again. She brushed curls from her eyes, then closed them again, taking a deep breath before pulling herself fully upright. She gulped at the water and gradually managed to fully open her eyes.

Scott still ranted on the phone in the next room. If her head would have allowed it, she'd have shouted to find out what was up. Right now, however, she only cared about making it to the bathroom for a shower and an overdue date with her toothbrush.

Thirty minutes later, she sauntered into the kitchen, hair still damp and in her comfiest jogging bottoms and vest.

Scott huffed at the table. "Took you long enough."

She stopped mid-way toward giving him a kiss. "And a good morning to you too, Sunshine. What was with all the yelling and the grump?"

"Don't pretend as if you don't know."

She sized him up for a moment, this was not a mood she had ever seen on him and it didn't suit his usually handsome, smiling face. "Okay, what did I say to upset you in my drunken state last night?"

"That's just the point, Stella. You didn't say anything. All I got was some drunken babbling about espresso martinis being the devil's juice. Oh, and let me see, how wonderful Alex was."

As she stood surveying the contents of the fridge, she paused, wracking her brain for memories of when she got home. Crap. Had she let something slip about Lori and Alex?

"Oh, don't panic," he said, as if reading her mind. "You didn't give away the fact that Alex is a bloody woman. It seems Andrew had the pleasure of meeting her last night too. He filled me in."

She slammed the fridge door shut and spun around. "Why do I not like the tone of your voice? Yes, Alex is a woman. So what? I didn't tell you because Lori wanted to speak to you herself. If you ever bothered to call her, that is."

"So the fact that your best friend is suddenly a lesbian doesn't concern you at all?"

"Concern me? Are you kidding? What concerns me is your reaction to the fact and that Andrew is calling to tell you, as if he's performing some kind of public service. It has absolutely nothing to do with him. Or you, for that matter."

"He didn't call to tell me that."

"Oh really? You're telling me that wasn't the first thing out of his mouth?"

"No, actually. It was more the whole situation in general. He thought Alex was just a friend."

"What situation? What has he done?"

"He showed up last night at Lori's drunk, hoping to talk. Seems he made an arse of it and got a bit rough with her.

He was calling me to see if I'd spoken to her. He's devastated about the way he acted."

"Oh my God. Is she okay? I'll bloody have that bastard if he's touched her."

"Calm down. He said he only grabbed hold of her arm. He was angry she wouldn't talk to him. Then, it seems, Alex stepped in."

Stella was searching for her phone to call and check Lori was okay, losing patience as Scott tried to justify Andrew losing it with Lori. "Are you even listening to yourself?" She looked around frustrated, quickly giving up the search, and too angry to be any good to Lori at that moment anyway. "If any other guy had 'only grabbed' her, you'd be knocking his door down right now, with me not far behind. Lori's been miserable with him and you know it. Is her being with a woman so incomprehensible to you? Would you rather she spent the rest of her life as Andrew's sad, obedient wife?"

He jumped up from his chair, knocking it over in the process. "Don't you dare question my loyalty to my sister. You know what she means to me and that's exactly why I won't let her make this mistake."

Although surprised at his anger, Stella wasn't about to let him intimidate her. She calmly crossed the kitchen toward him as he reached for her. Instead, she moved behind him, and picked up the fallen chair before heading out of the kitchen in search of her phone.

He followed her to the living room, taking a different tact. "Listen, Stella, I know she's your best friend and we both love her. You have to admit this is a bit out of the blue. It isn't her. Don't tell me you weren't surprised by this, as well. I really think if we got together and talked to her, we can make her realise all this Alex business is just some early mid-life crisis. It's Lori's way of finally rebelling and not being the good girl for once."

She saw right through him. She took a deep breath and let it out slowly, determined not to lose her temper. "You know, you and James are the only family Lori has left to love and trust. I wonder what she would think if she could hear the way you're talking, trivialising this massive change in her life, without even having a conversation with her."

He raised his hand, stepped toward her, and opened his mouth. "But—"

She banged her hand on the sideboard as he tried to interrupt. "Damn it, listen to me. She's already had her dad on the phone conspiring with Andrew to get her to take him back, I expected more from you. Do you realise since they split up, the pair of you have only ever considered Andrew's feelings and your own?"

He was pacing now, clearly upset by the home truths. "Maybe that's because Lori doesn't seem to have any feelings about it, not according to Andrew, anyway. He says she's like a different person these past couple of months. Has she been seeing this Alex woman all along?"

"See, once again you're only worried about Andrew and his side of things. I'll repeat myself. How about you actually call her and find out?"

"That's not fair. You know how worried I've been about her."

"Yeah, so worried you haven't even tried to see her this weekend? I mean, what is it, Scott? Did telling yourself that Andrew was looking after Lori help alleviate the guilt of deserting her? Of never being around? Is that why you and James are so keen to see them back together?"

His voice was low as he answered, "How dare you? I never deserted her."

She held up both hands, she'd clearly hit a nerve and that maybe wasn't a road she wanted to go down with him. "Okay, okay, I'm sorry. But, Scott, she's still your sister. The same Lori we both know and love."

Stopping mid-pace, he glared at her, his anger coming through. "Lori the lesbian is not my sister. I don't know that person. I mean, what, she has one bad relationship with a guy and suddenly women are the way to go?" The pacing continued. "How could she decide something like that and then lie and keep it from us? That's not my Lori."

Stella sighed, finally finding her phone down the side of the sofa cushion. She pocketed it and perched on the arm. Evidently, she was in for further arguments and, frankly, couldn't believe Scott's reaction. Sure, she had been mad at Lori for about two minutes, for hiding the fact Alex was a woman, but, after seeing the two of them together, she couldn't maintain it. And, of course, it was out of the blue, she couldn't deny that. But if this was what Lori wanted, it was up to Stella and her family to support her, not make things harder. It was Lori's life to live as she chose and so long as she was happy, Stella was only going to support her. Scott had fixated himself on the word lesbian, but this wasn't about that for her. It was about Lori and Alex, two people who had found each other and, right now, all she cared about was her best friend's happiness.

"It's not as if she purposefully deceived us. We made assumptions because of Alex's name and she didn't feel ready to correct us. She's still trying to figure things out. Give her a chance to explain to you how she's feeling. Can you imagine, all of a sudden finding yourself attracted to a guy? Right when the one and only relationship you've ever had is falling to pieces. How confusing would that be?"

Scott spun around and pointed his finger at her. "Don't be disgusting, as if that would ever happen."

"Disgusting?" She shot up from the sofa. "You can't be serious. The places you've been and everything you've seen in the world, all the horrors, the poverty, the wars, and hate." It was her turn to point the finger. "I'd have thought you'd be happy to see a bit more love in the world, in your life for that matter. Instead, you stand there judging and denigrating your sister's relationship because you can't wrap your tiny mind around the thought of two women in love?"

"Love?" he scoffed. "Don't be so ridiculous. This Alex has clearly taken advantage of her. Andrew's pillow is barely cold and now she's a lesbian running off with the first girl she meets? Please. It's a phase. She'll soon wake up and see what a fool she's making of herself."

Exasperated and angry, Stella knew she wasn't going to get anywhere the way he was acting. The Scott that stood before her was not the same man she'd thought, only the day before, that she was falling in love with. Deciding to give him an opportunity to cool off and think before he said anything else to regret, she stood and pointed at the door. "I'd like you to leave."

His face softened. "Stella, come on. Don't be like that." He moved closer to her.

She held his gaze and stepped around behind the armchair, putting it between them. "I'm not being like anything, Scott. It's you who has the problem here. Now leave."

"Surely you can understand why I'm upset?"

"Honestly, Scott, no I can't. I think you're being a dick and, I'm realising maybe I don't know you the way I thought I did. I've told you before, Lori's the number one Hunter in my life and whatever's happened between me and you won't change that. I won't stand here and listen to you being so hateful. You haven't even met Alex, haven't seen them together. You haven't given her a chance."

She pointed again towards the front door. "If we're to have any chance of salvaging something from this, you need to leave now."

He snatched up his coat and stormed into the hallway without another word.

"Scott," she called after him as he flung open the front door.

He stopped but kept his back to her. "What?"

"When you get home, I want you to think about something for me."

His shoulders tensed, but he didn't turn.

"I want you to think about how often you've seen Lori truly happy." His shoulders dropped and she heard him sigh. "Because last night was the happiest I have ever seen her and I won't let you get in the way of that."

He remained silent, only pausing a few seconds before walking out the door without a backward glance.

Chapter 35

Lori woke with a crick in her neck, having spent most of the night with Alex's arm tucked under it. She stretched slowly, groaning with satisfaction, and reached across the bed to pull Alex back to her.

Her hand slid along the still warm sheet, there was no Alex, but she couldn't have been gone long. Lori smiled, wondering if she was taking a leaf out of Frank's book with an attempt at breakfast in bed.

She allowed herself a few minutes to savour the memories from the night while she listened out for noises in the kitchen. Not hearing any, she gave in to temptation, the need to be near Alex was overwhelming. She pulled a baggy T-shirt from a drawer and tugged it on. Her head popped through the opening to the sight of Alex in the doorway.

"Morning, lovely. I was just about to look for you. Where's my breakfast in bed?"

Alex slowly padded into the room, stopped in the middle, and swayed slightly, not looking at Lori. Her brow was creased and she seemed shrunken and small, drowning in Lori's long dressing gown.

Lori glanced down and noticed Alex's white knuckles where she gripped her phone. She looked back up and her stomach dropped when she found tears in Alex's eyes.

"Alex? Are you okay?" Lori rushed to her as the tears fell. "Here, come and sit down. What's happened?"

She guided Alex to the bed, where she sat but didn't reply, merely shaking her head slowly and staring through Lori. She still held the phone and made no effort to wipe the tears.

"Alex, you're scaring me. What's going on?" Lori grasped her shoulders giving her a small shake. "Alex, talk to me."

As if only realising where she was, her gaze fell back to Lori, briefly meeting her eyes before looking away again. Her lips moved silently for a few seconds before she uttered one small word, "Beth."

Lori was confused. "Beth?" She took Alex's face in both hands, forcing her to come back to her, to focus. "Alex, you need to tell me what the phone call was about, tell me how to help."

Alex's face darkened then, and the tears abruptly stopped. Her gaze steely, she glared at Lori. "I couldn't fucking help her, so how the hell are you going to help?"

Lori recoiled at the venom in her words. "I...I..."

Then Alex was in tears again; she crawled onto the bed, curling into a ball. Sobs wracked through her body. Lori couldn't bear it, despite the outburst. Going to her, she folded her into her arms, feeling her T-shirt dampen almost instantly as Alex buried her face into her chest.

She drew the covers up over them and gently stroked the side of Alex's face. Replacing the phone with Lori's hand, she squeezed tight. In between soft kisses to the top of Alex's head, she whispered reassurance, meaningless because she had no idea what was going on, but soothing enough that the sobs eventually calmed.

Whatever had evoked such fierce reactions in Alex clearly needed to work its way through her system. Lori's mind whirled. She could wait for an explanation but, meanwhile, her mind spun in a circle of wondering. She couldn't understand what kind of call Alex could have gotten to bring about this situation so many years after her sister's death.

Alex's breathing gradually steadied, then deepened as she dozed from the exhaustion of emotion. Sure she was asleep, Lori slipped her arm from underneath her and quietly slid out of the bed. She wrapped the covers tighter around Alex and placed a light kiss on her cheek.

Okay, think, Lori. What could have happened?

She grabbed cotton shorts from a drawer and then crept through to the kitchen, found her phone, and called the one person she could always rely on.

"What?"

Lori held the phone away from her ear and her friend's harsh tone. "Um, Stella. It's me, Lori."

"Oh my goodness, I'm so sorry, sweetheart. I thought it was work. I've got the mother of all hangovers and I've just had a raging argument with—" she stopped short. "Oh never mind, you don't want to hear about that. I'm so glad you called. How's the head? How's the lovely Alex."

Lori couldn't help but smile at the suggestion in her voice. Ideally, this would have been a call she'd be making once Alex had gone; spilling her guts to her best friend and telling her how truly wonderful 'the lovely Alex' was. But it would have to wait.

"Actually, Stella, she kind of just freaked out on me and I'm really worried. I woke up and she wasn't in bed. Then she came back in the bedroom all dazed and crying, clutching her phone and not speaking. Well, apart from getting really angry and shouting at me when I asked how I could help. She was muttering about her dead sister Beth—"

"Whoa. Lori, slow down for me. Hangover, remember? I can tell you're upset so I'm going to save the grilling about you being in bed together for another day and, instead, I just want you to take a breath, calm yourself, then I can help you figure this out."

"Okay." Lori closed her eyes, took a deep breath, and heard Stella do the same. "I'm calm."

"Right, where is she now?"

"She's in bed. She was crying so much she eventually exhausted herself and fell asleep."

"Okay, you said you thought she took a phone call, did you look to see who it was? Was it maybe one of her friends that you met in Scotland with some bad news?"

"See, this is why I called you. I haven't checked. Hang on and I'll go get it."

She returned with the phone and thanked the stars it didn't have a pin code locking the screen. "Okay, the last call was 10.36am, not from a number in her address book. It's a 0131 code, isn't that Edinburgh?" She switched Stella to speaker phone and poured a glass of water.

"Yeah, it is. Read me the full number; I've got my laptop open. I'll see if I can reverse look it up."

Lori did as she was asked, waiting patiently, and listening to the tapping of Stella's keyboard. "Find anything?"

"Hang on, ah, here it is. Oh..."

"What?" The line was quiet.

"Stella? What?"

"It's a police station in the south of the city. Why on earth would they be phoning her about her sister? Didn't you say she died years ago?"

Lori could hear more tapping. She was losing patience. "I don't know, Stella. You're meant to be the detective. Alex said she died eight years ago. She was fourteen."

"What did you say her name was again?"

"Beth, Beth Ryan. What are you doing?"

"Okay, wait a minute, I can't run an official search, that would be breaking all kinds of laws, but we still have the internet. I thought I'd see if there was something in the news, an article about an accident maybe."

"Hang on, Stella, I don't feel good about this. I just wanted you to calm me down but we shouldn't be looking into this. Alex should be able to tell me in her own time what the deal is with Beth."

"And what if she doesn't? Don't you want to be able to help her?"

"Of course I do, but it feels weird prying like this. Last night was so amazing and I want to be able to help, but I don't want her angry at me for meddling in something she doesn't want me to be a part of."

"Listen, Lori, you are part of her life now, and you care about her. We're not looking out of some kind of morbid curiosity. We're looking out of concern for her given her current state. We can wait until she wakes up if you like. I thought it might help if we had some info, that's all."

Lori appreciated that Stella couldn't help going into automatic detective mode. Helping people was built within her, and to do that, she needed facts. But this wasn't a stranger; this was a girl asleep in Lori's bed. "I think we should wait until she wakes up. Whatever it is, I'm sure she'll tell me eventually. For now I'll let her sleep."

Stella sighed. "You're right. I'm sorry, sweetheart. I didn't mean to go off on one then, it's like autopilot. Will you call me later and..." She trailed off.

"What? What is it? You're still searching, aren't you? Stella, honestly, leave it. I'll go and try talking to her again."

"Shit."

The dread in the pit of Lori's stomach turned to a solid lump. She knew this was going to be bad. Her hand found the edge of a kitchen stool, and she sat. "Stella?"

Her friend blew out a long breath.

"Stella, don't you go fucking quiet on me. Tell me what you found."

"Sorry, darling. Look, I don't mean to hold out on you. I'd put her name in already, and the results were there as I went to close it. I don't want you to panic, but maybe it's not my place—"

"Stella, don't do that to me. You've looked now and, as my best friend, you need to put me out of the misery I am currently in. Now what did you find?"

"You're right. You're my priority which is why I looked in the first place. You need to know this one way or the other."

"Know what, Stella?" Lori's mouth had gone dry.

"Okay, okay. There's an open case on Alex's sister, Elizabeth Ryan, and her father George." Lori heard her suck in a breath.

"Lori, there's no way to sugar coat this. They were murdered at the farm eight years ago. The article says it was a robbery gone badly. There's a follow up on her mother, Annabelle. It says she committed suicide less than a year later."

It felt as if the solid lump in Lori's stomach had burst up through her chest and was now choking her. Shaking, she held on to the countertop with both hands, steadying herself.

Murdered?

Suicide?

Where was Alex in all this?

Stella's voice calling her name pulled her back into focus. She gulped down the lump, picked up the phone again and took it off speaker. "I'm here."

"Lori, I'm so, so sorry. I remember the case. I was in Edinburgh at the time. There was a massive manhunt for months across the country, and then it just ran cold."

"Tell me how it happened. I need to know everything."

"This won't be easy to hear, darling, but if you're sure."

Lori listened as Stella went on autopilot, sticking to the facts, relaying it to her automatically as a detective would. "Two men broke into the farm. They gagged and tied up her mother and father in their bedroom. It's presumed they checked both Alex and her sister's room but Beth was sleeping elsewhere in the house and Alex wasn't home. Mrs. Ryan's statement is quoted as saying while the men ransacked their room, Beth snuck up on them. She said their gun was propped near the door and Beth picked it up and turned it first on the intruder who had a knife held to Annabelle's throat and then the other. The other intruder lunged at Beth with a knife and she fired."

"So Beth shot one of the intruders?"

"No, it sounds as if there was some kind of scuffle and Mr. Ryan got in the way when Beth pulled the trigger. He took the bullet in his chest." She went quiet.

"Stella, how did Beth die?"

Stella's voice came through barely a whisper. "I'm so sorry Lori. She was stabbed. Nine times."

Stunned, Lori couldn't speak. She tried to ask for more details but the strength wasn't in her. She could only manage to choke out a sob. She couldn't take anymore and couldn't even begin to imagine how Alex had survived the aftermath.

"Sweetheart, please don't cry. I'm going to come over. Just give me half an hour..."

But Lori wasn't listening. She'd turned to find Alex in the doorway, fresh tears coursing down her beautiful face. Lori went to her, pulling her in tight, they cried together until they both crumpled to the cold, tile floor.

Chapter 36

Alex was vaguely aware of Stella coming into the kitchen after what felt like a lifetime since hearing Lori on the phone. She was aware of talking, something about struggling to get a taxi because of the rain and not being able to drive because of last night's alcohol. Was that only last night? Everything felt so long ago, everything but Beth. She was right back there again, back in the moment the police told her what had happened to her family.

She was numb, still on the floor, clinging to Lori. A blanket was draped around them and she heard the clinking of Stella making tea through the buzzing in her ears.

She let herself be guided to the sofa in the living room. Lori didn't leave her side, Alex's hand firmly gripped in her own.

A few minutes later she looked up, found Stella stood in the doorway, tea tray in hand, studying them. Alex saw the pity and wanted to scream at her not to do that, not to look at her that way. Instead, she focused on the reassuring feel of Lori's body close to hers.

She watched Stella put the tea down before sitting on the edge of the coffee table. She leaned forward and took Alex's free hand. "Alex, I'm so sorry."

Alex nodded but pulled away. She wasn't ready to talk about it but Stella clearly wanted her to.

Lori freed a hand from under the blanket to take a cup from the tray while still gripping Alex tightly with the other. Alex simply shook her head when offered a cup but did take a tissue from the box on the table.

"I realise you don't know me very well, but you do know Lori, and so I'm hoping her trust in me will be good enough for you."

Alex looked to Lori then. She still didn't say anything, just searched her eyes, the worry evident.

Lori reached out to cup her cheek gently in her palm. "Talk to her, Alex, she's on your side."

After holding her gaze a few more seconds, Alex turned back to Stella. "Do you know about the phone call I got this morning?"

Stella looked between Alex and Lori and then nodded. "I do. I hope you don't mind, I called the station and spoke to an old colleague and friend. I also read the file on your family."

"Do they really think it's him?"

Lori looked confusedly at them. "Who are you talking about?"

Alex took a deep breath to tell Lori but changed her mind. She couldn't find the words and, even if she could, she doubted she'd get them past the lump in her throat. Instead, she nodded to Stella. "Tell us what your friend said, I didn't get all the details."

Stella stood and paced. "I spoke to a police sergeant who's an old friend, Tim. He said that several nights ago, after getting off shift, one of his officers, Hannah, who's also his niece, had been driving home around the back lanes and came across an old guy wandering alone in his dressing gown." She stopped pacing and sat on the coffee table again.

"He was confused and had no ID so Hannah picked him up and took him back to the station where they then found some injuries and had him admitted to hospital. Tim said Hannah visited every day but the old man was talking nonsense initially. His conversation veered all over the place but one thing he kept repeating was that he had to get to the farm and help 'the girl.'

Lori said what Alex couldn't. "Beth?"

Alex began to cry again at the mention of her name. After all this time, it was no easier to think about, never mind talk about. The thought of this person out there with answers to what happened, but no way to get them, frustrated and angered her. She felt as helpless as she had trying to look after her mum while searching for answers in the aftermath of her dad and sister's death.

Stella kept going. "Apparently the old man has multiple brain tumours. No one has reported him missing and they're keeping him in hospital under police guard. Hannah interviewed him again last night and it was the most lucid he had been. She said he eventually became angry, though, shouting and saying she mustn't call Sean and then telling them they needed to help Beth, that Sean wouldn't stop, and it wasn't his fault. When they tried to find out what wasn't his fault, he just kept repeating the name Beth, then asked to go to sleep."

Alex watched Lori's eyes close for a moment as the pieces of the story came together in her head. She turned to Alex, sadly shaking her head. Alex didn't see pity there, just concern. Lori sagged back in to the sofa alongside her before speaking. "Stella, what else did he say? Did he have something to do with what happened?"

"We think so. Tim said that this morning the old man was slightly more coherent again. He kept repeating that he needed new slippers, so they ran out and got some, which settled him more. They called in a specialist to monitor and sit with him, then had a detective to take over the interview. The specialist suggested maybe the old man had witnessed or experienced something distressing which is why he'd left his home."

Alex was quiet. She turned away from Lori who was nodding along with everything Stella was saying, clearly trying to understand. She hated that this was happening now. Everything was meant to be getting better. She'd met a wonderful woman who, for some reason, liked her back and now, here they were. Alex wished with all her heart that she hadn't been the cause of the sorrowful look on Lori's face. She picked a spot on the coffee table and stared at it while she listened. Stella's voice faded and she was back in the music room, Beth was singing a ballad in the sweetest voice, her mum and dad looking on with such pride, and her own heart filling with the love for her little sister that had never faded.

Lori's living room came back to her as she felt an arm slip around her waist, and Lori sat forward again.

"Then the old man asked if they'd gone to the farm to get his slippers and did they find Sean, as well. He asked if they'd been able to help Beth. He said he was worried about her because there had been so much blood."

Alex closed her eyes. She thought she might be sick. Her hands shook as she took Lori's tea from her, taking small sips, trying to calm her stomach. Lori pulled her closer, rubbing her hands up and down her arms, but she still shivered despite the thick blanket.

"How did they make the link?"

"Mention of the farm and the name Beth sparked in the memory of the detective called in to interview him. You never forget an unsolved case like that." She continued. "Currently, they have a team of PCs going door to door in the area he was picked up in." Sighing, she got up to pace again. "He fits the description your mother gave of the old man involved in the pub altercation with your father the night of the murder. I know they wore masks when they broke into the farm but the file says your mother always swore it was the same two men and I'm convinced she was right."

Alex nodded, finding her voice. "I always believed her. It was too much of a coincidence."

"That's exactly why I believe her. The detectives investigating did too. They've got the artists sketches of 'Sean' from back then circulating with the PCs along with a picture they've taken of the old man. It's not much to go on but, until we can get a surname, it's all they have right now."

Alex knew crying wasn't the answer, but every word Stella spoke seemed to bring everything back to her as if the eight years between what happened and this morning had been erased. It was raw all over again. She was back at square one, could feel herself shutting down, blocking out the pain and guilt, along with anyone who tried to get in to help her. She still had no answers, no one had been caught yet and nothing was certain, apart from the cold hard fact her family was dead. She needed to get out of here. She needed to be back at her farm, away from the looks and attempts at consoling something that would never feel better.

She handed the tea cup back and extricated herself from under the blanket and Lori's arm, kissing her hand before letting go and getting up.

"Just give me a few minutes. When I come back you can ask me whatever you want."

As soon as the bathroom door closed, Stella moved to the sofa beside Lori, pulling her into her arms and hugging her tight. "Sweetheart, are you okay?"

"No, I'm not. Stella, I don't know what to do, what to say. Fuck. How on earth do I help her get through this?" Stella held her at arm's length and Lori pleaded with her eyes for an answer.

"You help her by being there for her, whatever she wants, whatever she needs, you provide. And I'll be right here for both of you."

"You make it sound so simple. I feel as if I've woken up to a nightmare that I can't begin to comprehend, but it seems Alex has been living it for the past eight years." Lori slumped back in the seat, flinging the blanket away in frustration.

She thought of the night before, how wonderful and perfect it had been, every moment of it so close to the woman she was falling for, feeling and experiencing a magic she couldn't have even dreamed of. She thought of waking up that morning, when everything had seemed so clear, but now it felt like a memory already consigned to the distant past.

"I don't even know where to start with helping. I didn't know Alex back then, I didn't know Beth. How do I begin to understand?"

"It's not about understanding, my love. It's about allowing her the time to come to terms with what's happening. You know her now, or at least you're getting to know her. I'm sure she'll let you know what she needs, but it'll be one day at a time, I imagine. In the meantime, I'm going to catch this bastard, Lori, be sure of it."

"How? You're not even working in Scotland anymore."

"I've spoken to my boss and Tim has put in an official request for my assistance. So I'm heading up there first thing tomorrow."

"I don't understand. Why would they agree to that?"

"Tim owes me a favour or two and he's not exactly going to turn down the extra help. I won't be able to lead on it, but I can at least help bring this animal down."

Lori met her friend's eye, could see the determination there. "I know you will, sweetheart, and I'm so lucky to have you."

Stella pulled her back into a hug. "From experience, when these kinds of things happen, all the family wants is answers, and for someone to pay for what's happened. I'll find those answers for her and hopefully that can be the beginning of her moving on."

Lori couldn't help the tears. Stella reached for a tissue and gently wiped them away, shushing her and then smiling.

"Why the hell are you smiling?"

"You love her, don't you?"

Lori looked down. When she'd woken that morning, she had been in no doubt that she was falling crazily in love with Alex. That hadn't changed, but Alex was going to be the first to hear it. "Stella I can't... I don't—"

"Shh darling. I wasn't expecting an answer." She squeezed Lori close. "I promise to do everything in my power to bring Alex peace. Then maybe you, my friend, can finally be happy too."

CHAPTER 37

There was nothing to pack. There'd been no chance to unpack the night before, and Alex was grateful. She quickly showered and threw on her clothes, eager to get back to the farm.

Lori came into the room as she checked for the essentials: keys, wallet, and phone. She hated seeing the disappointment that crossed Lori's face when she realised Alex was getting ready to leave.

"You're going? I thought we were going to talk?"

Her voice was small, and it made Alex ache that she couldn't stay, couldn't offer an explanation as to why she needed to go. "I think it's best. If the investigation is happening back home, I should be there. I'm no use here."

"Then let me come with you. I can call into work, take some leave. I'd be happy to come and stay and help any way I can."

"No." Alex didn't mean to be so abrupt and she saw Lori's face fall. "I mean, you don't have to do that. I appreciate the offer. But this isn't your problem and I need to just deal with it in my own way."

"You appreciate the offer? Who are you talking to here? And I think, after last night, I get to make it my problem. I want to be there for you, Alex."

"Well, I don't want you there." She hated being harsh, but she knew what Lori wanted wasn't an option. She softened her tone. "I'm sorry, that's just the way it has to be right now. Besides, trust me, you don't want to be around me, either."

She knew she was hurting Lori. The night before had been everything she had imagined and far more. She had finally let go and allowed herself to enjoy being with someone again, and not just anyone. Lori was special, she knew that. But her priority was putting away the man who had destroyed her family. She had no emotional capacity to deal with anyone or anything else right now.

"Isn't that a decision I should make, whether I want to be around you?"

Lori wasn't giving up easy but no matter what she said, Alex was resolute. "No, it isn't. Look, I realise this isn't how today should be ending. This isn't how I should be saying good-bye. You're just going to have to try to understand and respect my wishes. I don't want you coming with me. I don't want you following me to Scotland. I want to be on my own."

It broke her heart to watch the silent tears stream down Lori's face, but it was the right decision. No one else needed to be hurt, and she knew if Lori stuck around through this, that's what would happen. Alex would end up disappointing her. She would see Alex wasn't the person she thought she was. Inside, she was already falling to pieces and once she was back at the farm, she would let herself.

She threw the bag over her shoulder and brushed past Lori to get her jacket from the hall. Lori followed her. "Will you call me? Can I call you?"

Alex stopped at the front door and turned. She took in the beautiful face, the hair falling around Lori's shoulders, and her still bare legs, only partly hidden by the long T-shirt and shorts. She memorised every bit of her. She knew this was the last time she would see her.

She cupped Lori's face gently and brushed a tear from under her eye. "Please don't cry over me. I don't deserve it." And with a soft kiss, she was gone.

CHAPTER 38

Alex dropped her bag on the kitchen floor. She followed soon after. The dark surrounded her, along with the silence. The clock ticked and she counted each second, twelve, twenty-five, forty-six. When she got to sixty, she pushed herself back up again. Time, that's all she had, and she was alone with it.

Frank was still at her neighbours', wouldn't be back until the next day. She looked out the window down the track and considered going to collect him, but the questions around her early return would be too much and her breaking point was near.

She didn't need the light to see the memories. The Friday night dinners, Christmas mornings, birthday parties, summer barbeques, even the arguments that came from having two petulant teenage girls and protective parents. She also didn't need it to find the bar, or her favourite bottle of whisky. She took it and a glass and headed to the living room to flick on the TV. Her answering machine light blinked on the side table, but she ignored it. The police had her mobile number and would call it if they had any news.

Lori and Jess had both tried calling her mobile, and she'd left that to voicemail as well. She'd deleted the message that told her voicemails were waiting and put it on silent for the rest of the journey home. Lori's face came back into her mind as she knocked back the contents of her glass. How she'd left things and treated her was just another mistake she'd never forgive herself for.

The screen glowed, and she switched to the BBC news channel. She was on her second whisky by the time the photo fit came up. It was a sketch from a description given years ago but was coupled with the recent picture of the old man, frail and decrepit in his hospital bed. She shifted forward in her seat and pressed pause on the TV. Could this old man really be partly responsible for her family's deaths? He didn't look capable, but then some years had passed and his ailing health wouldn't have helped his appearance.

She had no doubt he had been there. All the questions she'd wanted to ask back then came flooding back. Why hadn't he stopped the other man? Had he enjoyed it? Had he helped? Had they planned to kill them all along or was it just a robbery. Her mum's statement had been littered with holes; she'd been in shock, devastated, and had hidden her eyes from most of what had happened. Alex couldn't blame her for that.

Then she asked the question he could never answer. What if she had been there?

Her phone lit up again on the arm of the chair and she saw Jess's name. It was quickly followed by Lori's once that had rung out. She nudged it with her elbow and it fell to the floor. The clatter was strangely satisfying. She picked up the bottle, poured another, pressed play on the TV, and turned up the volume.

Lori shouted at her phone in frustration as it rang out again. "Damn you, Alex." She'd just spoken with a worried

Jess and had filled her in on what happened earlier that day. They'd watched together as the photos of the unidentified men filled their screens and both resolved to try Alex again, to not let her retreat as she'd done before.

Jess was more forthcoming with Lori than she had been at the farm. She told her more of what had happened all those years ago. It was enough to convince her they should be worried about Alex's state of mind. Lori would defy anyone to come through that kind of pain unscathed, and talking with Jess had helped her understand that Alex's earlier reaction had been perfectly valid.

Jess had promised her if she had no luck getting through in the next couple of days, she'd head to the farm. She knew her best friend, and reassured Lori that Alex would need some time for herself initially, then it would be up to them to help pick her up and make her realise the world hadn't ended again.

In the meantime, she was glued to her screen, willing the police to identify the men. She had shared Stella's number with Jess and asked for her to be kept in the loop, particularly if Stella was unable to reach Alex.

A message came through from Jess. Unsurprisingly, Alex wasn't answering her calls either. Lori switched off the TV and tried Alex one last time before conceding for the night and heading to bed.

Sleep wouldn't come. Her mind couldn't leave Alex. From the little Jess had given away, it was clear Alex had taken a long time to come back from the dark place she found herself in after her family's deaths, and, with one phone call, she had been plunged straight back there.

She padded back to the living room wrapped in the same thick robe Alex had worn that morning, Alex's scent remained and it was a small comfort but nothing close to being able to wrap her arms around the real thing. She pulled it tight and shuddered, unable to shake the chill that had run through her and stayed since that morning in the kitchen.

Sat with the TV on mute, the photo fit came up on a fifteen-minute loop with the same stories repeated in between. She tapped her mobile phone screen, willing Alex's name to appear.

She texted Stella again, she knew she was being irritating, that Stella would call as soon as she heard anything, but the helplessness and sense of futility was infuriating. Stella's reply told her to get some sleep. Sleep? That wasn't happening tonight. Alex was going through who knew what four hundred miles away and there was nothing she could do about it.

The finality in Alex's parting words had scared her initially. She'd sat on the floor of the hall crying until she was dry. Then realising there were two people in this, no matter what Alex had said, Lori still had some say in their situation. She would follow Jess's lead because there was no one that knew Alex better. In the meantime, she had to stay strong, hope the police did their job quickly, and then be there ready, if and when Alex finally did answer her calls.

She hit the TV off button in frustration and headed for the kitchen and a half-finished bottle of wine in the fridge.

It wasn't like her to medicate with alcohol, and she poured it more from a lack of anything else to do.

She picked up her phone and scrolled the contacts, pressing the green button and hoping it would be answered. "Jess? It's Lori. I know it's late but—"

Jess cut her off. "It's okay, sweetheart. You don't need to say any more. I'm not planning on doing much sleeping either. What's up?"

"I want you to tell me more about Alex, about her family, about Beth, before all of this. I want to know what that Alex was like."

CHAPTER 39

Alex tried to go through the motions the first few days: showering, getting dressed, eating, feeding the animals, and walking with Frank after she picked him up. But each day another chore slipped, another thing was put off, another bill went unpaid.

She hadn't breathed since the call. She found herself falling deeper back into the well of emotions that had consumed her eight years earlier. She was sure to feed the animals but had spent the past three days with not much more than whisky in her own belly before Jess showed up, fuming that she'd ignored not just her calls, but Lori's as well. She didn't want to talk about Lori. She didn't want to talk about anything.

"Alex, I'm not having this. I'm not watching this happen all over again. I can't and I won't let you do it to yourself. Get up." Jess threw open the curtains and let in the morning sunlight.

Alex groaned into her pillow. Any small movement made her brain feel as if it was knocking around in her head. She wasn't even sure she was sober, more like drunk but with yesterday's hangover kicking in.

The covers were thrown back and Jess towered over her. "Don't make me do it, Alex. We've been here before and you know I will."

Alex didn't see she had much choice and thought she might as well make it easier on Jess. She held out her arms and, just like eight years ago, Jess easily scooped up the skin and bones that was her friend and carried her to the bathroom.

Alex raised her arms again, this time for her grubby T-shirt to be pulled over her head before the powerful jet of the shower assaulted her. She sat on the stall floor, knees pulled up to her chin, shivering under the spray which Jess had purposefully made too cold. She didn't protest as shampoo was rubbed into her lank, greasy hair, and shut her eyes tight as the lather ran down her face.

Jess grabbed her hand and put a bar of soap in it. "Your hair, I can do. But I'm not touching your other bits. Get scrubbing, Ryan."

Alex groaned again but made a show of lathering the soap until a satisfied Jess left her alone to wash. She stood up and held her face under the spray, willing the water to wash the past few days away, wishing to go back to London, to be waking up again in Lori's arms, for the phone not to have rang that morning.

She turned off the shower. Jess hadn't gone far and with the water stopped she reappeared with a large towel. Jess wrapped it around her and rubbed Alex's arms, warming and drying her at the same time before helping her into clean pyjamas and a dressing gown.

"C'mon, I'll make you some food."

Alex followed numbly. She was starving and her legs wobbled from exhaustion but the thought of eating made her nauseous. She'd maybe change her mind once Jess started working her magic in the kitchen.

"So have you spoken to Lori?"

Alex sat at the kitchen island as Jess unloaded the items she'd brought from the fridge.

"No, and I don't intend to. Leave it alone, Jess."

"What? I'm just asking. You know how worried she is, don't you?"

"Well, I told her not to worry so she shouldn't. Can't you just tell her I'm fine and not to keep calling?"

"I'm not lying for you, Alex. Besides, if I tell her you're fine, then what's your excuse for running off and ignoring her?"

"She's better off without me."

"Bullshit. Plus, shouldn't that decision be up to her? You're not even giving her a chance. You think it's the same as last time but it's not. You've changed, grown up, and you have people in your life who love you and want to take care of you. Every now and then you need to let them." She pointed towards the vegetables she'd begun chopping. "Case in point. Because of me, you won't starve and stink up this place."

Alex couldn't help but chuckle. "Okay, I'll call her. But not before I'm ready."

Jess stopped chopping and eyed her suspiciously. "Either I'm getting better at this or you just blatantly lied to me. It better not be the second."

Alex held up her hands. "Enough. Now, can I go lie down on the sofa while you cook?"

"On one condition."

"Jess, I said I'd call her." She was exasperated and just wanted the world to leave her alone.

"All right, snappy. I was just going to insist you agree to eat."

Alex sighed, sorry for being such a bitch when all Jess was doing was looking after her. She walked around the island, behind her friend, and wrapped her arms around her, kissing her cheek and nuzzling her face into Jess's neck. "I'm sorry, sweet Jess. Thank you. I promise I'll eat every bite.

CHAPTER 40

It had been nearly two weeks since the police had called Alex.

After Jess had shown up fuming, sobering her up with some real food and a much needed shower, Alex had taken the ass kicking and allowed her friend to hang around, only insisting she head home at night.

Alex knew she couldn't allow herself to return to those dark days. The drinking, the hatred, the blinding rage and anger that no one had ever been made to pay for her family's deaths. But it was hard to fight and she needed some space, some time to herself.

When Stella had called to tell her they had identified the suspects, she believed her and Jess when they said that was a positive step and they would find him, despite her initial scepticism.

"Stella, it's been almost ten days. Are you telling me he's even going to be in the country still?"

She had Stella on speaker and Jess hovered over the phone with her.

"Aye, I mean, he has a hell of a head start," Jess chipped in.

"Well, unless he got out somehow without a passport, he's still in the UK. He has a driving license but no passport, so he's limited with that. And there's no activity on his bank account, not that there's much in it."

"But you can't be sure he hasn't left the country? Damn it, he could be fucking anywhere in Europe with his driving license." Alex heard the impatience and anger in her own voice and was sure Stella had too. The stakes were too high and everything seemed to move so slowly.

"Alex, I get you're frustrated, I am too. But we can only go on what we have, be thorough and hope to catch a break. That's all I can offer right now."

"And what about vehicles? Have they found his car?" Jess continued the questioning, glaring at Alex and mouthing for her to calm down. Alex's mind was reeling with the possibilities of where he was. How far away? Who with? The thought that he might get away was incomprehensible to her at this point. She let Jess carry on, listening as Stella reassured them.

"No sightings yet that we've confirmed as him. We're getting calls all the time and I can assure you every one of them is being thoroughly checked out and we're continuing to monitor CCTV and traffic cameras, as well as going door to door, around his local area. And obviously the news outlets are running the full story hourly."

"Okay, we know you're doing everything you can, Stella, and we are grateful, even if Alex is incapable of showing it. Is there anything else we should know?"

"I know, and really, it's okay, Alex. I understand."

Alex muttered her thanks, still deep in thought.

Stella continued. "We do have some more background now, and I can tell you his past is colourful."

"Colourful as in criminal?" Alex said as she and Jess exchanged glances. They hadn't considered that he might have a record already.

"Exactly. I can't really give you any more than that but you can be sure everything we've learned will help."

Alex let Jess's arm slip around her waist. Hearing that others may have suffered at the hands of Sean Murphy only intensified her desire to see him behind bars, or better, dead. "I'm sure it will. Anything else?"

"Not at this point. Just sit tight and wait for my calls. I know that's hard, Alex, but trust me when I say we have the best there is working on this. We're going to catch this animal."

"I know. And I appreciate everything you're doing. Really, I do."

"Right, sweetheart, well I better get back to it. Jess, make sure you're keeping an eye on her. If anything significant comes up, I'll head out to the farm to talk. And remember what I said before: be vigilant. We can't be sure he hasn't stayed local and is planning a visit."

Jess was heading to the fridge and called out her good-bye, Alex took her off speaker phone, catching her before she could hang up. "Stella?"

"Yeah, I'm still here."

"It's just me now." Alex turned her back on Jess, lowering her voice. "Stella, how is she?"

She heard Stella sigh and a moment passed before she spoke. "You know I'm trying to keep personal and professional separate here, so when I say this, it's from Stella, Lori's best friend."

Alex nodded but realising Stella couldn't see her she forced an "okay" out. Afraid of what was coming.

"What you're doing to Lori, ignoring her like this, pushing her away when all she wants to do is be there for you, it's out of order, Alex. You're out of order. She's in bits."

Alex choked back a sob. "I'm sorry." She whispered.

"It's not me you need to be saying that to. Bye, Alex."

Still she couldn't breathe.

She poured a drink.

It had become a nightly ritual as soon as Jess headed for home. Pour a drink, sit, stew, beat herself up for every mistake.

Since the police had discovered Sean Murray's identity and put a warrant out for his arrest, he had disappeared. On Jess's insistence, Alex tried to avoid the TV and Internet, filled with stories regurgitating every detail of that night, the aftermath, and her mother's eventual suicide.

Sean's face had become the best known in Britain.

The possibility that he might show up at the farm, be drawn to the scene of his crime if he knew the chase was up was a concern for the police and her friends, but not Alex. If he was that stupid, then let him come.

She took her drink to the music room and ran a finger down the glass of Beth's picture, outlining her cheek. Tilting it to the light, her reflection flickered back at her. Dark rimmed eyes and hair badly in need of another wash greeted her. It had only taken a couple of weeks to undo eight years of rebuilding, despite Jess's best efforts.

She shook her head and toasted her glass in the direction of a sleeping Frank before downing it in one gulp and sinking back in to the armchair.

She waited.

She waited for the police to find Sean, for the search of his house to be over, for yet another detective to interview John Murray in an effort to break through his tumour-clouded mind. No surgery could help him, only medication could keep him comfortable, and in the meantime the doctors and detectives tried to get what they could from him.

Alex knew the Murrays had been there that night. Her mother had been convinced it was the men her dad had fought with in the village pub earlier that evening. She'd told the police that the younger man had been making lewd comments about her and had become angry when she'd sent back a drink he bought her.

They had chosen to ignore the insults until he'd followed her to the toilets, and that's when the fight had broken out. John Murray apparently had no part in it. Instead, he sat quietly at the bar, knocking back the booze until he'd been thrown out with his son.

After that, the rest became a theory and the word of her mum. A woman so consumed with the horror of what she'd witnessed in her bedroom that night, she never again saw light. Annabelle Ryan left Alex to pick up the pieces alone.

And now where was she? Alone again. She stared into the empty glass, but there were no answers there. She hadn't found them in the bottom of a bottle all those years ago and knew she was a fool to think she'd find them there now. It was habit, and there was no reason she could see to break it. The numbness it offered would do instead of the answers she couldn't find.

She wondered what Lori would think of her if she could see her now. How could she love her like this? Remembering the bothy brought a rare smile to her face. She could have never have imagined when she set off that day, that a random meeting in the mountains would be the moment to bring her back to life.

That's how Lori made her feel: alive. Their night together in London had awoken feelings in her she thought were lost long ago. Feelings that Rachel had never ignited and she realised what an idiot she had been to settle for Rachel's version of love.

She clung onto the memory of London, replayed it nightly, moment by moment. She closed her eyes, conjured the honey scent, the feel of Lori's skin beneath her lips, and the softness of her hair as it tickled Alex's body. How she felt at home, tucked in against her; there was nowhere she'd rather be.

And now it was gone. She'd thrown it away and didn't imagine Lori could forgive her or would want this person she was becoming. She had lied to Jess. She had no intention of calling and dragging Lori through the pain and despair with her. It would beat her down and Alex would never forgive herself for it.

Her phone flashed, the loud ringtone kicking through her thoughts. She checked the caller ID and her pulse quickened when she saw it was Stella. Squeezing her eyes shut she tried a deep breath before answering. "Please tell me you've found him?"

CHAPTER 41

Stella pulled up outside the farm and took a deep breath. She'd kept her call brief, insisting, instead, that she come out to the farm to speak to Alex in person. Her reasons were two fold, she had some big news and wanted to give it to her in person, but Lori had also asked that she visit and report back on Alex's state. She felt sneaky about the second reason, but her own curiosity had led her to agree.

Alex had refused at first but relented when Stella stated point-blank she wasn't talking on the phone so Alex might as well agree. However, now she was here, a part of her wished she had just stuck to the phone.

The farmhouse was in darkness, apart from a small light flickering at the end of the building. She approached the side door as Alex had told her, the darkness hid the figure behind the glass and Stella jumped as it opened before she knocked.

"Sorry, I didn't mean to scare you. I saw the headlights."

It was worse than Stella had thought. She could smell the booze coming off Alex and her demeanour suggested she'd had more than one already that night. Alex turned and headed back into the house without another word, her clothes hung at her hips and shoulders and Stella wondered how much she was eating, never mind drinking.

The flicker of light she had seen turned out to be a couple of large candles, centred on a coffee table littered with magazines, playing cards, and poker chips. A photo of Beth sat next to them, not far from a near empty bottle of whisky.

A dog she assumed was Frank, curled up at the foot of an armchair which Alex now settled herself into, pulling a tartan throw down over her shoulders.

"So I take it they haven't found him?"

She sounded defeated and Stella wished that wasn't the news she was bringing. "I'm afraid not." Stella pulled over an ottoman and sat close, Frank separating them, his chest rising and falling rhythmically in sleep. She whispered across him. "They have found something, though."

Alex adjusted the throw and reached for the bottle. She glanced at Stella then and must have thought better of it, instead putting her empty glass on the table. "Well?" She spoke impatiently, making Stella feel as if it was an inconvenience for her to be there.

Stella put aside her own feelings, swallowed back a retort, and gave Alex some slack. Yes, Stella was working her ass off and had travelled across the UK pulling every string possible to get on the case. But what was she expecting from Alex at this point? Gratitude? Her family were still dead and she hadn't asked for the help. Stella was doing this for Lori.

"The dogs found a bloody handkerchief folded up inside a small tobacco tin. It was hidden underneath a floorboard in John Murray's bedroom. It's going to take some time to test it but we're pretty sure it's from that night."

"I remember something about a handkerchief from Mum's statement."

"So did I. She said the man who covered her mouth did so with a hand wrapped in a bloody handkerchief. If we only find John Murray's blood on it, it won't be much use but there's hope he will have picked up your mum's DNA, maybe even Beth's if he was involved in..." She couldn't finish the sentence.

Alex had shuddered and pulled the throw tighter around her.

"The way we're looking at it, Alex, is that it was either some kind of trophy or an insurance policy. Either way it's our best chance at tying at least John to the scene that night. Our guess is it's the latter, considering which room it was found in and, at this point, going on what your mum said, we don't think John was part of what happened to Beth."

"Of course he was fucking part of it," Alex spat the words. "He was there. He was part of the plan. He tied and gagged my parents just the same as his animal son. He might not have..." She stopped, looked at the picture, and took a breath. "He might not have been the one to stab her, but he was part of it. He's as much to blame for this."

Frank's ears twitched at her tone and he rose from his sleep, sniffing around Stella lazily, he seemed satisfied she was friendly and resumed his position.

The tears came then, and Stella had never felt so helpless. She was clinging to the small hope that came with the handkerchief, but she could see that all hope was lost for Alex.

She moved to the arm of the chair, put an arm across Alex's shoulders, and tried to pull her in for a hug. Alex attempted to shrug it off at first, but then the tears came harder and she let herself be comforted. She grasped on to Stella's jumper, burying her face in it. Stella held her, smoothing her hair and uttering promises she wasn't sure she could keep.

Frank jumped up suddenly, startling Alex. She pulled away, wiping her face with both sleeves, unable to look Stella in the eye.

"I'm sorry. I don't know where that came from." Frank leant his chin on Alex's knees and she scratched him automatically, still sniffing and wiping her face.

Stella moved back to the ottoman.

"You never have to apologise. I can't even begin to imagine how you're feeling. You know I'm doing all I can, don't you?"

Alex smiled her way. "Aye, I do, sweetheart. I know I'm not great at showing it, but I appreciate everything."

"You know who else wishes she could help?"

Alex's face dropped then. "Please, Stella, don't. Look at me. How can I have her see me like this? I'm a mess. This whole thing is a mess. I don't want her dragged into it."

"But don't you realise she already is in this, just by the fact that she cares about you, Alex. You're hurting her more by not letting her in, not letting her help. And how do you know she can't help? My girl is strong. She's survived crap of her own, you know? Have you thought that maybe having her is what's different this time? What can make the difference to you this time?"

"Okay, now you're just quoting Jess. And I'll tell you the same thing I told her. Lori just needs to forget about me, forget about all this, and move on. There have been too many tears already because of this and hers shouldn't be added to them."

Stella stood then. She wasn't going to get anywhere, she knew. The vulnerability she had witnessed only moments ago was gone. The wall was back up and no one was getting in.

"I like you, Alex. I don't profess to know you, but I can say with certainty you're wrong about this. And it's too late. She's already drowning in her tears."

Stella turned and didn't look back. If she'd been harsh, it was because Alex needed it. She also needed Lori. She got into her car and held down *one* on her speed dial. Lori answered after the first ring. "So? How did it go? How is she?"

"Oh, Lori, I don't know what to say. I wish I could tell you she's holding up all right but I'd be lying. She's a mess."

She heard Lori choke back a sob, and her heart broke for her. "Hey. Don't do that, sweetheart. Please. She's got Jess so I'm sure things won't get as bad as Jess said they were before. There are stages to this and she'll eventually move on from this one and, hopefully, it'll get better."

"I just want to hear her voice, Stella. That's all I want." Her voice broke fully then and Stella pictured her beautiful face stained with tears.

"I know, darling. I have the feeling that's all she wants too, but she's stubborn. She's set on her decision and it's going to take something more for her to pick up the phone."

"You know my application for New York is due by the end of this week?"

"Really? So soon?" Stella felt her own voice crack. She was fighting hard not to be upset at the potential that Lori was leaving, but she couldn't stand in her way. Besides she loved New York and combining it with her best friend was going to make for some amazing visits.

"Yeah. Adam has pretty much filled mine out. He's knows me better than anyone professionally, our careers have run so parallel to one another."

"Are you sure this is what you want? With things how they are with Alex."

Lori signed down the line. "I've no idea. But there's a deadline and I don't want to regret not at least finding out if

I would have had a shot. This isn't something I can put on hold. I guess I'll deal with it if and when."

"You're right." Stella cleared her throat. She needed to be supportive, not pour more guilt on Lori for simply trying to find happiness and fulfil her dreams. "This is about you Lori and for too long that hasn't been the case. There's no harm in putting the form in and seeing what happens."

"I knew I could rely on you. I told Adam to send it over so I can check it before Friday. I wish I could talk to Alex about it though."

"I know, darling." Stella felt despondent for her. She'd waited so long for this opportunity and now it was soured with uncertainty and heartache.

"But what am I meant to do when she won't answer my calls? Text and say 'Hey I might be moving to New York, thoughts?' and I'm certainly not putting you or Jess in that position."

Stella smiled to herself that Lori's sense of humour was at least partly intact. "I think what you're doing is best right now. I'm certain you're going to get that interview, and I'm convinced one of the jobs is yours, but now isn't the time to tell Alex. What do we say? One day at a time."

Lori went quiet and Stella didn't interrupt the silence. "I thought she was falling, the same as me. I thought I meant something to her. Have I been a fool, Stella?"

The tears were back, Stella knew, but anger was creeping into Lori's voice. "You're no fool, Lori. She's the one fooling herself."

"I find that hard to believe."

"She needs you, Lori."

Lori was quiet and Stella heard the tears start afresh. "Do you really think so?"

"I'm positive. Call Jess. She'll tell you the same. I think it's time you made her realise it. Come to Scotland, Lori. Come now."

Stella hung up and glanced back at the house. She could swear there was a shadow in the window watching her, but she didn't stick around any longer. She texted Jess and briefly told her what was happening and that she should phone Lori for more details.

Once back at the station, she scrubbed her face with dry palms, giving her cheeks a hard pinch and a couple of slaps in a vain attempt to wake up. She glanced up at the images flickering across the TV high in the corner of the open-plan office space, the volume had been switched off and she saw a more recent photo taken from Sean Murray's driving license appear. It filled the screen next to an old mug shot as details of the case scrolled underneath. A reporter appeared and mutely relayed what they knew. The text below stating the headlines, a nationwide alert was out on Sean Murray, he was deemed dangerous, potentially armed, and not to be approached.

Stella waited, buzzing with nerves, anticipation and frustration at every dead end they ran into. He was so far doing a good job of hiding, but he had to rear his ugly head at some point and Stella was determined she'd be the one there to cut it off.

She read the stilted subtitles of what the reporter was saying for what she was sure was more than the hundredth time that day. Her mobile vibrating across the desk pulled her attention from the TV.

She grabbed the phone and let her shoulders drop when she saw Scott's name on the caller ID. She slipped it into her back pocket, letting it go to voicemail, tucked a file under her arm and headed for the grubby staff canteen and the last dregs of the coffee pot.

Scott had called incessantly since their argument, but she refused to even acknowledge his calls. He could wait. If he bothered to call his sister as she had suggested, she might have confided in him and he'd be aware of the situation.

But selfish arse that he was, he still hadn't. So she'd decided he could stew in his ignorance until Lori and Alex were taken care of, and she found some breathing space to deal with him. He didn't even know she was in Scotland.

She sweetened two cups of the tar-like coffee before taking them along the corridor to the audio-visual room. Her contribution to the case so far had been one endless shift, scouring hours of CCTV footage from in and around businesses and streets where they'd had sightings of Sean Murray called in to the hotline. Boring work, but it had to be done and she was happy to put her skills to use in any way possible.

The officer assigned to help her was the same one who'd picked John Murray up, Hannah Wallace. She stared watery eyed at the multiple screens, yawning already. Hannah smiled gratefully as Stella passed her a cup.

Stella pulled up another chair. "We have more on Sean Murray's background. Want to recap?"

"Sure." Hannah stilled the images on the screen and turned her way. "What do we know so far?"

Stella pulled the file from under her arm and got as comfy as was possible on the cheap office chairs. "We know he's an ex-soldier with a failed building company under his belt. He's divorced with two children but they've been cut off from him for the best part of a decade. He got some tour medals, the Gulf, Bosnia, Northern Ireland, and Afghanistan, that's where it gets colourful."

Hannah was nodding. "The assault charge."

"Exactly. We have an accusation of assault against a female RAF officer while on tour. The charge was never proven but it forced him out after nineteen years of service and, with a man like this, that's got to have hurt his pride. He accepted a deal to go quietly when she decided not to pursue charges and he was discharged honourably with his pension intact."

"So we know he had previous. Unproven, but that doesn't sound like the way to treat an innocent man." Hannah voiced the scepticism Stella was thinking.

"Yeah, it doesn't sound good." Stella agreed.

"So what happened with the wife and kids? Do we have any more on that yet?"

Stella couldn't imagine someone going home and living a happy family life with the weight of the crime they'd committed. No sane person anyway. But unfortunately she knew it happened, every day, everywhere. She'd seen it enough times herself. "Yeah we've got court records now on his divorce. His marriage wasn't as lucky as his pension." She smiled wryly and returned to reading. "Soon after his discharge, his wife took the kids and moved back south to her family in Bristol. Took a chunk of his payoff with her but it doesn't look as if she's claiming any other form of child maintenance. A local went to speak with her, but she claims not to have heard from him in years."

"I'd say that's a good thing for her." Hannah noted and Stella agreed.

"It looks as if he moved in with his dad and got into the family business soon after she left, but the recession didn't do the business any favours. His tax records are sporadic at best over the past five or six years; doesn't look as if he's held a job for more than six months. No credit cards. No savings account."

"No trail to follow."

Stella nodded her agreement. "He's not exactly a ghost though. There might not be much financially but there's a past here, links, ties, reasons to stay in the country. We're not done with the ex-wife and kids, I can't believe he would walk away from that without a fight."

Hannah's brow creased. "Is it worth having someone watch them? If he thinks he's about to get caught, his kids might be a draw?"

"Already on it. The locals down south are helping all they can. I guess in the meantime we keep going with what we're doing. Any joy?"

Hannah spun back around toward the screens, shaking her head. "Sorry Detective, and the list of sightings doesn't seem to be diminishing."

Stella ran her hands through her thick curls, resisting the urge to tug it all out in frustration. "Okay." She picked up her coffee. "Let's do this." She pulled her chair under the desk and settled in beside Hannah for another long night.

CHAPTER 42

Lori had spent two weeks wondering. Two weeks pacing between her living room and kitchen, between the sofa and the fridge. Two weeks staring at her phone, willing Alex's name to appear. Two weeks typing and then deleting message after message to Alex, only sending a handful. Two weeks of tears, of anger, frustration, and confusion. Two weeks of not knowing.

Through it all, one thing overrode all those other feelings, kept her awake at night, made her ache in a way she had never experienced.

She missed Alex.

Her head told her to forget it, she was a one night stand, and Alex had moved on, had more important things to deal with. Her heart told her Alex missed Lori just the same, but had spent so long on her own she'd forgotten how to ask for help.

Stella's lecture about tick boxes and settling for safe rang in her ears. Of doing what was expected rather than what she wanted. Well, this was the moment she took that advice, took a chance. Alex might decide to turn her back on Lori, but that was a risk she was willing to take.

Andrew had inadvertently helped her make the decision to head north. Listening to another message from him the night before, when she'd heard his defeated tone she'd let it play through. He had apologised for being an idiot and for the scene at her house, he admitted his ego had done the talking and he knew that's what had pushed them apart in the first place. He still wanted an opportunity to talk, but knew it was too late to salvage anything more than friendship. She could live with that, and felt lighter knowing he had taken a step towards moving on. She felt free.

She couldn't deny she was also sad at the loss of what they once had and empathised with him, it wasn't only his fault. They had simply lost sight of what was important and what would make them happy together. She knew he was a good man, but he wasn't good for her anymore, and it seemed he was coming to realise that.

At the office, she had given Adam a quick rundown of things to cover before leaving, but he'd been fussing around her, his excitement over New York growing now both their applications had been submitted. He had word from a buddy that they both had been shortlisted and would get an interview date in the next few days.

The New York opportunity was moving faster than she expected. Alex was just a daydream when Adam had first told her about the job, but now she was very real and Lori couldn't deny she was still having second thoughts about a potential move to the other side of the ocean.

She vied between missing Alex deeply, the thought of moving unbearable, but then the anger at being shut out bubbled over, and in her mind she was telling Alex to go fuck herself, while resolutely telling herself she was moving to New York.

Then she would imagine never seeing Alex again, and the tears would come. It was a pattern, a cycle that had consumed the past two weeks and she was exhausted by it. The circle had to be broken.

She should have been excited with Adam but couldn't muster it. She'd shot him down rather cruelly in frustration when his constant chatter had become too much. Telling him she hadn't made a decision but definitely wasn't going if it meant putting up with him.

Her words should have hurt him but instead, they seemed to bring him back to earth where his friend of more than five years was struggling, and he hadn't taken a minute to notice. The way he sat back in his chair and appraised her, his head slightly tilting while pulling at an ear lobe told her there were more questions to come. She knew that look. And his questioning was relentless.

Despite his prodding she couldn't talk about it. If she did, it was possible it would break her too, and she knew now, for Alex, she had to be strong. There was no more time for her tears. Instead, she gratefully accepted his offer to cover some meetings with a promise that they'd talk properly when she got back.

Walking to her car after work, Lori's suitcase weighed heavy, as did her heart. All day, her mind had been firmly in Scotland with Alex. She'd made the decision to be bold after her last calls with Jess and Stella. Alex needed her, whether she knew it or not.

Checking her phone had become an obsession; waiting for an update from Stella on the search or a response to one of the few texts she had sent Alex. Geography was the least of her worries when it came to the distance between them, and she was fed up of relying on Stella and Jess to keep her up to date.

She wasn't going to let Alex push her away anymore, isolating herself, and no doubt drinking herself into oblivion if what Jess told her was true. Jess knew the signs of Alex withdrawing and had told her she wasn't prepared to watch it happen all over again, but she needed Lori's help.

So Lori had booked a flight at the last minute, and Jess had promised to pick her up and take her to the farm. They'd agreed not to tell Alex, hopeful that once she saw Lori, she wouldn't turn her away.

She dropped her case in the boot of the car, slid into the driver's seat, and checked her phone again as she attached it to the hands-free. Still nothing.

Even Stella had been illusive, only texting with official updates and, when she did call, it was all business, straight to the point, only talking about Alex, and her worries about her and the case. The only flicker of her real friend had been when they had discussed Lori's potential move and she had told her to come to Scotland.

Otherwise, she wasn't feeling the usual warmth from the friend she had come to rely on over the years, and she was desperate to talk to her properly. She wanted advice and reassurance. She wanted her best friend, not Detective Roberts.

There was something niggling at the back of her mind, but Lori gave her the benefit of the doubt that her distance was just her way of trying to stay focused and cope with the emotion of the situation, given her professional involvement with the case. She wasn't very familiar with 'work' Stella so maybe this was how she operated.

She tapped off a text to Jess to let her know she had arrived at the airport. Despite the circumstances and the potential that Alex wouldn't have her, now she was free from work and on her way, she was excited with the anticipation of seeing her.

She pushed the darkness that surrounded them to the back of her mind and allowed herself some time to think again of their night together, of the weekends they'd shared and what Alex had come to mean to her. This was her go to when she was ready to give up.

The depth of feeling frightened her. After just over a month and only one night together, she couldn't comprehend the monopoly Alex had over her thoughts or the overwhelming sense of loss she felt not having her near.

Was it obsession? Infatuation? Could she so easily dismiss seven years with Andrew and fall straight into the arms of not only someone new, but a woman? Would her family approve? Was she ready?

She'd tried contacting Scott but had only gotten through to a generic voicemail message and she worried it might not even be his current number. She needed to speak to him because when she wasn't thinking about Alex, she was imagining how everyone else would react to her and Alex being together.

Her and Alex.

She jumped as a flight attendant put a hand on her shoulder. She looked around the departure lounge and realised all other passengers had boarded unnoticed. The attendant smiled. "In your own little world there?"

Lori smiled but had no other response. Instead, she followed her to the counter and mutely watched as her boarding card was scanned, and she was free to head to the aircraft. The wind whipped across her face and she tilted her head to the clouds, closing her eyes and allowing her hair to tickle her face as she queued to board the plane. She could smell the fuel in every gust and the hum of engines near and far seemed to vibrate through her, quickening her heart rate with each step she climbed towards the cabin.

She opened her eyes and glanced across the greenery between runways. She watched a wild rabbit join a mate, seemingly oblivious to the industrial roar around them as they munched on grass and played.

As she settled into her window seat, she looked for the rabbits again but the wing cut across her view. She studied each panel and screw, wondering at the flimsiness of a machine about to lift them thousands of feet into the air.

She sat back and buckled up. "Okay, that's how you end up panicking."

The man next to her glanced up from his crossword puzzle. "You okay, love?"

She nodded but was lying, and not because of the wonder of physics. Did she really believe there was a future for her and Alex? Did Alex even feel the same? She had pushed her away when life had turned ugly. Hiding out in the countryside and reverting to a version of herself that Jess had thought was consigned to the past. Lori couldn't blame her for that and was doing her best to understand why, to put herself in Alex's position, no matter how impossible that was.

Did Alex not think enough of her to trust and accept her help and support when she needed it most, when Lori was so obviously offering it? Surely if they were to have a future together that was where it started. It wasn't all about chemistry and attraction. She wanted more. Needed more. And they both deserved more. Did Alex still want that? Would she let her in...not just in the door, but into her heart? There were four hundred miles between her and answers.

Her feet tingled with vibrations as the engine gathered momentum and the pilot pulled up the nose. Lori blew out a breath and looked down past the wing, as the patchwork greenery of England was enveloped in cloud.

CHAPTER 43

Stella slid her chair back, stood, and paced the length of the room again. The last of the coffee was long cold and her glasses weighed heavily on the bridge of her nose. They were no longer helping her to focus on the numerous monitors before her.

She pushed them up on her head and massaged between her eyes, then dropped back into the chair and offered up a silent prayer that something on Sean Murray would materialise soon.

The door opened, making her jump. Hannah Wallace, appeared in the gap. "Stella, sorry, Detective Roberts."

Stella waved her off. "After the hours we've spent in here together, Stella's fine when it's just us. What's up?"

Hannah grew serious. "We have a reported robbery at a farm in the Borders. There's reason to believe it's Sean Murray."

On her feet again, adrenaline kicked her brain back in to action. "Why? Was there a sighting? Has he hurt someone else?" She ushered Hannah into the room.

"No, thankfully the owners were away at a wedding when then think it happened so no one interrupted him. They only discovered the robbery this afternoon when the wife went to take her car out of the barn and it was gone. She says she hadn't used it since last weekend."

"He stole a car? That's brilliant news. I'm assuming a call's already gone out with a description?" She was pacing again, thinking through the next move.

"Aye, finding the vehicle has been made a priority but that's not all he took."

Stella stopped pacing, bringing her attention back to her colleague. "Why do I not like the sound of where this is going?"

"The officers that attended the scene became suspicious and called it in when they realised nothing else valuable had been taken from the house. In fact, it looks as if he was after specific things."

Stella held out a hand impatiently. "And those things were?"

"It seems the only items missing are the old second hand car from the barn along with some tools from their workshop...and a shotgun."

"Shit." Stella pulled the glasses off her head and threw them on the desk.

Hannah nodded her agreement. "If it was him, at least we now know for sure he's armed. What his intentions are is another matter."

Stella sat and gestured for Hannah to do the same. "Okay, what's the property's proximity to Alex's farm?"

She watched as Hannah's brow furrowed. "Wait, you don't seriously think he'd go there?"

"Something isn't sitting right here, Hannah, and the fact that after more than two weeks on the run, he's now potentially still in Scotland worries me. I think that's exactly what he might do."

"Why? Returning to the scene seems like the best way to get caught. Why risk it?"

"I can't be sure, but from what we know about him, I think knowing Alex exists might seem like unfinished business.

Those appeals she did, for witnesses, were everywhere. I've been wondering from the start if Beth was his only victim so I did some digging. I thought some flags might rise around the east coast near his home town, but there was nothing to suggest a link with other unsolved murders."

"You think he got a taste for it after Beth?"

"I don't think he went to the farm intent on killing anyone, but the manner in which Beth died doesn't suggest someone who went at her only because he feared for his own life or getting caught. If he'd stabbed her once and ran, I might have assumed that. Put it down to him reverting to survival mode, like an animal cornered. But he stabbed her nine times, Hannah. Nine." She emphasised the word and Hannah winced. "That's suggests fury, he relished it, but I think it was also an opportunity he'd been waiting for and he took it. It was overkill."

She watched as Hannah's head bowed, no doubt at the imagery, remembering the crime scene photos they'd pored over earlier that week. She scrubbed her hands over her face as Stella had done so many times herself. It wouldn't remove the visions that she knew would be forever ingrained in her memory. Stella knew that from her own bitter experience.

"I still don't understand why he might go back to the farm? To relive it through Alex? Or get some sick kick by returning to the scene?" Hannah picked up a pen and scribbled notes Stella couldn't decipher upside down, her handwriting lopsided in the way that most lefties wrote, she used some kind of shorthand that was obviously her own.

"Well, I didn't stop at the east coast. When I heard his ex-wife lived in the Bristol area and I heard John Murray talking about Sean taking trips, I got in touch the detectives down south. They have at least five unsolved murder cases in the past eight years that fit a similar MO. Young women, all with few or no family ties, known prostitutes and drug users, with a variety of charges on their records; solicitation, petty theft, and possession. All of them last seen around the city in areas known for nefarious activity but no witnesses to a car or person with them. Unfortunately, where these women are concerned, if there's no one pushing for justice, other cases end up taking priority when the trail runs cold."

"So because no one gives a shit about them, neither should we?" Hannah shook her head. "I hate that." She was circling her pen around and around, the black spot on the page getting darker until the paper ripped and she threw the pen down. Stella felt her frustration, watched her foot tap with impatience.

"I know. It's cruel but reality. One detective I spoke to is convinced it's the same killer in each case and also thinks he can link at least two others to the same person. They were women picked up in bars, with husbands or boyfriends, but the method was the same. There's been a lot more press and resources put into those cases, but he says, although they recovered DNA in both, which matched to confirm the same killer, they didn't get any hits on the database. And the other victims, given their line of work had numerous profiles left on them and the money wasn't spent to compare them all with these two other cases. No one wants to believe their beautiful, loving wives and girlfriends could be in the same category as runaways, addicts, and prostitutes. Not even the police."

"It makes me sick." Hannah stood. It was her turn to pace. "Are there any witnesses in those cases?"

Stella flicked through a thin file containing the bullet points that her counterpart had e-mailed. "There's nothing concrete. Both women were out with friends, were seen talking to a male but alcohol always seems to be involved, as well as it being late, in a dark bar or club. The description given by friends is of a generic white male, medium height, heavy build, dark hair, nothing distinguishable."

"So what links them? Do you really think they could all be Sean Murray?"

"It's a theory and it's loose right now. All the women were bound with duct tape to their wrists and ankles. All were stripped from the bottom down, raped, most likely strangled into unconsciousness before bleeding out from multiple stab wounds to the torso. All were wrapped in plastic and dumped in woodland or fields at various locations that have no pattern. No attempt was made to hide the bodies, just enough time to dump and run."

"Wow, this is crazy. How do you go from armed robbery to a serial killer? Like, I get shooting someone if things get sticky and you panic, but the way he went for Beth, I understand what you're saying. You think he always had it in him?"

"I do. I think it started in the military, maybe with the rape accusation. I think that chip on his shoulder has fully formed into rock inside. And don't forget there's the mother who left him. I think each one is revenge, for his ruined career, his marriage failing, the loss of his sons. Each woman represents another who has wronged him."

"So Alex going on TV to appeal for witnesses, for help, that's just one more person out to ruin his life?"

"Exactly. I think he's furious right now that he's been caught. He thought he was smarter than all the women he murdered, he was untouchable. And now there's this other woman on the TV, describing him and what he did, telling the nation he's evil. In his mind I bet he thinks he's done nothing wrong. That they all deserved it."

Hannah blew out a breath. "Shit. It sounds crazy, but you're the detective. I'm buying it and I think we need Alex to believe it as well." She sat in front of a computer and pulled up a map. "Both farms are south of Glasgow, it's got to be less than forty miles between the two I'd say. Do you think he's that stupid to rob a farm so close to the original crime scene?"

"No, I certainly don't think he's stupid. I think he's desperate and took an opportunity. He's a born hunter and a trained soldier, used to far worse conditions than the Scottish countryside. I wouldn't be surprised if he's been on foot up to this point, camping out in the hills, which is why it's taken him two weeks to get this far. I think he couldn't resist when he came across the empty farm, it was just the bit of luck he needed."

Hannah echoed her earlier expletive, "Shit."

"That sums it up perfectly."

Hannah stood again, ready for action. "I found that old man and made him a promise. No matter his involvement, I told him I would help Beth. If catching her killer is how I do that, then I'm ready for it. Tell me what you need from me?"

Stella smiled, silently thanking Tim for his choice of officer to help her. The fact it was his niece no doubt played a part in his decision. "Right, I need the past seven days of CCTV footage from every petrol station within a fifty-mile radius of Alex's farm. We need to confirm Murray took the car and there's a good chance he will have needed petrol at some point. Prioritise those on routes between where the robbery took place and Alex's farm."

Hannah threw her a careless salute. Stella appreciated her attempt to relieve some of the tension. "Anything else I can do, Detective?"

Stella laughed at the gesture. "Yes. Prepare yourself for many more hours of drinking bad coffee, stuck in this tiny room with me."

Hannah winked and started toward the door. "Ah, there're worse ways to spend an evening, I'm sure, and, if you're lucky, I'll even treat you to a fancy coffee."

She was gone before Stella realised she'd been flirting. Flattered and amused, she pulled her phone from the depths of her bag where she'd put it so she didn't have to see Scott's name flash up every hour when he tried to call.

Debating whether to worry Lori and Alex just yet, she flicked through to Jess's number. She didn't want to panic her before they'd confirmed it was Murray so, instead of calling, she tapped off a vague text.

> Possible break, we may have an ID on the car he's driving. Hope Lori gets there okay. Keep them safe and I'll keep you up to date. S x

> Great news. Fingers crossed this nightmare ends soon. Picking Lori up in a couple of hours, I'll let you know when I've dropped her off. Oh, and of course I will. My part is easy. Hope you've had some rest?

> Thanks Jess. Still stuck in the AV room. The coffee is terrible but the company is good, a pretty, young officer who I think has taken a liking to me. She's all blonde hair, blue eyes, and bouncing with enthusiasm. Remind me to introduce you.

> Ha! I knew I liked you! Behind every cloud...x

Stella couldn't help but laugh. Jess had become her messenger and friend over the past two weeks, relaying information to Alex when she failed to answer her phone. She pulled up her call log. Twelve missed calls from Scott. Sighing she threw the phone back in her bag.

He could wait.

A few hours later, Lori and Jess bumped along the gravel track to the farm. Lori couldn't be sure whether it was nerves or Jess's driving making her stomach lurch.

She reached into the foot well for the phone in her bag, bashing her head on the dashboard as a particularly big pothole got the better of the tiny car.

"Ouch, merda. Jess."

"Sorry. I'm just excited to get you there."

Lori rubbed the top of her head. "Yeah well, in one piece would be good."

Jess eased off the accelerator. "You know, I think the only reason she doesn't get this track paved properly is because she gets sadistic pleasure in watching me bounce along it."

Rummaging in the dark foot well to gather the contents of her bag, Lori had to laugh despite the sore head, and felt some of the tension in her stomach dissipate with the banter. "More like she's scared at just how fast you would drive given a smooth run."

Jess laughed with her. "You're probably right. Oh, and by the way, it's rude to call people names in a language they don't understand."

Lori sat up again having retrieved everything, reassuringly patting Jess's knee. "As tempted as I was, don't worry I didn't call you anything. I just know the word for 'shit' in about ten different languages. I'll teach you for your travels if you like?"

Jess looked at her wide eyed. "Holy crap, I hadn't even thought of that! You are totally my new best friend. If Alex sends you away, screw her, you're coming home with me. In fact, I'm turning the car round right now." She laughed, and Lori knew alarm was plastered all over her face. "Clearly I'm kidding. Like I'd get in the way of you two lovebirds."

"Hey, let's not count on anything just yet. I may still get a door slammed in my face for showing up like this."

Jess hit the brakes, and they skidded to a stop outside the farmhouse. It stood dark all around except for a lone bulb over the side door.

They both took a deep breath at the same time.

Jess reached across the console, took Lori's hand, and squeezed it tight. "She might not know it, but she needs you. You're the ray of sunshine she didn't have in the past, and I know you can help bring her out of this."

Lori squeezed back. Not trusting her voice, she simply nodded and climbed out of the car.

CHAPTER 44

The darkness surrounding Sean Murray was suddenly cut through by the headlights of a car turning onto the track. Even before he saw the car up close, he knew who it was by the way the lights jumped up and down as it hit every pothole speeding toward the farm.

He sat tucked behind some hedgerow, his boxy, dark car was invisible from the road. He ducked down in the driver's seat, and risked only a brief glimpse from under his hat to confirm it was the pretty blonde girl again.

Satisfied he was right and she was alone, he glanced at the dashboard clock and waited for the car lights to go out at the end of the track. Now it was a waiting game. The waiting didn't faze him; the army had taught him well. The situation was his to control so long as he was patient and kept his temper in check. Besides the anticipation was all part of it. It brought him to life and heightened every sense.

He'd been watching the farm for nearly a week, trying to discern a pattern to visits from the blonde and find out whether there was a boyfriend or other family members to worry about. So far, she was the only regular visitor, and he wondered if she was a girlfriend. The thought was a pleasing addition to his fantasy. Otherwise, it seemed the last of the Ryans was a bit of a recluse, and he'd only seen her stray from the house to go to the barn to feed the animals.

As always while he waited, he allowed his mind to go back to that night. The anger he had felt when that silly little bitch had pulled the gun on them was the same as the night his wife had left him. That whore had thought she could walk away from him. Take their sons and go live with her piece of shit on the side without any consequences. Beth thought she could get the better of him, that a gun could stop him.

He slouched further in the seat, allowing his eyes to close for a few minutes. The blonde would be a while and it was silent. He'd hear her coming. He remembered how innocent Beth had looked, a child caught up in something she wasn't ready for. He saw the fear on her face and, despite the gun, the tremble of her shoulders. The rest of the room had faded until it was only the two of them. When the gun had turned his way, he hadn't felt fear, but excitement. He saw the face of every woman who had tried to bring him down in hers.

Reaching into his trousers, he pictured the sweat on her brow as it trickled into her hair line. The waft of strawberries was there with him in the car. As he straddled her lifeless body, even the blood couldn't overpower it. He inhaled deeply and the same rush he felt the moment he made his move washed over him again.

This close to the farm, his faded memories had reignited, become vivid again. Every ounce of anger had poured out of him with the first plunge of his knife into her chest. It was instantly addictive and he plunged again. He could hear Beth's screams. He could taste her blood in his mouth and feel it slipping through his fingers like silk, her wide eyes looking past him, unseeing, her light extinguished. He could feel the pressure building in his trousers as he remembered each strike, until the sound of his blade cutting through flesh one last time made him jerk with satisfaction.

She'd thought she could get the better of him. She was wrong.

She was the first, but not the last. A sweet cherry that topped a pile of nobodies, there had never been anyone like her since. He had quickly realised the exhilaration of his first time couldn't be replicated, but it didn't stop him trying.

He rested his head back, pulled a handkerchief from a pocket, and cleaned himself up. He opened a window and lit the rag, watched it twist and turn as it burnt, before letting it flutter to the ground in burning wisps of ash.

He reconciled with himself, not for the first time, that she had deserved it. She had left him no choice once she had pointed the gun at his old man.

And now his face was the most famous in Britain, and he knew it wouldn't be long before his time was up. He'd seen Alex on the cover of a newspaper, and the resemblance to Beth had caught him by surprise. He knew she was too good an opportunity to miss. He thought about his ex-wife. His only regret was that she would probably never experience the consequences of what she had put him through, but Alex would.

He was still in control, after all.

He could still choose his ending.

Chapter 45

Alex heard the engine before the headlights flashed across the front windows of the music room. She sighed when she recognised the sound of Jess's tiny car and braced herself for another lecture.

She padded through to the kitchen in the dark, dumped her whisky in the sink, and poured some water in the glass. Knowing her friend would let herself in, she thought it best not to give her any ammunition. *It's not as if she doesn't have enough already.*

She was surprised to hear the murmur of voices as the side door opened. She crossed toward the hallway as the light flicked on, and Jess and Lori were illuminated in the doorway.

Even the constant drip feed of alcohol hadn't helped to put Lori out of her mind, and Alex had come to realise that she was the only thing different in her life from eight years ago. When her nightmares put Alex in Beth's place that night or conjured revenge plots against the Murrays, she was able to bring herself down with thoughts of Lori.

At first, she had tried not to dwell on the night they'd spent together. The feelings she had brought out were overwhelming on top of everything else. She couldn't give Lori her full attention, the time, and energy she needed, that she deserved. She'd resigned herself to losing Lori, along with everyone else she loved.

But over the past couple of nights, Stella's words had cut through the fog and she'd allowed herself to imagine the simple pleasure of sleeping on her shoulder at the bothy or feel the tingle again like when Lori had kissed her dimple that first time. Her mind had wandered back to their night in London, and she could almost feel Lori's body pressed tight against her own. She relived that night over and over when sleep wouldn't take her, and wished she was back there. The memories brought comfort. Helped her take a breath and cleansed her mind of evil, if only for a few seconds.

She knew she'd pushed Lori away. Away from the ugliness of her past and the person she was turning back into. She hadn't asked to be saddled with so much hatred and despair. How could Lori ever love someone so damaged? One night together, no matter how special, did not obligate her to have to deal with Alex's never ending nightmare.

She'd thought about what they could have had and what she had hoped for them whilst lying in Lori's arms, feeling her warm breath on her neck. Her stomach churning and her chest tightening at the loss.

She hadn't slept again that night and had instead found herself barefoot on the cold tile floor of the kitchen, sipping water and looking out at the night sky, with Frank laying at her feet. That and concentrating on the moon helped to ease her away from an impending panic attack. She'd imagined Lori standing behind her, reassuring arms wrapped around her waist...

Alex blinked.

Lori stood in front of her. Real and solid. Right here. Right now. Eyes glassy with tears, they did their sparkly thing as she chewed her lip in nervousness.

The barriers Alex had tried to erect dissolved in a moment. None of the reasons not to see Lori again mattered. How could she have been so stupid to think ignoring her was the right thing to do? She didn't say a word, just moved into the arms that Lori held open. Relief rushed through her as she breathed the familiar honey scent and felt the warmth of her body as it enveloped her.

"I'm sorry, Lori. I'm so sorry," she repeated into her shoulder before the tears took over and her body shook with sorrow.

Lori held on tight, planting soft kisses to the top of her head.

"Shh, sweetheart, it's okay. I've got you now."

Alex glimpsed Jess smiling their way and she returned it, mouthing a thank you before wrapping her arms tighter around Lori. Even as Jess blew her a kiss and headed for the door, she didn't let go.

CHAPTER 46

It was close to midnight, but no matter how tired she felt, the furthest thing from Stella's mind was her cosy hotel bed. She tried Jess again and cursed when it went straight to voicemail. She knew she was probably still driving, but her patience was wearing.

She tapped off a text.

How did it go? Are you all still at the farm?

When her phone beeped almost immediately, her fingers fumbled putting in the pin, she got it wrong twice before taking a breath to calm down and entered it again with less urgency.

Jess had arrived home.

Stella immediately rang her number again, clicking a pen top while waiting for Jess to pick up.

"Jeezo, a little impatient?" she answered. "I was going to call once I'd had a chance to pee. I just bloody fell over trying to catch your call."

"You fell over, how on earth—"

"My room is a frigging mess. Listen, you can't say anything to Alex but before all this happened, I'd finally booked my trip away. I've got the next year as sabbatical from work and I'm due to leave in a few weeks. Hence the mess, I'm a terrible packer."

"You're leaving?" Stella was surprised. From what Lori had said, Alex and Jess were inseparable and Jess wasn't the kind of person to leave her friend alone in a crisis.

"Well, no, of course I'm not going to leave now. But when this is over, then yes, I'm out of here. I've waited so long for this trip."

"Of course, that came out wrong. I guess from what Lori said, it sounded as if you and Alex came as a pair."

"Yeah well, normally we do and I'm pretty sure I'm going to miss her terribly and be home within a few weeks, but I've got to at least try. She's my number one but, you know, she has Lori now. Once this bastard is in jail where he belongs, they can start to move on together and I'll be able to leave knowing she's being taken care of."

"I understand, Jess. I do. I take it things went well at the farm then?"

"Stella, you should have seen Alex's face when she saw us both. I didn't stick around but I'm not worried. Anyway, I didn't mean to side track you. What's up, Detective?"

"It's okay. I'm glad you're looking out for yourself too, Jess."

"Well, I'm not going to get excited just yet, unless you're calling to tell me you've got him?" There was hope in Jess's voice but Stella could tell she really wasn't expecting her answer to be yes.

She switched back into work mode, remembering why she had called. "We've got some information on Sean Murray's possible whereabouts and I wanted to speak to you first to see how things had gone with Lori and Alex."

"Christ, Stella, why didn't you shut me up about my stupid bloody travelling? What's going on? You sound worried."

"Did you notice any strange vehicles parked up around the farm, maybe off a lane or down a track?"

"No. Will you just tell me what the hell you know? Where is he?"

"Sorry. Okay. Right, I don't want to panic you, but we think Sean might have plans to go back to the farm. In fact, it's possible he's been watching it all this time and is in the area."

The line was quiet and she could only imagine the thoughts running through Jess's mind. "Stella, how do you know?"

"Well it's a theory at the moment, but, first off, a nearby farm was broken into and whoever did it only stole a car, some tools, and a gun."

"Shit."

"That's exactly what I said. Hannah and I have been scouring hours of CCTV footage from local petrol stations and supermarkets, and we might have a match. The guy seems to go out of his way to keep his back to the camera, but the car and the physical description matches even if we can't see his face. What sealed it for me was a statement from the garage attendant. He says he remembered the car because the driver left without paying but when he ran outside after him, he found cash left on the pump. He thought it was someone who didn't deal well with people."

"I don't understand."

Stella could hear the panic creeping in to Jess's voice.

"Why would he go back to the scene of the crime? Alex wasn't even there that night so it's not as if she could identify him."

Stella blew out an angry breath and threw a hand up in frustration. "Who fucking knows, Jess? My guess is he wants to be caught and plans on going down in a blaze of glory. He must have seen Alex on the news or in the papers."

The phone muffled a moment and she heard scuffling about. Jess came back on the line. "I'm on my way back out there. Have you called Alex or Lori? Have you warned them?"

"No, Jess, don't go. I tried them both already. Both rang out to voicemail."

"Shit."

"Don't panic. I know Lori has a tendency to turn hers on silent when she doesn't want to be disturbed. I bet she's done the same with Alex's to give them time to talk."

"There's a maniac out there."

"I know, but Lori definitely has other things on her mind right now. You saw her, Jess. Her priority is Alex."

"That doesn't make me feel any better, Stella."

"Well, this might. I'm heading out there now, I'll call again when I'm on the road. I could be wrong and I don't want them worrying unnecessarily. We don't have actual proof that's what he's planning, it's all circumstantial and conjecture. I couldn't even convince those that matter to get a local patrol car out to the farm—"

"Are you kidding me? Do you really expect me to just sit about and wait for another call like the one I got from Alex all those years ago?"

Stella closed her eyes. She couldn't even imagine a call like that from Lori. "No I don't, Jess. You're right. I'll be at the farm in around an hour or so, traffic should be fine this time of night getting out of Edinburgh."

Stella grabbed her keys and was on the move and from the sounds of it, so was Jess.

"I'm on my way. Just hurry. Okay?"

"Okay. Drive safe, Jess. Apparently you're a terrible driver."

"Yeah, yeah, I will. Oh and, Stella?"

"What?"

"Bring that hot, young officer with you."

Shaking her head at Jess's cheek despite the circumstances, she pocketed her phone and grabbed PC Wallace on her way out the door.

CHAPTER 47

Alex ran her hands back and forth under the hot water. She lifted a handful of bubbles and blew them Lori's way. "This was a good idea. Thanks."

Lori smiled down at her from the edge of the bath and wiped some bubbles from her cheek. She waved her phone in front of Alex. "I've put them both on silent. I don't know about you, but I need a night with you, and you alone. I hope that's okay?"

"That's more than okay with me."

"Good, and this," she pointed to the bath and continued, "is only phase one. Phase two involves a hot meal and a large glass of red wine."

"Wow, you're allowing wine? Don't tell Jess or she'll be packing you back off to London."

"Well, I figure if I have to deprive you I'm going to have to deprive myself, and I really need a glass of wine."

Alex chuckled and sank into the water up to her chin. "Jess's driving?"

Lori traced a finger through a puff of bubbles, her brow creasing. "More like worrying that you wouldn't want to see me. But yes, Jess's driving can't be ignored."

Alex couldn't take her eyes off her and Lori looked down to meet them. They glowed like hot coals in the candlelight, bright and filled with fresh tears. "I'm so sorry, Lori. I know I've treated you badly and I shouldn't have run out on you that weekend. In fact, I still don't understand why you even came after how I've been these past few weeks."

Lori crouched down on the floor beside her, reached into the water to find her hand, and linked their fingers. "I'll be honest. When you stopped replying to my texts, I almost gave up. I told myself it was only a one night stand, and you were back here with your real friends, and you didn't need me. That I was a mistake that you obviously regretted, and didn't want to have to deal with along with everything else."

The sorrow on Lori's face cut Alex to her core. That she'd made her feel so worthless and used was something she'd never forgive herself for. Because the opposite was true, that night had changed her life, and she knew now it was only for the better. Lori made it better. "You must know that's not true?"

Kissing the back of Alex's hand, Lori squeezed it tight in both of hers. "Of course I do. I've never felt anything like I did that night and I knew it couldn't be all one sided. Although the cold shoulder was hard to take, and did make it easier to believe it was a one-off, in my head I understand why you ran. I can't say I know what you're feeling, because I honestly don't think anyone can unless they've been in your shoes. But I do know how overwhelming it must be for you. But I won't lie to you, Alex, running the way you did made me feel like shit."

Alex cringed. "I don't think I can say sorry enough times for making you feel that way, Lori. But I truly am. I wasn't seeing clearly, and it never crossed my mind that my actions were reducing our night to something so sordid. In my mind, it was anything but, it was special, and you're special. You must know that?"

"I know, but at the time—"

Alex arched an eyebrow. "Confusing, eh?"

Lori smiled at her. "I don't want to dwell on all that. I'm here now, we're together, and I'm so happy to see you. But yes, confusing, as well as a million other jumbled feelings."

"Want to talk about it?"

She watched as Lori puffed out her cheeks before blowing out a slow breath. Alex wasn't sure if she wanted to hear what was coming.

"I felt as if...oh, I don't know, Alex. I guess I felt as if this wasn't meant to happen to me. There was suddenly this completely different story playing out in my head of what my future might be and it was so different. It was overwhelming."

Now it was Alex's turn to be confused. "Fancy explaining that one to me?"

Lori sighed. She stared at the flame of a candle as she seemed to look for the right words. "No, c'mon, let's just enjoy this right now. We can talk later. I'm meant to be the one looking after and listening to you." She smiled down again at Alex. "How about I go get you that wine?"

She made to get up, but Alex kept hold of her hand and pulled her back. She sat up again in the bath and reached out to tuck a lock of hair behind Lori's ear. "Lori, I'm fine. It's just you and me in the world right now. Tell me."

Lori sat again, drawing circles in the water. "I suppose before things went sour with Andrew, I used to look at him and see my future, see my life mapped out just like everyone else's. I thought eventually I'd be ready to give up my independence for something I was always told would be better. I saw a husband, and a house, and a couple of kids. There were pets and school runs, arguments about where to spend Christmas. I was going to be the model parent and wife. I would be willing to sacrifice weekends in the mountains and happily relinquish ever being spontaneous again because all those other things would fulfil me. I felt secure in those thoughts because I was going to have the regular traditional family I didn't have as a child." She looked down at their linked fingers. "I guess what I'm saying is, the thought of letting all that go was daunting, in my future you weren't meant to happen. And I certainly didn't see you coming."

Alex let go of her hand and cupped both of Lori's cheeks with soapy hands, forcing their eyes to meet. "But don't you see, Lori, that you can still have all that. I mean, obviously not the husband part." She chuckled. "Tell me what's stopping us from having a future like that? What you've just described is all I've ever wanted since I lost my own family, even if I couldn't admit it to myself. The only difference is I saw it with a woman."

She watched Lori's eyes fill with tears. "I know that now. Now I'm here and I'm with you. But I was scared, Alex. Although now I feel ridiculous seeing how brave you are about everything that's happened."

"Me? Brave? Are you kidding me, Lori? All I've done is hide out. You just crossed the country for someone who's done nothing but push you away. You said it yourself that you were scared. But you still came. You're the one who hasn't given up, so compared to you, I'm a coward."

"But—"

"I'm not finished." She ran her fingers through Lori's hair, caressed her neck, and pulled her face closer. "I have spent the last eight years freefalling through my life with nothing solid to grab onto. All this time, I've pretended to be part of the real world by filling my house with friends and animals in the hope that one day the numbness would pass. But at the end of the day, they go home and I'm still alone. I'm left with the same anger and pain to keep me company, along with the question that still haunts me every day. Why my family?"

Alex stroked her hair as Lori choked back a sob. She needed her to realise how important she was, because in that moment, Alex was finally realising it too. It really was only the two of them in the world, and, suddenly, the only thing that mattered was Lori being there with her, and them being together. She wasn't beaten yet. He hadn't won. Because sat before her was someone that still wanted to be in her life, that made her realise life still would go on, and she could be happy living it.

"The darkness always came back, Lori. The void and the self-doubt and the fear that having everyone I cared about stolen from me had created."

She gently wiped the tears from Lori's cheeks and brushed their lips together, closing her eyes at the tenderness she felt in the kiss, sinking into it like the hot bath.

"Wow," Lori breathed into her mouth. Her own eyes still closed.

"Wow, back," Alex whispered, smiling as she pulled away. She kept her hands where they were and stroked her thumbs across Lori's cheeks, her eyelids, her lips. "Losing your mum at five years old wasn't meant to happen to you, Lori. Being isolated and abandoned by your dad wasn't meant to happen either. Both were terrible things that I'm so sorry you had to go through. But you were brave and came out stronger." She smiled again. "You say this wasn't meant to happen but I'm inclined to disagree. I just need you to keep being brave and trust me that we can get through this. I need you to put your faith in us. Do you know why?"

"Why?" Lori sniffed, the tears falling again.

"Because I love you," Alex whispered through her own tears. "And I believe you were meant to happen to me."

Chapter 48

Sean had watched the blonde drive away, singing as she went, clearly oblivious to his presence. Over an hour went by as various lights flicked on and off throughout the house until only a faint glow came from one he guessed was her bedroom. He knew the house. Knew that end was the one with the bedrooms they'd checked through his first time there.

It was after 1am. Surely too late for any more guests to show up.

He unzipped the sports bag in the boot of the car he'd stolen, checked his supplies again, laid the shotgun inside, and zipped it closed as far as it would go.

The hinge of the boot groaned as he slowly lowered it, letting it drop the last inch so the latch caught and locked. Not that it mattered if it locked. There was nothing of his worth stealing and he wouldn't be back. He hoisted the bag over his shoulder, drew the knife from his belt, and set off on the familiar track. He never dreamed he would be back where it all began, about to relive his first kill through her sister.

Keeping his pace and breathing steady, he stopped every few metres and listened. He knew there was a dog on the farm and couldn't be sure it would be locked inside the house.

He reached the shadows of the barn and wondered if the rabbit was still on the back door step. He didn't think it would be that easy this time.

He took a breath, ready to sprint across to the side porch but a familiar clunking sound in that direction stopped him.

The door had a dog flap. He heard the bark before he saw the blur of brown and white running in his direction. With his back to the barn, he braced himself, and when the dog lunged so did he. The blade stiffened in his hand on impact, but he held fast, holding on as the weight pulled him down. It was over in a moment.

The dog fell with a yelp at his feet. He slowly withdrew the knife from its torso, wiping the blood on the thigh of his combats. A gentle cry came from the back of the dog's throat before its eyes closed, and he began whining quietly through ragged breathing. He took no pleasure in killing the dog. It was insignificant, a mere obstacle to overcome. He listened. It was just like that night. Water trickled in the burn and owls called across the fields.

Goose bumps rose on his arms, but not from the cold. There was a mild breeze that carried the scent of damp hay, but otherwise the night was still. He waited a moment, unsure if there was anything or anyone else out there. Hearing nothing more than the high pitch of a bat, he continued inching along the edge of the barn. The dog wouldn't last long and certainly wouldn't be barking anymore.

A light flicked on to the left of the courtyard.

A woman's face appeared in the window, looking out into the darkness. He was sure she couldn't see him, but he kept his eyes on the window as he felt along the barn wall until he reached a small door. Holding his breath, he slid the bolt across, the hinges whined, high pitched like the dog, as he pushed the door open. He paused, had she heard? Keeping still, he let the breath out slowly, and, satisfied he had gone unseen, slipped inside the barn.

While he peered through a small crack, he heard a final moan and the dog begin to pant heavily. The woman took one more look around before pulling the curtains closed.

He was angry at himself. Clenching and unclenching his jaw, he swallowed back the bitter bile in his throat. The dog he had prepared for, but the woman he saw wasn't Alex Ryan and he didn't understand how she had got there undetected. Fuck. He allowed himself a moment to pace the width of the barn, spitting out the foul taste in his mouth. The bile had risen again with the fear of being prematurely caught. He would just have to make her part of the plan. He was a soldier; had fought in wars and learned a mission rarely went to plan, but he was smart enough to make it work.

He stopped, pulled a torch from his pocket, and flicked the narrow beam around the barn. A pen in the corner housed what looked like a goat, laying down asleep amongst hay. Chickens clucked quietly in their house, the flap that released them outside was closed so he knew no one had reason to come out to the barn.

He noticed a stack of tables and chairs in a corner and he lifted two chairs into the middle of the room, along with a table for the tools in his bag. He unloaded them, leaving the shotgun on the table for later. Instead, he chose to tuck a handgun he'd had since his army days into his waistband, along with the knife that never left the sheath on his belt.

He flicked off the torch and a woman's voice stopped him in his tracks with one hand on the barn door handle.

"Frank," she shouted. "Where are you, boy?"

He peered through the crack in the door again as the dark haired woman he'd seen in the window headed towards the barn.

"C'mon, Frank? The boss lady left your flap unlocked, and you have permission to stay in the house tonight, so don't blow it. Are you out here tormenting, Pedro?"

He watched her suddenly sprint in the direction of the dog's now motionless body, calling his name again before letting out a cry, no doubt when she noticed the blood.

"Oh shit, Frank, what happened boy? Who did this to you?" He watched her look around frantically while pressing her hands against the dogs gaping wound. She pulled off her hooded sweater, and wrapped it carefully around the dog before interlocking the sleeves and giving them a yank to tighten against the wound. The dog yelped, and Sean saw her wince with it. He couldn't believe the damn dog was still alive.

She had her back to the barn door, and he heard her call out to Alex only once before he watched her body stiffen and still.

Too late.

He clamped one hand hard over her mouth while he put the handgun to her head with the other.

"I dare you to fucking try something," he spat the words out low and close to her ear. He pulled her to her feet, and she didn't struggle. He felt the power course through him, just like that night. He felt invincible. He'd never done two in one night before.

He kept her mouth clamped shut by pressing the gun under her chin as he dragged her back through the barn door. He threw her to the floor in the direction of the chairs and aimed the gun at her head. "Sit down," he growled. He kept the weapon trained on her as she did as he asked and made his way to the roll of tape on the table. "You and I need to talk."

CHAPTER 49

Alex climbed wearily into bed. Her head snapped up at a shout from outside. Was Lori still out looking for Frank? She crossed to the window and peered around the courtyard; no sign of either of them.

She opened the window and listened for Lori calling out again. It was quiet. The hairs on her neck bristled. It was too quiet.

"Lori?" She called from the end of the corridor, but knew she wouldn't get an answer. "Frank?" She waited another moment, but he didn't appear either.

At the window again, the darkness outside enveloped her, closed in and tightened its grip, as her stomach clenched with it. She forced her eyes to focus on the yard, but all she could see were shadows. She listened but the silence was broken only by her shallow breaths. She remembered the way her mum had described the quiet after the men had left, as her husband and daughter lay lifeless before her. How she had frozen, willing herself to wake up from what had to be a terrible nightmare.

Swallowing back the panic Alex forced her mind to concentrate. The fear of loss was creeping in again. Would it always feel like this? Every time Lori left the house or wasn't with her. Would the fear ever leave her?

She shook herself. Lori had probably gone chasing after Frank, who, no doubt, had picked up the scent of a fox or a badger.

The lie calmed her momentarily. Straining to distinguish the shadows she knew from the ones she didn't, her skin pricked again and the adrenaline kicked in. It felt wrong and she had to trust that feeling. It wasn't paranoia.

Deep down, Alex had always feared that whoever killed her family would one day return. So she had prepared. She had trained. She had learned. To fight, to shoot, to hunt. She'd prepared herself for the day she'd meet Beth's murderer. Would she kill or die? She didn't know. In her deepest, darkest moments, she wondered if she'd be strong enough to pull the trigger—as Beth had—knowing what had befallen her sister in those fatal seconds that followed. Would she be able to look a man in the eye and end his life? A man she knew to be a killer...could she stand as judge, jury, and executioner? She didn't know. She'd hoped she'd never have to know. But one thing Alex did know for sure, she wouldn't go down without a fight.

She pulled on jeans and a jumper, left the bedroom light on, and made her way along to the music room. Keeping low away from the windows, she left the other lights off.

Lori definitely wasn't in the house.

She caught Beth's face in the dim moonlight while she pressed lightly on a narrow panel in the cabinet below. After pulling off a key taped to the back of the picture, she opened the metal gun case, and withdrew the handgun hidden there. She checked it over quickly before loading it and pocketing an extra clip.

She took off her jumper, opened another one of the cabinet cupboards, and removed the bulletproof vest a pal she'd made on the force during the initial investigation had helped her get hold of. He'd also trained her to use her gun properly. She quickly donned the vest and pulled her jumper back into place before she added a knife to an ankle holder, secured it in place, and pulled on the trainers she'd grabbed from the hallway.

For months after her mum's suicide, Jess had come to stay with her, but eventually she'd had to return to university leaving Alex feeling alone and vulnerable. She'd barely slept and jumped at every bump in the night. Every shadow in the corner was the man returned to murder her like the rest of her family. At her lowest points, she thought it would be a welcome relief. Some nights she wished for it, to be put out of her misery. To be gone with them rather than being left alone with the guilt and questions.

She knew she had to push those thoughts from her mind. She had someone to live for again. She wanted the life Lori had painted. This was the fight she'd been waiting for and, more than ever before, it was one she wanted to win.

She'd bought the gun first, and at the time it had made sense to hide the weapon in the room she found herself sleeping in most nights. The music room. Later she added the vest after doing her first bit of work with the police and reconnecting with one of the detectives, Simon, assigned to her family's case. The knife came last, and with great reluctance. Alex didn't think for a second she'd ever be able to use it but apparently you can never be too prepared. As her fear gained momentum and the adrenaline spiked in her bloodstream again, she had to admit that she was grateful of any advantage she might gain right now. She wiggled her foot and felt the strap of the ankle holster scrape against her skin. She'd have to remember to thank him the next time she saw him. If she saw him again. *Stop that. That*

*kind of thinking will only ever get you into trouble. Remember
what the big ape taught you. APE. Assess, plan, execute. You
can do this, Ryan, you're ready, so get the fuck out there.*

She allowed one last glance at Beth's face and was
resolute. If he had finally come for her then she was all he
was getting. Lori would survive this. That bastard was not
getting anyone else that she loved. Not today.

She crept through the hall to the back door and began to
inch it open when headlights bobbed in the distance. "Shit."
She quickly realised it was Jess and rushed back towards
the kitchen where she'd left her mobile phone. Fumbling
with it and the gun still in one hand she hit the call button.
"C'mon, Jess. Pick up the phone."

The phone rang out to voicemail. "Fuck." She dialled
again, watching over the kitchen countertop as the car sped
nearer. It rang out again and she threw the phone in the
sink before grabbing it back. "I'm God damned brain dead,"
she whispered as she dialled nine-nine-nine. In her urgency
to help Lori, common sense had left her.

The panic threatened to take over as she rushed out her
name, address, and reason for calling to the operator as
Jess's headlights got brighter. She gave Stella's name and
heard the operator tell her to "stay inside the house and
lock the doors. Do not under any circumstances approach
the suspect."

Not a chance.

"That's not happening. I suggest you stay on the line."
She slipped the phone in her back pocket and headed for
the door.

Stella hit speaker when Jess's number flashed up on her phone. "Where are you?"

"I've just pulled up in the courtyard. It seems quiet and I can see Alex's bedroom light is on."

Stella breathed a small sigh of relief, and felt Hannah relax next to her. "Did you notice any cars along the lane, anything parked up or unusual?"

"No, nothing at all. Hang on, my phone is beeping with another call."

Stella waited for Jess to come back. She didn't slow her speed, she needed to reach the farm and see for herself that everything was fine. The line clicked and Jess came back.

"Stella there's two missed calls from Alex on my phone. Both were made just a minute or so ago."

"No message?"

"No. And now I'm wondering why she hasn't come out to meet me. There's no way she wouldn't have heard me arrive."

Stella's skin prickled. "Fuck. Fuck. Fuck." She cussed to the rhythm of the pounding in her heart. "Can you see anything, Jess? Any sign of someone else in the house?"

Jess's voice came through again in a whisper. "I can't see anything but shadows. No sign of either of them or Frank. How far away are you?"

Stella felt the blood rush from her face to her heart as her body went cold. "About twenty minutes. Listen, Jess, you need to get out of there."

"Stella, I think he's here. I don't know where, and I don't know if he's tried anything, but I feel it. There's something wrong."

"Shit. Jess, start the car and go. Wait for us somewhere nearby but get out of there."

A low laugh came through the speaker. "If you knew me you would know I'm not going anywhere. Not while Alex is still here and in danger."

"Jess, you don't know what you're getting into. Just wait a little longer for us. Don't do anything stupid."

"I'm sorry, but I can't leave her. She needs me. Please. Just hurry."

"Jess!" Stella shouted for her to listen, but she had hung up. She pressed her foot harder on the accelerator. "Hannah, if we don't make it there in time..."

"Stop it. We'll make it."

Stella glanced her way and saw her determination. She gripped the wheel, pulling off the motorway into the darkness of the country roads, repeating Hannah's words. "We'll make it."

CHAPTER 50

The only sound he could hear, beyond his own steady breathing, was the dark-haired girl, whimpering through her gag.

Sean watched as the blonde talked on her phone, still in the car. She seemed oblivious. "Fucking idiot. Of all the nights I could have picked, it's the one she decides to come back." Berating himself, he paced. The adrenaline was flowing. He needed to reassess; he could handle this.

He stopped, shook his head, and glanced at the girl tied ten paces from him. "See? See what you whores do to me? I'm here blaming myself again when it's your fault you're tied to that chair. My plan was perfect. And now it's her turn to fucking try to ruin it." He peered through the gap in the door towards the house. He could see the bedroom light still on, but no movement. The rest of the house seemed still. It'd been long enough that he was sure Alex Ryan knew something was wrong. What he hadn't predicted in all his fantasies was what she might do if she knew he was coming. What would the bitch do? Would she be stupid enough to try to take him on? Or would he be hearing the sound of sirens very soon?

He watched the blonde in the car put down her phone. He needed to think. Two girls were manageable...but three? How could he cope with three? What was the best plan of attack? His mouth watered at the thought, at the challenge. He could take out three. There was no one better at taking out upstart bitches like these. Make it fast. Make it hard.

Grab her as soon as she opens the car door. He balled his hands into fists and felt his lips curl into a sneer. Grab her and hold the knife to her throat. Easy. As long as she's not expecting him, it would be easy.

Then an unsettling thought occurred to him. What if that was Alex on the phone warning her? What if it wasn't a surprise? Would his approach work if she was expecting him? He pictured the woman, tall, slender, and weak. It would work. Besides, surely she would have sped out of there if she knew he was there. Staying was pure lunacy. *Maybe the Ryan bitch thinks that Princess Posh over there is just out walking the dog. Maybe she's passed out drunk and doesn't even realise what's going on.*

Maybe. Maybe not. Was it worth taking the chance?

He strode over to the woman, held a finger to his lips and the gun at her head before removing the gag. "What's your name?"

She licked her lips and stuttered, "L...L...Lori."

"Okay, Lori, you're going to do me a little favour." He pulled the knife from its sheath on his belt and chuckled as her eyes widened. "You're going to call to Blondie, out there in that stupid, little, red car."

She dared to shake her head at him but the knife at her throat soon stopped her.

"Let me rephrase that." He pressed a tiny bit harder, until the steel bit, but just before the blood would start to trickle. "Call out to the fucking blonde or I will use this knife to cut that pretty face of yours ear to ear."

He watched her eyes close as she gulped at the air and knew she was close to tears. "No one's coming to save you so be a good girl now, and do as I say."

She opened her eyes and glared up at him.

"Do it."

She leant forward into the knife, pressing it tighter to her neck, challenging him. The slow trickle of red was hypnotic as it traced a path to her collarbone. Oh how easy it would be to pull the knife across, and watch the gush of life leave her, watch her eyes dim. He savoured the thought but held firm, the anticipation burned in his stomach. He would enjoy it more with an audience.

He watched her jaw work as she gritted her teeth, her eyes never leaving his. "Do it."

She licked her lips again and called out.

Alex chewed the inside of her cheek, and resisted the urge to call out to Jess. She watched her movements in the car as Alex cracked open the side door and risked a small wave, even though she knew she was more than likely hidden from Jess's view in the darkness.

She was unsure of what was out there, or where it could be hiding, and she was reluctant to give away the fact she was on to him. She had to control the almost overwhelming urge to run out into the courtyard like a mad woman, waving her gun and demanding to know where Lori was.

No, that's not right, Alex knew. There was no doubt in her mind. Sean Murray was somewhere on her farm. And wherever he was, he had Lori. She could feel it in her bones, like the chill that was seeping into her from the cold, hard floor of the kitchen. She knew with utter certainty that Lori's life now rested in her hands. Just as her mother's and father's had rested in Beth's. The weight of the responsibility was crushing. It sucked the air from her lungs and drained the blood from her brain. And the world shrank to the tiny point of light that came from the car when Jess picked up her phone. *Both of them. Both of their lives are in my hands.*

Alex pulled her own phone out of her pocket, the volume was low and she could hear voices at the other end from the dispatch centre. "Please, stay on the line and get someone here as fast as possible," she whispered. She kept the line open, and shoved it back in her pocket. She wished she'd grabbed Lori's phone too. Then she could have tried Jess again. But she hadn't, and it was too late to worry about it now.

Alex peered around the door and watched as Jess's lips started to move, as she started speaking to someone else. "Dammit, Jess, what are you doing?"

Alex slid further out of the door, behind a low bush, and scanned the courtyard for anything odd. Anything out of place. Her eyes had adjusted and she knew the topography as well as she knew her own face in the mirror.

It was maybe thirty metres to Jess's car and she weighed up whether it was worth the risk of running to it. She had no idea where Sean Murray was. She readied herself to sprint when a familiar voice called Jess's name, called to her for help.

Alex twisted toward the sound and her heart rate tripled to a roar in her ears.

Lori. She's in the barn.

The world slowed down as she watched Jess get out of the car. Lori called out again. She could hear the pain in Lori's voice and tried not to imagine what that bastard had already done to her. Emotion would do no good right now. Emotion would make her careless. Emotion would make her easier to kill. Emotions were for later. She choked back the fury rising in her throat, and waved toward Jess, who seemed to finally have spotted her in the shadows.

She pulled the gun from her waistband and held it up for Jess to see. In the moonlight, the whites of her eyes shone bright with surprise. Jess knew about the knife but not the gun.

"Jess, please. Help me."

Both their heads snapped back toward the barn door. It's a trap. Alex knew it and so, it seemed, did Jess, but she squared her shoulders and started for the door anyway.

Alex whispered as loud as she dared, begging for her to stop, but Jess shook her head. "I have to," she hissed back.

Alex crept sideways and found a position closer to the car, putting it between her and the barn door. She gave herself a better angle to glimpse through the door when it opened.

Maybe she could get an idea of what kind of weapon she was up against or at least his position in the barn. Then she saw it. Frank. Lying motionless on the ground. Her fears were confirmed: Sean Murray was here, and Frank wasn't taking a nap. The lump she'd been swallowing back rose up and threatened to escape, bringing with it bile. For a moment, the urge to vomit took hold, but she pushed it down, took some breaths. She was torn between fury and sorrow, and neither would do her any good. She needed to focus. There was nothing she could do for him now without giving herself away. He loved Lori and Jess, and would want her to protect them as he had so obviously tried.

She wasn't the only one to see him. Pulling her eyes away from Frank's lifeless shadow, she watched Jess's hand fly to her mouth and the small cry that escaped told Alex what she saw wasn't good. Meeting Jess's eyes she held a finger to her lips and motioned for Jess to calm down. Even across the distance Alex could tell she was on the verge.

Pulling off her ankle sheath, Alex made sure the knife was clipped in place before holding it up for Jess to see. He might be watching them. He might know she was going to arm Jess. But she couldn't let her go in there with nothing, and if he wasn't watching, he wouldn't be expecting it.

Jess called out as Alex threw the knife, covering the sound of it hitting the gravel. "Lori, where are you?"

Alex watched as she grabbed it, discarding the sheath, and holding it with the blade pointing up her arm in an attempt to hide it.

Alex's stomach clenched as Lori's strangled voice called out again. "I'm in the barn, Jess. Please help."

"What's happened? Should I go get, Al—"

"No," Lori cut her off. "She's sleeping. I came to find Frank and I think I've twisted my ankle. Don't disturb Alex. She needs her rest."

They both took deep breaths. Alex's tightened her grip on her gun while Jess grabbed the door handle of the barn.

Jess nodded to her and Alex saw Jess mouth, "I love you," before pushing the door open and disappearing from view.

Chapter 51

Sean kicked the door closed as soon as the dumb bitch was through it. He followed up with a sharp blow from his gun, putting her face first on the floor.

He watched in amusement as Lori strained against the tape that bound her while screaming at him through her gag. She fell sideways to the floor, the chair clattering noisily with her.

They were his now. Both of them were his, and it was just too fucking easy. *Let's hope the main prize isn't as disappointing.*

Blondie started to roll over, groaning with every movement. He pushed a knee into her spine and stopped her before she got any further. He grabbed for her wrists, and caught the flash of steel before it was embedded in his thigh. "Fuck!" He fell back in shock and kicked out in fury, managing to catch her hard in the stomach.

He stood and pulled the knife from his leg with a grunt while the bitch in the chair cried out. Towering over Blondie, he looked between them both, writhing and helpless on the floor.

Fucking whores always thinking they are so smart when all they do is ruin everything. They destroyed his career, his marriage, his relationship with his sons. They always thought they knew better than him. Always thought they were better than him.

He offered her a smile before he charged back at the bitch who'd just stabbed him. He grabbed her by the hair and dragged her to the waiting chair next to his other conquest.

"Do your worst, you fucking pointless piece of shit." He shouted at the closed door, loud enough for Alex to hear as he yanked Blondie's arms behind her back and taped them in place, laughing at her pathetic attempts to kick his shins. "Because I'm not going anywhere until you're sitting in a chair with your bitches here. Tell me, Alex, which one of them are you fucking? Or is it both?"

He pulled the princess and her chair upright again and replaced the gag.

"Shall we play a game, Alex?" He listened. Waiting. Nothing but silence. He smiled. Finally. A worthy adversary. He knew she was out there. Probably armed. He shrugged. *I would be.* He could guarantee that the police were on their way, but what else was left? This was his final stand, what he'd be remembered for. Seemed his wife was wrong all along, he wasn't good for nothing. There was something he'd always been good at. In the army, and now here at the end. He was always good at killing.

He waved the small blade back and forth between the two women as he shouted out again. *She can hear me. I know damn well she can hear me.* "It's a game I like to call, 'Which of your little whores should I kill first?'" He laughed. "I'll count to five to give you a bit of thinking time before I make the decision for you." He stepped closer to them. "One." He tapped the posh bit on the nose with the blade. "Two." He shouted. "Will she pick you, do you think?" He asked quietly. "Three." He shouted without waiting for a response. "Or will she pick Blondie? Four." He winked at Jess. "Gentlemen prefer blondes they say, don't they?" He pressed the steel against her cheek. "But I'm not a gentleman. Five!"

No response.

"Dear, oh dear, oh dear. Time to up the ante, I guess." He stood up straight and tilted his head from one side to the other, making his decision. "Have it your way, Bitch. But remember, Alex, this one's on you." With a sharp jab he drove the knife into Blondie's stomach. The rush flew from his head to his groin when she screamed. He laughed, seeing the pure hatred in the posh bird's eyes as she tried to shuffle closer to help her friend. Futile.

"I've started without you, Alex. You should probably get your skinny arse in here if you want to stop me putting holes in your girlfriends."

He stepped behind them. "Now, sit still, 'cos this is gonna hurt." He reached out and pressed on the wound. She screamed beautifully before she passed out.

"It's up to you now, little Alex. Your choice. Which one do I kill first?"

CHAPTER 52

Jess's scream was too much. Alex drew the gun and ran across the courtyard, charging the barn door, she shouldered it open and finally came face to face with the monster that killed her sister. She raised her gun and aimed it at his head.

He was ready for her, though. He stood behind the two most precious people in her life and she had no choice but to keep her distance. The knife at Lori's throat and the casual way he waved his gun in the direction of an unconscious Jess as her life bled away ensured it.

"Ah, at last you decide to join us. A little late for Blondie here but your posh princess might have a chance." He chuckled. "Well...maybe."

Maintaining her aim, she fought to keep her voice steady. "Put the weapons down, Sean. I will shoot you."

He forced Lori's head back with the knife and exposed her throat further. He pressed it tight to the jugular releasing another bloody tear. "Shoot, and it's the last fucking breath she takes." Sneering, he tapped his forehead with his gun. "Unless you really think you're good enough to hit me here?"

She flicked her eyes briefly to Lori's and held firm. She needed to be brave for them both. "I know I'm fucking good enough. Put your weapons down. I won't ask you again."

He laughed and moved the gun to Lori's temple. His voice was soft when he whispered words into the chasm between them. "Your little Beth wasn't good enough."

Alex's breath left her at the sound of Beth's name on his lips. "You don't get to say her name." *Emotion will not help.*

"She had a shotgun and half the distance to cover, but she still missed."

Her hands shook as she slowly started to inch in his direction. "Stop talking and step away from them." *Assess, plan, execute.*

"You know this all feels very familiar. My dad was holding the knife to your mother's neck just like this. Your father bound and gagged next to her."

She tried to block out the words, concentrating on her aim, picking her target. *Assess...we're all in fucking trouble.*

"Let me ask you something, Alex. Do you ever wonder if you'd still have your family if Beth hadn't missed?"

She felt the rage build, but kept eye contact, refusing to blink. "I already said you don't get to say her name." *Plan... shoot the bastard.*

He looked away first, down at the gun now pointing at Lori. "Okay, just one more question then, Alex." He said her name with a sneer.

"Stop talking." *Execute.*

When he looked up at her again, his lip curled with satisfaction. "Ask yourself what might happen if you miss?"

Her gaze fell to Jess and Lori. Jess's head was bobbing slightly, she groaned as she started to come to. Lori's neck was still exposed, fresh blood from it joining the trail from her cheek.

"I only want you, Bitch. Put the gun down and they're free."

Lori shook her head regardless of the bite of the steel. Her eyes welled up as she held Alex's gaze, pleading with her to risk the shot.

This was the moment. Judge, jury, and executioner. Now was the moment to execute. To survive. To save.

She shook her head. "I will not be you." She whispered and dropped the gun on the ground knowing she couldn't have made the shot without at least one of them falling victim to Sean Murray. *Better to bide my time. Keep him talking.* "I've lived too long in your shadow. I'd rather die than live in it one more second. I will not let you control me anymore. I'm not a puppet for your amusement, or a doll for you to play with."

"Not even got the guts to fight. I'm disappointed, Alex. Your baby sister had more mettle than you."

Alex shook her head. "Maybe. But I have an advantage she didn't."

"And what's that?"

"I got to make a phone call." The sound of sirens in the distance grew louder quickly.

"Bitch."

"You've still got time."

"I knew it. Knew you'd fucking chicken out of facing me. You spineless fucking Bitch."

The rage that coloured his face scared her. In that instant, she realised what a mistake she'd made. She'd miscalculated his reaction to the approaching police. It seemed self-preservation wasn't on his list of goals for the evening. "Please just let them go. There's still time for you to run."

He stared at her, his eyes cold and hard. "You must think I'm a fucking idiot, just like the rest of the whores who've ruined my life did."

"I don't, Sean, I don't. It doesn't have to end like this. Please."

She glanced at the gun in front of her and tried, in desperation, to calculate in how many steps, and how quickly she could reach it.

"Haven't you learnt anything yet, Alex. Everything good ends."

Alex watched as he leaned in close to Lori, making a show of smelling her hair as he removed the gag. Pressing the gun to her temple, Alex winced with her as he kissed the top of her head.

"Say your last words, Princess."

All Alex could see in Lori's eyes was determination. She smiled at Alex. "I love you."

No sooner had she said the words before a roar escaped her as she launched herself upward with the chair. Smacking the top of her head into Murray's chin, the chair broke under her as she toppled and fell back on it.

Alex watched in slow motion as he reeled backward, blood spraying from his mouth. She watched as he staggered momentarily as Lori kicked out at his ankles from the floor, before landing his own kick to her ribcage and spitting a piece of bloody flesh from his mouth next to her head. Then his focus was back on Alex. He spun around and, in her mind, his arm moved as if it was breaking through water, recovering his aim on her. It was a slow blur in her peripheral vision, because she was moving too. Her focus shifted.

Assess, plan, execute.

Four.

That's how many steps it took Alex to reach the gun.

Gunshots deafened them all.

CHAPTER 53

Alex couldn't stop hitting him.

Aware of shouting at first, then someone pulling at her, trying to grab her wrists, it wasn't until Lori's arms wrapped fully around her that she came back to the room and realised what she was doing.

She straddled Sean Murray's lifeless body, arms and legs were thick with his blood, from the chest wounds where both she and Stella had shot him, and his face from her blows.

She let Lori lead her away while still holding her tight, everything a blur through the tears. Was it really over? Were they safe? Her mind couldn't process the past few minutes, wouldn't allow her to believe he'd finally paid for his monstrous crimes.

Hearing her name called, she suddenly remembered. Jess.

Lori guided her to the gurney about to be loaded into the ambulance with a young police officer glued to its side.

"Oh shit, Jess." Alex grabbed her hand. "I'm so sorry, sweetheart. This should never have happened. I'm so sorry you were dragged into this."

Jess held up her other hand. She shook her head and lifted her oxygen mask. "I think I deserve a holiday after this."

Alex laughed through her tears and nodded. She kissed Jess on the forehead and placed her mask back. "A really long holiday, I'd say."

They were about to climb into the ambulance with her when the paramedic stopped them. "Sorry only one person can go with her."

Stella came up behind them and gave Alex a nudge. "I think PC Wallace here will be happy to escort her. I can follow on behind with you two."

Hannah smiled at her superior, and eagerly jumped into the back of the ambulance with a grateful nod to Alex. "From what Detective Roberts has told me this past few weeks about Jess and the conversations I've overheard, I don't think you need to worry about her, but I promise to take good care of her."

Alex raised her eyebrows, unsure of what she'd missed, but she trusted Stella's suggestion, and the thought of leaving Lori so soon caused her a small panic.

She squeezed Jess's hand in acquiescence. "We'll be right behind you, Jess. I love you."

Jess squeezed back, her eyes closing as the paramedic shut the doors.

"There's something we have to do before we follow them to the hospital." Lori fought the tears again as she took Alex's hand and led her toward a patrol car.

A police constable stood sentry next to the tartan blanket wrapped around Alex's faithful dog in the back seat. They crouched down together and Lori smoothed his fur. "He was so brave, Alex. I just know it."

Alex gently stroked his head and kissed him. "That's Frank. Brave until the goat chased back..."

The PC spoke. "I've offered to take him into the emergency vet's so you can head straight to the hospital, Miss Ryan. The paramedic wrapped the wound tight and gave him something for the pain." Nodding at Lori's bloodied face and neck he continued. "You should probably let them look at you as well."

Alex nodded at his offer, grateful to the kind officer. "Thank you—"

"PC Allen, Steve Allen."

"Thanks, PC Allen. You're a gentleman."

Hiding his blush, he bent to stroke Frank one more time before closing the car door. Lori's arm went round Alex again as they watched him drive away.

Lori reassured her. "We'll take care of Frank tomorrow. I have a feeling PC Allen won't leave his side, and right now Jess needs us."

For the first time since she fired the gun, Alex saw Lori. Saw the raw cuts to her cheek and throat, the streaks where tears had run a path through the blood. She took her hands, ran her thumbs across the angry purple bruises where her wrists had been bound.

The shock hit her and she felt her legs go numb. Her whole body tingled, and the chill cut to her bones. It all could have been so much worse.

"Are you okay?" She ran her hands over Lori, looking for other injuries, touched the skin under her cut cheek, felt her arms, her sides, lifting her chin to look at her neck, before taking her face in her hands. "I'm so sorry, this is my entire fault. Refusing to leave, hiding out on my own. Determined I could deal with it myself—"

"Hey!" Lori shook her and stilled Alex's hands. "Stop that right now. The only person who's at fault here is Sean Murray. And now he's paid the price."

"But—"

"But nothing. No one is asking you to carry the blame, Alex. That needs to end tonight. You said yourself, you were determined to deal with this yourself?"

"Yes."

"Well, look around. Tonight proves you don't have to. Me, Jess, Stella, Hannah, Frank, the whole team of officers, and paramedics here now, you might not have asked for help, but we came anyway."

Alex tentatively traced a finger under the cut on Lori's cheek again. "I can't believe I nearly lost you."

Lori brought their foreheads together and enveloped her in her arms again. "Ditto," she whispered. "But you didn't." She kissed new tears from Alex's lips and smiled, holding her gaze. "I'm not going anywhere, Alex. It's time to let people back in."

CHAPTER 54

In the small hours of the morning, Alex looked around the waiting room at her family. That's what they were now. Bound together in the tragedy of that night, she made a silent vow to them all.

It was only forward from now on. There was no looking back. No more hiding. No more blame. No more bitterness.

She would honour their bravery, their friendship, and their love for her over the years, by taking every opportunity to be happy from now on. She'd make Beth proud.

James Hunter entered the room with a tray of coffees. He smiled as he handed her one. Lori sat between him and her brother, who sat scowling at his feet. Both of them had turned up unexpectedly after a call from Stella telling them what had happened. It seemed they were already on route to the farm but no more explanation had been given. It could wait.

She watched Lori look back and forth between them through the steam of her coffee and imagined the whole situation to be as surreal to her as it was to Alex. Catching her eye, she smiled. "You okay?" she mouthed, aware of the silence in the room.

Lori mouthed back, "Yeah." Nodding either side of her with a small shrug, signalling her own confusion at their sudden appearance.

Stella squeezed Alex's hand before leaning in close to her ear. "I've already told Lori, I'm pretty sure you two are busted." She chuckled at the small groan that escaped Alex's lips and stood. "Don't look so worried. I've heard their intentions are honourable and I'm about to have a conversation."

Alex watched as Stella nodded in Scott's direction before stepping outside of the room with him. A look of confusion passed between her and Lori and they could only shrug again and wonder.

Reaching to her left, Alex stilled Hannah's jiggling leg and smiled her way. "She's going to be fine, Hannah, I know my Jess, and she'll be stronger than ever after this."

She watched Hannah down her coffee. "I hope so." She got up and paced before heading out of the door after Stella and Scott. It seemed Jess's magic had already captured the young PC's attention and she made a note to get the scoop from Stella on what her intentions were toward her best friend. For now though, her presence with them all waiting for the outcome of Jess's surgery didn't feel out of place, considering the hours she'd put in alongside Stella to help solve the case. She'd also been the one who volunteered to call Jess's parents. They had retired to Spain a few years before, but were booked on the first flight home later that day.

Lori got up and took the seat Hannah had vacated as her dad went to refill their coffee cups. "So according to Stella we're busted."

Alex nudged her shoulder but kept her eye on the door where, hours before, they had taken Jess. "And how do you feel about that?"

She felt Lori's hand slip into her own and turned her way. Her expression was soft and Alex could see no worry or apprehension, only love. "I feel lucky to have my family all here together, and to have you by my side."

"So you called your dad?" Stella paced, not willing to let Scott try and placate her, she needed the full story, wanted to understand.

"Yes. I called him yesterday from the airport. Stella, I realise now how wrong I've been. That wasn't me that day in your flat. You have to believe me."

"Tell me why, Scott? Tell me why I should, because right now you're still just an asshole homophobe."

She watched him hang his head. He scrubbed at his face with rough hands and the sound against the bristles of an unshaved face almost masked the sob that escaped him. But Stella heard it and her heart broke a little. She felt herself soften, but she still knew no more than that day in her flat.

She knelt in front of him and pulled his hands away, heard him take a breath before eventually lifting his eyes to hers. "I'm so sorry, Stella. Those things I said were unforgivable, but I hope you can understand. Hearing those things about Lori took me back to a place in the past, an unhappy place. And I couldn't bear to think of her going through the same thing I did."

"Scott, you're not making sense, what happened to you?"

He took another breath and the words Stella least expected came from his lips. "A boy broke my heart."

The tears came harder. Stella rose to sit beside him, taking his hands and turning him towards her. "Tell me."

She watched him swipe at his face with his sleeve, collecting himself and stemming the tears. "Ah, it all seems so stupid and insignificant now, but at the time, my life was hell. It was at boarding school, I was fifteen and there was this older boy, Jacob, who started paying me a lot of attention. We were on sports teams together, shared a dorm, hung out in the village when we had our free time, his gang were sixteen and seventeen, and I felt special as the only one in my year to break into it. You have to understand, these were the lads the girls all fancied and all the boys wanted to be."

Stella nodded. "I think every school has one of those gangs. So what happened?"

"Well, at first, I just got invited to the odd thing. I'd been performing well on the football pitch, was starting games regularly, and I guess that's when it began. But after a while I noticed Jacob finding reasons to spend time only with me. Like going to the cinema and saying it would be a group of us, but then only he would show up. Or getting two tickets to the local football game and inviting me. It felt good, and slowly I started to wonder if he was interested in me more than as a friend."

"And did that bother you? Did he hurt you, Scott?"

"No. No. Not in the way you're thinking. I think he was interested in me, and I felt the same. It never crossed my mind that either of us was gay, I just liked hanging out with him. I was in awe. There was a connection between us, we got each other, and talked in a way that was different when we were alone to when the other guys were around. Back then, I was more interested in sports and my camera than girls and he was the first person who seemed to appreciate my photography. He would come with me on hikes and I loved taking his picture."

He laughed then and Stella urged him on. "What's so funny?"

"It's not funny at all. It's more that it's much clearer now how events conspired. We'd stayed out past curfew one night but there was a way to sneak in through the kitchens. When we got there, Jacob decided we should steal some of the teacher's wine. We ended up drunk in the basement and..."

"And?" Stella knew what was coming but wanted to hear it from Scott.

"And I kissed him."

"Wow. I take it that didn't go well."

"Oh, it went well, for about thirty seconds. The next thing he's pushing me across the room and then he's punching me. Calling me all these dirty, disgusting names, and accusing me of forcing myself on him."

"That little fucker." Stella was raging now. He had no reason to lie to her, and she ached for a young Scott, how traumatising and confusing the situation must have been.

"Yeah, I tried to reason with him, said it was the booze, it was a joke. I tried everything. But he told all the guys in our dorm. Used the photos I'd taken to say I was obsessed with him. Word spread, just whispers, no one wanted to talk about that kind of stuff out loud. Fortunately, Lori never got wind of it, or if she did, she never said anything. But that was it. In the dorm, the changing room, on the pitch, in class, in the dining hall. Until Jacob left the following year, I was the faggot who liked to get guys drunk so I could take advantage of them."

"I'm sorry, Scott, that's awful. Why didn't you talk to someone? Have him expelled, moved?"

"I've wondered that myself and looking back I think it's because I genuinely did care about him, he was my first real crush. I looked up to him and he treated me like shit. But the saddest thing is I think he really liked me too. But he wasn't ready to admit it. Social media has since informed me that he's not so shy about it now." A wry smile crossed his face.

"So all those things you said about Lori, that's where those came from?"

"I guess, but it doesn't excuse them. I was upset because it brought everything that happened with Jacob back, but I also had these horrifying images of Lori getting branded in the same way. I know it's a different world now, but it's been so tough for her already. I couldn't cope imagining bastards like those guys subjecting her to what I went through."

Stella took his arm, lifted it around her shoulders, and sat in his lap. Stroking her fingers down a spiky cheek, she wiped away the last of the tears. "I'm sorry that happened to you, Scott. And I understand more why you reacted that way. You need to talk to Lori about this. And we need to talk to her about us."

His smile made her happy and she didn't fight it when he kissed her. It was tentative and gentle, as if she might change her mind. She pressed into him and made sure he knew she meant it.

"So there's still an 'us' to talk about?"

She kissed him again in answer, and felt her own tears coming. There was no going back, she loved this man and was willing to take a risk to make it work.

Hannah's appearance broke their spell. Stella noted the smirk on her face when she saw them and put a finger to her lips in warning. "Later."

"A nurse said the doctor will be out soon with news."

Stella extricated herself and pulled Scott to his feet. "Come on, I want to be there."

Scott led the way out of the room, but Stella caught Hannah's arm. "Have you got a minute."

She nodded for Scott to carry on. "I'll be there soon."

She turned to Hannah and saw the smirk was back. "Isn't that Lori's brother?"

Stella prodded her with a sharp finger in the shoulder but kept her tone light. "You know fine well it is and I'll trust you to keep quiet until I can talk to her, okay?"

Hannah gave one of her salutes. "Aye, Detective, whatever you say."

Stella swatted her hand down but laughed. "Seriously, Lori is going to be pretty mad with me so I need to do this my way. Anyway, you can't talk. I see the feisty Jess has got your attention. What's going on?"

"Aye, you could say that." A wistful look washed over her face. "Let's just say an affinity was discovered in the back of the ambulance."

Stella turned up her nose. "How on earth do you make that sound dirty?"

Hannah laughed. "It's an art. Obviously I barely know her but I'd like to change that. So I'll keep your secret if you keep mine?"

It was Stella's turn to salute. "Deal."

Hannah and Stella returned as Jess's doctor entered the room. They all stood expectantly. Alex spoke for the group. "How is she?"

He smiled and she felt her shoulders slump in relief. Lori's hand slipped into hers again as she joined her side.

The doctor spoke matter of factly. "We had to remove her spleen but that's a perfectly manageable situation these days, with medication. Although we did have to perform it open, we couldn't use keyhole surgery due to the extensive bleeding, so with the additional tissue damage, some contusions to her liver, and bruising to her kidneys, she's going to be very sore and need a lot of rest. But she should be back on her feet in six to eight weeks."

"Can we see her?" Alex asked.

"She's in recovery right now, but a nurse will come to get you when she's properly awake and in her room. There's no doubt she was a lucky girl."

Alex reached to shake his hand. She looked around the room at the relieved faces and agreed with him. "She and I both, Doctor. Thank you."

Her legs finally gave up and she dropped like lead into a chair. Lori was at her side in an instant, along with Stella, but no words would come, only tears. They both reassured and held her hand and rubbed her back, and the relief flooded through her from head to toe.

She'd almost lost her Jess. That Jess had put herself in the line of fire for Alex was overwhelming. To have someone willing to sacrifice themselves, just as Lori had risked her life attacking Sean in those final moments, filled her with love and guilt in equal measure. She loved them both but didn't know if the guilt would ever leave her, that they were put in that position because of her past. *How strong and fallible we are all at once. That we have the power to hold someone else's life and happiness in our palm.*

She looked up then, into the face of someone capable of doing just that with her life and happiness. "He's really gone. It's over isn't it?"

Lori enveloped her into her arms. "It's over, my love. It's over."

EPILOGUE

Four months later, Alex and Lori were about to see Jess and Hannah off at the airport. The first few weeks since that night at the farm had initially passed by in a blur of police statements, hospital rooms, vet appointments, and calls and visits from friends. The farm hadn't seen so much activity in years.

The three women's version of events, along with the call that was recorded from Alex's phone, and Stella and Hannah's statements on what happened after their arrival at the scene, had been told and retold a dozen times over. Forensic evidence confirmed Sean Murray as Beth's killer and the case was finally closed.

There was no one to bury him, his ex-wife had been informed but had no interest in associating herself or her sons with her murdering ex-husband. He was given a pauper's funeral and Alex was satisfied not to know where his body lay.

John Murray was diagnosed with terminal brain cancer and placed in a palliative care facility. His blood, along with Beth's, was found on the handkerchief and, although he wouldn't see the inside of a jail cell due to his condition, he had, instead, relived the crime almost daily in his head until a massive stroke took him in the night a month previously.

"We've come a long way, eh?" Alex looked at each of the women in turn, Lori, Jess, and Hannah. They'd hardly been separated since 'that' night at the farm and today was going to be hard on them all.

"If it's possible, Hannah, I think I'm going to miss your cooking more than Jess's." Her comment elicited a pop on the shoulder from Jess.

"Oi, it was me that filled your freezer again don't forget. I guess the heroine badge has faded already and I'm back to chores," she pouted.

Hannah laughed. "Aw, you'll always be my hero, even if you were the worst, most demanding patient in the history of patients."

"Hey, I didn't force you to stay at my bedside all those weeks. Just admit it was my awesome bravery in the face of adversity that kept you coming back."

"Okay, okay you two. Break it up, I'm feeling nauseous." Alex winked Lori's way. "Besides, we all know who really saved the day here with her kick ass moves."

"Yeah, yeah, yeah, Lady Hunter wins." Jess rolled her eyes.

They'd had an ongoing argument about who had played the biggest part in bringing Sean Murray down and Alex knew it was for her benefit. That Alex had pulled the trigger and ended his life had never been spoken about in jest. Only in the dark of the night, when the moment returned and haunted her dreams, when Lori lay by her side, comforting her and listening. Only then did she speak about it.

She smiled around the circle again and each woman seemed to sigh. "I'm glad we can talk like this. We won, ladies. We get to carry on. We get to be happy."

Alex's smile was returned and she knew each one of them was reflecting on her words.

"And we get to go on great adventures." She looked at Jess and Hannah. "You two better bloody take good care of each other. I'm serious. The other side of the world is far away, but not so far that I can't come kick your asses if I hear of trouble."

Hannah's salute came out. "I promise. I've spent the past four months listening to her whinge and moan about every ache and pill. I think I can handle her in holiday mode."

Jess feigned hurt, but Alex could see past it to her smile. She was smitten and in Hannah had finally met her match. Alex wasn't worried at all. They would have a fantastic time, and Jess going on her travels was long overdue. Alex couldn't stand in her way any longer.

Lori linked arms with Hannah. "Let's go get some coffee and leave these two to get all soppy on their own." She blew them both a kiss and wandered in the direction of a coffee cart.

"What's it like?" Jess slipped an arm around Alex's shoulders and nodded in the direction that Lori had just gone.

"What's what like?" Alex didn't follow.

"To have someone you love that much by your side?"

Alex smiled and hugged Jess to her, thinking on her answer. "It feels like when you get caught in the rain, miles from home with no money, and chance intervenes when a friend happens by and picks you up. You're still cold and bedraggled, battered by the forces of nature but it doesn't matter because you're safe, and you know you're on your way to getting warm. So you count your stars that that person was there at the right time to save you, and vow never to get caught in the rain again." She nodded towards Hannah as they wandered back with coffee.

"But I think you know that feeling."

A short time later, Alex and Lori waved good-bye as they watched Jess and Hannah queue at the doors of airport security. Holding hands, Alex leant a head on Lori's shoulder, sighing as she watched their friends, still feeling tearful after their farewell. "They're so ridiculously cute. Do you think they know that?"

Lori chuckled. "Oh, they know it. They also know they're not as cute as us." She pecked Alex on the head as she wiped away her own tears. "C'mon we need to get going to the train station."

Alex glimpsed the back of Jess's head as they disappeared from view. "I hate this day."

Lori had taken a leave of absence and stayed with Alex until Jess was properly on the mend and her own wounds had healed. Well, the physical ones anyway. She had taken just a few small stitches to her cheek and neck that had left only two tiny, white scars, along with a couple of cracked ribs and a concussion from her heroic head butt.

"I can't believe it's time already. Where did it go?" Alex pulled her in tight, oblivious to the world around them, the myriad of people rushing around them on the station concourse. She needed to feel Lori close before the time came to say good-bye.

"Hmm...well, I recall lots of getting better, talking into the small hours around our nightly bonfires, lots of wine, terrible attempts by you to cook, oh, and my favourite part... hours that led to days in bed with you."

Alex groaned. "Can't we be there right now? Please, I've changed my mind. You're not going anywhere apart from back to my bed."

Nowhere did Alex feel as safe as when Lori's warm body was tucked close. She felt at home, supported, and cared for. The fear of what came next had left her. They looked to the future together with excitement instead of the previously felt trepidation, and she knew that love and support had to be returned on her part. No matter how hard it was.

Lori replied with a kiss. Alex could kiss her all day and all night. She melted into it the same way each time, and each time, it only got better.

They broke apart, leaving Alex breathless. "Have I told you today how much I hate Adam?"

Lori laughed and looked at her watch. "Two o'clock and that's the first time. We're making progress."

"He knows I blame him entirely for this, doesn't he?"

"He does, but still can't wait to meet you when you come to New York. And you promised you'd play nice, remember?"

"Aye, okay. But that was until I stupidly made you go for that interview and talked you into taking the job. It was all lies, damn lies, I tell you." She stamped her foot, and Lori laughed again.

"You're such a drama queen."

"Yes, I am, but I'm being serious now. I don't know if I'm ready to let you go."

Lori's arms circled around her, and she was back in that safe space, reassured and happy with the decision they had made.

Lori had gotten an offer from the UN for a year's contract in New York. She had turned it down at first, but Alex could see a part of her regretted it. She had reassured Alex, she was where she was meant to be. But it had been a dream not so long ago, and Alex wanted nothing more than to see her dreams come true, to be part of them.

They had talked about relocating together but decided there was time enough for that. Alex wasn't ready to leave the farm quite yet, and it had become home to Lori as well.

Adam was heading to New York with Lori after bagging the permanent job, which had reassured Alex. She would at least have a friend there. In a year, they would reassess. They had already dreamt together that maybe Alex would be ready to join her then, or Lori might make Scotland her permanent home.

If they'd learnt anything, it was that the rest of their lives didn't need to be decided now. It was Alex and Lori, now, in the future, forever. They'd take each day together as it came.

"It's only a year. It's only a year," Alex repeated what had become her mantra in the weeks leading up to Lori's departure.

"See that's where you're wrong. It's only three weeks. Three weeks and you and I will be in the Big Apple together and I'll have you in my arms again. Think of the adventures we're going to have."

The call came over for Lori's train, and Alex blew out a breath. "Shit. I still can't believe it's time already."

"You're sure I can't persuade you to run away with me?" Lori pulled her in tight.

Alex laughed despite the tears that were threatening. "Not today, my beautiful Lori. Maybe tomorrow?"

Lori smiled. "There's no *maybe* about it. You're still mine tomorrow, no matter where we are."

Kissing her, Alex felt it. Felt the truth of Lori's words in her heart. This was just the first step towards their future, and she felt excited, not sad. They were in it together and always would be.

The final call for the train broke them apart.

Leaning in close to Alex's ear, Lori whispered, "I'm going to marry you someday, Alex Ryan." She followed it with a soft kiss to Alex's cheek, just the way she had done that first night on the farm.

Lori started walking backward, her eyes never leaving Alex's, shining with happy tears that mirrored her own. Before Lori turned to pass through the platform gate, Alex mouthed, "I love you," and already couldn't wait for that day.

About Wendy Hudson

Originally from Northern Ireland, Wendy is an Army kid with a book full of old addresses and an indecipherable accent to match. As a child she was always glued to a book, even building a reading den in the attic to get peace from her numerous younger siblings.

She's always enjoyed writing and turning thirty was the catalyst for finally getting stuck in to her first novel.

By day Wendy is a trade union officer, campaigning and fighting the good fight. By night you'll find her with a laptop dreaming of becoming a full time writer and doing her best to make that happen.

Now settled in Scotland, her summers are all about wild camping, sailing, golfing, and drinking beer at as many festivals as possible. This is normally followed by a restful winter of eating out, skiing, avoiding the gym, watching ballet and football, and not dancing at gigs.

CONNECT WITH WENDY:

Website: www.wendyhudsonauthor.com
Facebook: www.facebook.com/wendyhudsonauthor
Twitter: @whudsonauthor

Other Books from Ylva Publishing

www.ylva-publishing.com

Collide-O-Scope

(Norfolk Coast Investigation Story – Book #1)

Andrea Bramhall

ISBN: 978-3-95533-573-1
Length: 370 pages (90,000 words)

One unidentified dead body. One tiny fishing village. Forty residents and everyone's a suspect. Where do you start? Newly promoted Detective Sergeant Kate Brannon and Kings Lynn's CID have to answer that question and more as they untangle the web of lies wrapped around the tiny village of Brandale Stiathe Harbour to capture the killer of Connie Wells.

Welcome to the Wallops

(The Wallops – Book #1)

Gill McKnight

ISBN: 978-3-95533-559-5
Length: 242 pages (67,000 words)

Jane Swallow has always struggled to keep peace, friendship, and equanimity within the community she loves, but this year everything is wrong. Her father has just been released from prison and is on his way to Lesser Wallop with the rest of her travelling family. Her job is on the line, and her ex-girlfriend has just moved in next door. Only a miracle can save her.

Conflict of Interest

(Portland Police Bureau Series – Book #1)

Jae

ISBN: 978-3-95533-109-2
Length: 466 pages (135,000 words)

Detective Aiden Carlisle isn't looking for love, especially not at a law enforcement seminar, but the first lecturer isn't what she expected.

After a failed relationship, psychologist Dawn Kinsley swore to never get involved with another cop, but she immediately feels a connection to Aiden.

Can Aiden keep from crossing the line when Dawn becomes the victim of a brutal crime?

The Red Files

Lee Winter

ISBN: 978-3-95533-330-0
Length: 365 pages (103,000 words)

Ambitious journalist Lauren King is stuck reporting on the vapid LA social scene's gala events while sparring with her rival—icy ex-Washington correspondent Catherine Ayers. Then a curious story unfolds before their eyes, involving a business launch, thirty-four prostitutes, and a pallet of missing pink champagne. Can the warring pair join together to unravel an incredible story?

COMING FROM YLVA PUBLISHING

www.ylva-publishing.com

The Lavender List

Meg Harrington

After the Second World War, Amelia Maldonado opts to live a quiet life bussing tables at a diner during the day and going out for auditions at night. The one bright spot is her friendship with the charming Laura Wright, a well-heeled woman with a mysterious war-related past.

When Laura shows up outside the diner barely conscious and spitting lousy lies, Amelia takes it upon herself to figure out the truth. From mobsters to spies, Amelia quickly finds herself forced back into a world of shadows she thought she'd escaped long ago and thrust into partnership with the one person she's sure can ruin her—the enigmatic Laura Wright.

Four Steps
© 2016 by Wendy Hudson

ISBN: 978-3-95533-690-5

Also available as e-book.

Published by Ylva Publishing, legal entity of Ylva Verlag, e.Kfr.

Ylva Verlag, e.Kfr.
Owner: Astrid Ohletz
Am Kirschgarten 2
65830 Kriftel
Germany

www.ylva-publishing.com

First edition: 2016

Credits
Edited by Andrea Bramhall & Cheri Fuller
Proofread by Jacqueline McCarthy
Cover Design by Adam Lloyd
Vector Design by Freepik.com

Printed by
booksfactory
PRINT GROUP Sp. z o.o.
ul. Ks. Witolda 7-9
71-063 Szczecin
Poland
tel./fax 91 812-43-49
NIP/USt-IdNr.: PL8522520116